HEATWAVE

HEATWAVE

Jane A. Adams

This first world edition published in Great Britain 2004 by
SEVERN HOUSE PUBLISHERS LTD of
9–15 High Street, Sutton, Surrey SM1 1DF.
This first world edition published in the USA 2005 by
SEVERN HOUSE PUBLISHERS INC of
595 Madison Avenue, New York, N.Y. 10022.

British Library Cataloguing in Publication Data

Adams, Jane
    Heatwave
    1.   Ex-police officers - Fiction
    2.   Blind - Fiction
    3.   Hostages - Fiction
    4.   Detective and mystery stories
    I.   Title
    823.9'14 [F]

    ISBN 0-7278-6141-7

Typeset by Palimpsest Book Production Ltd.,
Polmont, Stirlingshire, Scotland.
Printed and bound in Great Britain by
MPG Books Ltd., Bodmin, Cornwall.

Prologue

Naomi had been half expecting Alec's proposal, but even so, it came as a shock to hear him actually say it. It was probably inevitable though, considering they had spent the better part of the day attending the wedding of a friend and one-time colleague. Naomi had chosen her dress with care; something suitable for an afternoon wedding, a formal reception and then far less formal dance, and the simple blue silk that felt so wonderful when she stroked it, and clung emphatically to every curve, had, she knew, been something of a triumph. Alec's pride in having her beside him had been unmistakable and the little exclamations of envy and admiration from several other women had been very gratifying.

It wasn't that Naomi was vain, or that she particularly wanted to score points. It was simply that two years, no, maybe even a year before, she would have been horrified at attending anything so public, so exposed. As it was, her thorough enjoyment of the day, and even her anticipation of the event – the shopping trip with her sister to find just the right dress and the careful matching of accessories – was such an important marker of how far she had come. The fact that she could not *see* the rich blue-green and that she had to trust her sister's judgement on which shoes and bag did or didn't 'go' had not diminished in the slightest her pleasure in knowing that she looked good and felt better. The accident that had taken her sight, her career, her entire way of life from her, had seemed finally to be receding, if not exactly into the background, then at least to a manageable distance.

But now the day was ended. Naomi's sense of triumph had been given the chance to wane and weariness had taken over.

1

It all seemed a little hollow. The occasion had been so over-whelmingly filled with memories. Colleagues – Alec's still, once hers – had flocked to them, told her how wonderful she looked, how great it was to see her. How well they thought she had coped with it all . . . and that was the problem, really. Yes, she had . . . *coped* . . . whatever that meant. Naomi had long since been of the opinion that you played the hand life dealt you and didn't waste time and effort bemoaning what might possibly have been. But that didn't mean that it was easy. It didn't mean that the pain went away.

Lately, as she had rebuilt her life and settled in to the changes this new hand had dealt, she found that now her time was not merely spent learning how to cope, that she was actually bored. She felt restless, ready to move on to a new challenge, and that new challenge, so far, had failed to materialize. To have these shadows from her previous life pressing in on her all day, sitting next to her and talking shop, only served to remind her of all the things missing and profoundly missed.

'Naomi, you know how I feel?' Alec sounded uncertain that she did. 'You say yes now and I'll be the happiest man alive.'

'Will you?'

'Sure I will.'

'Alec, I don't know. I don't think I'm ready for this. For marriage and all that.'

'I all but live here, at your place. We could move into mine. It's plenty big enough.'

And that had been what did it. The idea of her leaving this carefully chosen asylum she had moved to after her accident was more than she could bear. They'd all thought she was crazy, starting off somewhere new, but for Naomi that had been the beginning of everything. The fact that she knew this space inti-mately, had chosen everything in it, had designed it around herself and her new set of priorities, was something, she figured, those well-meaning friends and family could not bring them-selves to understand, and for Alec to suggest she might abandon that . . . it was too much. Too much to even contemplate.

'I can't, Alec. Not leave home. Not yet.' She spoke more sharply than she'd intended. 'Alec, I love you, but I'm not ready to be anyone's wife.'

He sighed and she felt him sink back into the sofa. 'But you'll think about it?'

'I'll think about it.' She smiled. 'Take it as a maybe? Huh?'

'I ask the woman to marry me and she says maybe.' He laughed and reached to clasp her hand. 'I don't suppose Harry has anything to do with your indecision?'

'If Harry asked me, I'd tell him no. Does that make you feel better?'

'A maybe is better than a straight no,' he agreed. 'I'm rushing you, aren't I?'

She nodded. 'Yeah, you are. Alec, it just came home to me today that I don't know who I am any more. In here –' she touched her temple – 'I'm still the Naomi I used to be. Out there, I'm . . . I don't know what I am. If I said yes to you tonight, it would be because I could then say, I'm Alec's wife. It would be because you were giving me some kind of identity. Not because I wanted to say yes.'

'Is that such a bad thing?'

'I think so, yes. Ask me again?'

He kissed her. 'You know I will. Again and again until I get the answer I want.'

'You'd better do.' She paused, not sure what the etiquette was when you'd turned someone down, though she suspected that Alec had almost expected her response and knew it would make no difference between them. 'Are you staying?'

'No, I've got a long day tomorrow and I'd never get up in time to go home and change. Still on for tomorrow night though?'

'You know it is. I'll be home for about six.'

'You're off out with Harry and Patrick tomorrow, aren't you?'

'Don't grouch about it. Harry is one of my oldest friends, so don't play jealous.'

'I'm not! Well, maybe just a little. Anyway, I thought Helen was the friend. Harry, as I recall, was just the big brother. OK, OK.'

Naomi could imagine him holding up his hands in mock surrender.

'Just as long as I'm sure you'd say no, if Harry asked you.

Look, tell Patrick I've borrowed that game he wanted to try out. I'll drop it in for him.'

'Will do.'

He got to his feet, pulling her up with him, then kissed her again, the kiss more passionate this time. Reluctantly, she pushed him away. 'Go, or you'll be turning up to work in your best suit.'

'Would it matter?'

'Go! I'll see you tomorrow night.'

'That's far too long. OK, I'm going,' he added as she pointed at the door. He kissed her again and her resolve almost melted away. Almost, but not quite. She needed to be alone now. To think about the day. As she heard the door close and the engine of Alec's car as he drove away, she stood still in the middle of her living-room floor and thought about it. Would she say no, if Harry asked her to marry him?

Yes, she was pretty sure she would, though the comfort she derived from his solid, reliable presence sometimes made her wonder. If he should pounce at a weak moment . . . She laughed, the thought of Harry pouncing amusing her. He'd need his son, Patrick, to prompt him, and he'd probably still mistime it.

Alec on the other hand . . . She loved him, certainly, but did she love him enough? Frankly, at that moment, Naomi really didn't know.

One

Constable Andrews was suffering from the heat. August had begun with heavy rain and days cold enough to feel like October. Then, the second week had begun and all had changed. The past nine days had produced heat enough to melt the tarmac and have the local authority mumbling about a hosepipe ban.

Andrews was patrolling in shirtsleeves. Regulations supported the wearing of a stab vest at all times, but Andrews, after suffering his for the past week, had succumbed to temptation and left it back in the patrol room. Even stripped down to basics, his white shirt wilted and sweat ran from the back of his neck, trickling down his spine and soaking the waistband of his trousers. His slow march had taken him from the promenade and down the high street and he was just looking forward to a quick chat with Molly at the café, before he turned back towards the seafront and the sea breezes once again, when he noticed the car. Quite what attracted him, he wasn't certain. The black Ford Granada prowled along the high street, driver searching for a parking space large enough to accommodate him. Five men could be glimpsed inside.

Air conditioning, lucky sods, Andrews thought, noting the closed windows. The driver seemed to have given up on his search for a parking spot and accelerated into a side road opposite to where Andrews was standing.

The police constable watched as the front-seat passenger and those from the rear got out, straightening themselves up and glancing around as though to get their bearings. They were dressed casually in jeans and T-shirts – one in a faded pair of red shorts. Three looked younger, in their twenties. The older man carried a dark-blue holdall with a Nike motif, white against the dark background. The driver stayed put,

5

engine running, heat haze from the exhaust blurring across the number plate.

Andrews frowned. This didn't look right. Nothing wrong with five men sharing a big car, of course, or a friend dropping others off for a quick errand – and the air conditioning would need the engine running, he supposed. But Andrews didn't think that was it. He keyed his radio and slipped back into the shadow of a fruit-shop awning, watching as the men came back on to the main road and turned left, walking purposefully now, heading past Andrews on the other side of the road.

'Can you give me a PNC check,' he asked control. 'Ford Granada, black, registration . . .' He listened, keeping the men in sight. Moments later, he was hearing the report of a stolen car. Keeping in the shadows and the men in view, Andrews prepared to follow.

Inside the bank, Naomi relaxed in the chill of the air conditioning. It was cold enough to raise the hairs on her arms and send a sudden shiver down her damp spine. She wore a bright-blue summer dress, short and fitted. It set off dark hair that had been allowed to grow since winter and a figure, newly honed from the last several months of gym workouts.

The boy behind her slouched in baggy jeans. His one concession to the weather was the fact that his black T-shirt, emblazoned with a Celtic dragon, had short sleeves, instead of the usual long, covering-the-hands style that was his regular out-of-school wear. He clutched a skateboard in a grubby fist, a permanent fixture through the summer months when the bright weather had dragged even Patrick out from his computer games and away from his drawings.

'The queue's moving,' Harry told Naomi. Patrick's father took her arm gently and eased her forward. Napoleon, Naomi's glossy black guide dog, huffed reluctantly to his feet.

She dropped her hand to stroke the dog's ears. 'Poor old boy,' she said. 'Just find a cool spot and we make you move.' He wriggled against her, beating his tail heavily, but rather half-heartedly, against her leg. They had already agreed that after the bank they'd head inland to Morton Park, with its

6

massive lake and old shade trees – and skateboard run. Take a picnic and spend the rest of the day being utterly lazy.

Harry was at the start of his annual holiday. He and Patrick planned to go away for a few days later in the week, taking Mari, Patrick's grandmother, with them to visit relatives in the Lakes. But today nothing important was arranged and Harry, as he had confided to Naomi earlier, felt guiltily content, as though he were playing truant from his job.

'Is it usually this busy on a Monday?' Harry asked.

'Um, can be. How many tills have they got open?'

'Two,' Harry told her. 'Out of five.'

She smiled at his disapproval. 'Never mind, we're moving now and at least it's cool in here. I've just got some stuff to pay in, shouldn't take any time at all once we've got to the counter.'

'Listen to this track, Nomi,' Patrick said. He'd brought his Walkman, another part of his summer uniform. He detached one small black plug from his ear and lodged it precariously into Naomi's. She reached up to adjust it, then smiled. 'Chili Peppers,' she said.

'Yeah. The cover version of this was crap.'

'Language, Patrick,' Harry said sententiously.

'I only said . . . OK. Good, though, isn't it?'

'Is er . . . is that the track I kind of like?' Harry offered.

'Yeah, it's . . .' But whatever Patrick had been about to say was drowned out by a roar of sound. A sharp crack and then a blast followed by screaming and a falling, like a shower heavier than rain, as plaster from the ceiling cracked and hit the floor.

'Nobody move and no one's going to get hurt. Understand me? Now, on the floor. I said, on the floor.'

'Harry? What—?'

'We're being robbed,' Harry told her. He sounded so affronted she almost laughed despite the fear that gripped her.

'Harry, I figured that one . . .'

'Dad, Naomi, just get on the floor, will you?'

She felt Patrick tugging at her skirt and dropped down beside him, good sense finally kicking in. 'Napoleon, come here.' She pulled the dog close and reached both arms around

7

him, holding him tight. He whined softly, but seemed otherwise remarkably unconcerned, and Naomi marvelled, not for the first time, at the equilibrium of her sleek-coated friend.

A woman continued to scream. Not a scream of pain, but a repeated hysterical squealing, regular and oddly controlled. Like a car alarm, Naomi found herself thinking, and just as irritating. Others could be heard, crying, whispering, trying to soothe.

'I said, shut the fuck up.' The man's voice again, closer this time.

'She's scared. What do you expect?' The woman's reply was firm and cool.

'I expect her to shut up.' This time the voice was level with them and the clump of feet near enough for Naomi to edge back instinctively at their passing.

'In the bag. Now. I said, in the bag.'

'How many are there?' Naomi whispered.

'Four, all armed,' Harry told her. 'Faces covered with those SAS-type balaclavas. God,' he added, 'I wish she'd shut up.'

Naomi had already tuned the woman out. Training had taken over. Training and experience of the twelve years she'd been a serving officer. Ex DI Naomi Blake was focussed on the voices over at the counter. The man in charge, calling the shots, his voice the slightest bit muffled from the mask, but clear and authoritative for all that. Barking his commands and expecting them to be obeyed. A new voice, softer, more uncertain, echoing his master's orders. Must be at the second window, she thought. No sound from the other two men, or at least nothing she could discern above the woman's squeals and the urgent murmur of other voices all around her.

'Where are the others?'

'Near the door,' Patrick told her. 'They've not moved since they came in.'

'Just hold on,' she told him. 'They'll be out of here in no time. Try to remember as much as you can. OK?'

'Hey you. Shut your mouth or I'll shut it for you.'

Startled, Naomi realized from the sudden tension in Harry's body that the man was talking to her. And just as suddenly, she knew that his was a familiar voice. She'd heard it before.

8

Then, 'What the fuck?'

Sirens heard from outside on High Street. One, two, three, maybe four cars, she counted, trying to differentiate between them, screeching to a halt and doors slamming hard.

'Police!' a different voice shouted from over near the doors.

'Damn!' Naomi cursed softly.

'Isn't that a good thing?' Harry questioned.

'No, Dad, I don't think it is,' Patrick told him heavily. 'We're in here with four armed men and the police are blocking their one way out. Personally I think that's a crap thing.'

Naomi closed her eyes and exhaled slowly, trying to calm the sudden attack of nerves that pounded at the pit of her already knotted stomach.

'How many people in the bank?' she asked quietly, her words almost drowned by the sirens.

'About a dozen, I guess,' Harry told her. 'Then there's the counter staff and whoever—'

'Hostages.' Patrick filled in what Naomi was thinking. 'They've got themselves hostages, haven't they, Nomi?'

She nodded slowly, not feeling able to confirm Patrick's words aloud.

Two

Outside the bank, back-up had arrived and Andrews found himself the centre of attention.

'There were four of them got out of the car,' he explained. The driver must have cut loose when he heard the sirens. I didn't see him go,' he shrugged uncomfortably. 'I couldn't be everywhere. Anyway, I called in with the index number and control told me the car was stolen. So I kept them in sight and kept the commentary going. They went into the bank, paused just inside the double doors there, pulled on masks and took weapons from the bag.'

'What kind of weapons?' Sergeant Peel, the most senior officer present, asked him.

'Two shotguns, one a sawn-off. And I think two sidearms, I couldn't see enough to say for certain.'

'Descriptions?'

'Two white males, one in his forties, thinning hair. Light-blue T-shirt and faded jeans. The second was younger, early twenties, I'd say. Fair hair, white shirt, short-sleeved blue denim shirt and jeans. He looked jumpy; at one point I thought he'd clocked me but . . . Other two, one black, one Asian male. Both in their mid to late twenties.'

'No one you recognized?' Andrews had been pacing the streets of Ingham for a lot of years.

Andrews shook his head. 'Not local,' he said. 'But the descriptions and MO fit what we've had so far.'

Peel nodded briefly, then turned as a dark-blue Mondeo pulled up beside him. There'd been four similar robberies in the past month, the difference being, *they'd* been successful and the thieves had been in and out within minutes. Not like this.

10

Looking at the set of Peel's shoulders and thinking about the people now trapped in the bank, Andrews half wished he'd never even been there. It could have been done and dusted by now. Another robbery, the bank a little lighter on its take and a few shaken people to comfort and maybe arrange some counselling for. Now, because he, Andrews, had been on the ball, been doing his job, there were people inside that bank with four armed men.

The Mondeo door opened and two CID officers got out. DI Alec Friedman and DCI Dick Travers.

Travers spoke briefly to Peel and then came straight across to Andrews. He patted him briefly on the arm. 'Good observation,' he said. 'Now, talk to me.'

Friedman stayed where he was, staring at the entrance to the bank. 'Any movement from inside?' Andrews heard him say.

'Nothing, sir,' someone told him. Andrews glanced at his watch. It seemed like forever, but less than fifteen minutes had passed since he had first noticed the car.

'Control said a shot had been fired.' Alec Friedman fired the question towards Andrews without looking his way.

'That's right, sir. Single shot. I heard screaming, then the outer doors were slammed shut.' He came over to where Alec stood and pointed. 'There's two sets of double doors. The inner ones are automatic. The old doors, see, they're generally left wide open. There's an ATM just inside and a camera facing it.'

'So, there's a chance our men will have been caught on film before they masked up?'

Andrews nodded. 'It's possible, but they were fast and kept their heads down. My bet is we'll get a lovely picture of someone's bald patch. Not that we can get to the camera anyway.'

'Any idea how many hostages they have?' This from Travers.

'No way of knowing. It's a Monday, not the busiest, and it's still early, before the lunchtime queues.'

'Negotiators are on their way,' Travers said. 'Meantime, we sit tight.' He glanced across at Andrews. 'We have to assume they know we're here?'

Andrews nodded and cast a sideways glance at two of his fellow officers, standing sheepishly beside their patrol car.

'Control said no sirens,' he told Travers. 'Seems someone didn't get that particular instruction.'

Travers followed his gaze and then nodded. 'No point crying over it,' he said brusquely. 'We'll hold the inquest later. Meantime . . .'

'Back behind the vehicles,' Alec Friedman ordered.

'What?'

'Look. The doors.'

He watched officers beat a hasty retreat, finding what cover they could and dragging the odd member of the public back with them.

The doors cranked slowly open and a figure stepped out. He held a young woman in front of him. She wore the bank's blue uniform and she was crying noisily. The man – the older one whom Andrews had identified as leader, had his hand beneath her chin, gripping her face tightly enough for her features to deform. In his right hand he held a gun.

Alec felt in his pocket and extracted his mobile phone. He had no idea if he'd get a decent picture at this distance, but he felt he had to give it a go. He watched as the man slowly raised the handgun. From the shape, it looked like an automatic rather than a revolver.

Replica or real? Alec wouldn't have placed bets.

Moving as unobtrusively as possible, he began to take his pictures, watching all the time, lowering the phone abruptly as the man looked his way.

'Alec, for God's sake.' Travers grabbed him and pulled him down. Alec shrugged him off, impatient, but also shaken. Just for that instant, before Travers had yanked him away, Alec had been staring straight down the barrel of the gun and, even from that distance, street and pavement and bank steps in between, it was enough to freeze him up inside.

'You stay fucking well away,' the man was shouting. 'We've got hostages in here and, personally, I don't give a damn if we have to lose a few, just to prove a point. You get me?'

'We get you,' Travers shouted back. 'But you're not doing

12

yourself any favours. Put the gun down, let the woman go, we can—'

'Look, copper. Why don't you shut the fuck up?' He shifted position, turning himself and the woman to face Travers. Then he moved again, the gun now at the young woman's head. Her cries turned to whimpers, animal-like and desperate.

'Christ!' Travers said. 'Where the fuck's my ARV?'

Personally, Alec thought this would be a lousy time for an armed response vehicle to arrive, but he did not get the chance to say so. The shot, thunderous at such close range, its crack amplified by the buildings, had them all on their bellies.

Alec heard the bank doors slam.

The woman? Was she dead?

As the sound of the shot died, her keening was the only sound left in the narrow road. Alec lifted his head and peered over the bonnet of the car. She knelt on the pavement, still dangerously close to the now closed doors, in the line of fire from the windows above.

He heard Andrews shouting to her, telling her to run towards the cars, but Alec could see that she couldn't move. That moment of frozen-in-the-headlights fear he had experienced when the gun had pointed straight at *him* flooded back and he knew she'd stay there until someone went to bring her in.

'Bugger!'

He rounded the front of the car before Travers could stop him – or he himself had the time to think. He ran, bent almost double, to where she crouched, then grabbed her by the shoulders and pulled her on to her feet. Near as he could tell, she was physically unharmed, but her body was rigid with fear and she was beyond listening or even hearing him. Beneath her, the ground was wet and she seemed to notice this as he pulled her away, clutching at her damp skirt and wailing ever more loudly as though her shame at having pissed herself was almost the worst thing.

'Move!' Alec told her. 'We've got to move.'

He realized that he was shouting at her. The calm, reassuring presence he would have liked to project, lost, somewhere, in the knowledge that in all probability they had a gun pointing at their heads.

13

Somehow, he struggled halfway across the street. Andrews met him, grabbing the woman. They bundled her between them into the partial shelter of the blue Mondeo. She lay on the ground, moaning softly. Alec could hear Travers summoning an ambulance.

Still crouching, he opened the back door of the car and dragged a plaid travel rug off the back seat. He kept it there for when Naomi's dog travelled in his car. It smelt of Napoleon, was sprinkled with shiny black Labrador hairs, but he didn't think the woman was in a fit state to notice and her skin was icily cold despite the heat.

Travers scooted up beside him. 'She all right?'

'Shock. Other than that, I think so.'

'What the bloody hell were you playing at? No, never mind. Ah, finally.' A police car appeared around the slight bend in the road and Alec recognized the ARV. 'About bloody time.'

Alec glanced at his watch. Twenty-five minutes since Andrews had first called in about the car.

Three

'Do you think she's dead?' Patrick whispered.

'I don't know. He might be bluffing,' Naomi told him.

They kept their voices as low as possible, but in the silent aftermath that followed the shot and then the slamming of the heavy doors, their voices sounded impossibly loud.

'Hush,' Harry warned.

From somewhere to her right, Naomi heard a child whimper and its mother try to calm it. She felt Harry move beside her and his hand reach out to clasp hers. Patrick, absent-mindedly, flicked the wheels on his skateboard. The whirr as it spun grated on her nerves. He stopped the sound almost as soon as it began and murmured an apology. *To her?* Naomi wondered absently. Or to the hostage-takers.

The tread of heavy footsteps on the polished wooden floor. They stopped close by.

'Shut up and behave yourselves and you'll be all right,' a voice told them.

'Like that young woman is all right, I suppose?'

Naomi lifted her head and turned in the direction of the new voice.

'Thought I told you to shut up?'

'And if I don't? I suppose you'll shoot me too?'

A low cry drifted from over on her right. Momentarily distracted, Naomi glanced sideways, responding to the sound with her sighted body language as she still so often did.

The heavy footsteps moved away, towards the person who had interrogated him. 'Look, lady, I don't want to shoot you. I don't want to do any frigging thing except get all of us out of here with as little fuss as possible. Now, shut up and stay shut up.'

15

He was dangerously edgy, Naomi thought. Edgy and confused. No way had he expected this or even mentally prepared for the possibility.

'You,' he snapped at someone else. 'Is there a back way out?'

'Yes . . . yes. Into the yard then over the wall. It comes out in Trimball Street.'

'Take a look,' the man demanded. A second set of foot-steps, these lighter and accompanied by a slight squeak like hard rubber soles against the polish.

Trainers, Naomi thought. She wanted to ask Harry or Patrick what they could see, but dare not draw attention. A door opened, then slammed closed. Another beyond that, the sound muffled, then the steps again, but with an urgency to them. The voice was slightly breathless. Muffled. Was he still wearing the ski mask?

'They're out back as well.'

'Shit. You. Help him get something jammed against that back door.'

'I told you this was a stupid idea.' A young voice, this time. Young and scared.

'You didn't have to tag along. I was doing you a bloody favour, so don't frigging well forget it.'

Sounds of something large being dragged across the office floor grated from the rear of the bank.

'Well, no one's going to sneak out without paying,' Patrick commented.

Harry shushed him again.

Naomi stifled the sudden and singularly inappropriate desire to laugh. She bit her tongue, recognizing the reaction for the nervousness it was. She forced herself to breathe deeply, though the air no longer seemed as cool and refreshing as it had been after the outside heat. If anything, it seemed almost painfully cold.

'How many of us are there?' she whispered softly.

'Four of them and about a dozen of us,' Harry told her. 'Including two children, and Patrick, of course.'

'I'm not a kid.'

'Shut up back there.'

16

They fell silent. Naomi squeezed Harry's hand suddenly, selfishly relieved that she was not alone.

Outside, the ambulance had arrived. It glided silently into the street, the crew having been told no sirens and the minimum of fuss. There was a slight incline from the top of High Street down towards the bank, and the driver cut the engine, allowing momentum to take them past the tight-shut doors and, hopefully, out of direct range of shots fired from the windows.

The officers from the armed response vehicle covered the crew as they got out, using the riot shields they kept in the vehicle to give a semblance of protection. Even so, it was a nervous moment. Alec watched as they came around to the side of the car. He still crouched there, supporting the woman now swaddled in the blanket, trying to get her to respond to him. She was a little calmer now, but when she realized she was going to have to leave the cover of the car and walk round to the back of the ambulance, panic set in once again. She clung to Alec, begging him not to let her go. In the end, he had to half lift, half drag her, cowering behind the police officers with their body armour and transparent shields, and bundle her into the back of the ambulance with the paramedic. The driver ran around to the front and scrabbled in, starting the engine and speeding away in a racing start that would have looked good at Le Mans. He had just departed when the second ARV and a van came through the cordon.

'Finally, some proper back-up,' Travers grumbled. 'Right, first priority, we get these people out.' He jerked his head towards the greengrocer's behind. They had herded all civilians into the back room awaiting the arrival of the ambulance and the serial of a dozen men now filling their way cautiously out of the back of the van. Alec glanced across to see who was in command, recognizing the Inspector, Tom Hemmings. He nodded a brief greeting. Hemmings was from Pinsent, a few miles up the coast. Alec wondered who'd be appointed senior investigating officer on this one. *He* was the local man, but Travers might prefer to bring someone else on board, someone with more experience of this type of incident.

'Hemmings,' Dick Travers noted with dissatisfaction. 'Arrogant bastard.'

Alec smiled. 'But he gets the job done.'

'Keep him on a tight rein,' Travers instructed.

Alec glanced at him, questioning.

'I'll have to clear it with the super, but as far as I'm concerned, you're in charge. Small-time heroics, I can live with.'

Well, Alec thought, that answered that one. Alec Friedman was SIO until someone argued otherwise. He wasn't sure if he should be pleased at Travers' decision and the trust it showed, or annoyed that it meant breaking tonight's date with Naomi. He decided that the two emotions were not mutually exclusive and settled on both.

Hemmings had ushered his crew into the greengrocer's. It was, Alec noted, something of a tight squeeze. Hemmings then dropped down beside Alec and DCI Travers. He nodded briefly when Travers informed him of Alec's seniority.

'OK,' Alec said, feeling that he should do something to deserve his new role. 'Let's get on.'

Four

A lec glanced at his watch. It was eleven o'clock, an hour, give or take, since Andrews had first reported this incident. Everyone was in position and it was time to make the next move.

The two armed response units had moved back, reinforcing the cordon, their estate cars pulled diagonally across the street. Rifle officers had been positioned on the flat roof of the King's Head pub, allowing a clear view of the rear of the bank. Two others had been positioned in upper rooms facing on to the front of the building. One in the greengrocer's, which had been taken over as the central control room, and the other two doors down in an attic flat, the residents having been hurriedly evacuated. A second incident room had been set up in the school hall – PC Andrews being put in charge of that one. He was well known in the locality and Alec felt he needed someone familiar to oversee the interviews of potential witnesses and to calm those who'd been so rudely turfed out of their homes. Fortunately, High Street was mostly small shops, many with the proprietors still living over the premises. Those flats that were let out were largely empty, people already having left for work before the robbery. They'd need dealing with, but not until late in the afternoon, when they'd arrive home to find their street blocked off.

Of course, it could be all over by then, Alec thought hopefully.

Then dismissed the thought. This situation was unlikely to enjoy a swift resolution.

Travers had left, gone to make his report to the superintendent. Hostage negotiators were on their way, a team of two, only one of whom Alec knew, and the undermanager had just been escorted through the roadblock, clutching plans of the bank and work rosters. At least they would then know who'd been on duty that morning. To complete the picture, Hemmings had just told him that the local press had arrived. A reporter along with a photographer.

'Says he knows you. Spotted your car, so he knows you're here.' Hemmings grinned.

'Let me guess,' Alec said. 'Simon Emmett?'

Hemmings jerked both thumbs upward in a congratulatory gesture. 'Give the man a peanut. Likely to be trouble?'

Alec shook his head. Simon was OK; it was the rest he was worried about. And they'd come. Alec knew that. It was just a question of how quickly.

'I've got four of my lot either end,' Hemmings told him. 'Then there's the ARVs ten yards in. Anyone stupid enough to break the cordon, they can bloody well get themselves shot.' He glanced round as the door opened. 'Who's this then?'

'Mr George Tebbutt. Undermanager,' Alec told him. He advanced and shook the newcomer's hand. Tebbutt's palm was damp.

'Thank you for coming so quickly,' Alec told him. 'You've been told what happened?'

Tebbutt nodded. Alec led him over to the table – this was normally the dining room in the upstairs flat – and sat him down. Hemmings followed.

'I need to know,' Alec told him, 'who was working today. How they're likely to react to this situation and as much information as possible about the layout of the bank. We want to work out where the hostages are likely to be held.'

'Hostages,' Tebbutt said. He seemed awed by the word. He stared at Alec, then shook himself. 'They told me that a member of the female staff has been released?'

'A Maria Childs. Yes.'

'She's all right?'

'Very shocked. They're checking her out at the hospital, but that's just procedure. I expect she'll be home later today.'

'Her family know?'

'Her husband was to meet her at the hospital.'

'Was she able to tell you what happened?'

'When she's feeling a bit more like it, we'll get a statement from her. A police liaison officer has been assigned,' Alec told him. 'She was very shaken.'

Tebbutt nodded. 'I should have been in later today,' he said, 'but I had an appointment elsewhere.' He seemed sobered by the thought.

Hemmings shifted impatiently. 'If we could have that information, sir.'

'Of course, of course.' Tebbutt pulled himself together. He produced a sheet of paper with five names written on it. 'I'm sorry, the writing's a bit shaky. I did it in the car when I was being brought over.' He pointed to Maria Childs' name. 'You don't need to know about her, of course. He glanced up at Alec. 'Did you know she was pregnant?'

Alec shook his head.

'They only found out on Friday. Everyone was so delighted. She and Mick have been married five years, trying for nearly as long. I hope it's going to be . . .'

Silently, Alec swore. That explained her hysteria. She had said nothing and it hadn't crossed his mind to ask. He made a note to mention it when he called the hospital.

'Then there's Mr Machin. Brian, he's the manager. He's calmness itself, most of the time. Of course, this isn't most of the time.'

'Quite.' Alec agreed.

'The other three are customer advisors. There's Megan James, Tim Barron and Audrey Shields. Megan and Tim should be fine. Young but sensible. They'll keep their heads down and say as little as possible. That's what they've been told to do. Audrey's coming up for retirement and her health hasn't been so good.'

'What's wrong with her?' Hemmings wanted to know.

'Her heart. Angina, I believe. She cut down to part-time hours a year ago. She's been with us . . . forever.'

'And how is she likely to react?'

Tebbutt shook his head. 'She's a sensible woman. The sort you can rely upon in the usual sort of crisis.'

But, Alec filled in for him, this isn't the usual sort of crisis. 'You mention training,' he said.

'We have regular orientation sessions. What to do in the event of a robbery, that sort of thing. We've got a video which is supposed to show the kind of scenario that might happen.'

'And your staff are told to do what?'

'Oh, cooperate,' Tebbutt said. 'We don't want anyone hurt. Give them the money. If it's feasible, put a dye stick in the bag, and observe as many details as possible. Then raise the alarm as soon as it's safe to do so.'

'Any instruction on what to do if you're a hostage?' Hemmings asked.

Tebbutt shook his head. 'General instructions to stay calm and not to provoke, but nothing specific. I mean, robberies happen, but something like this, it's pretty rare. We weren't prepared for it. Not at all.'

Alec didn't think the robbers had been prepared for it either.

He called a PC over to the table. 'Go with this officer, Mr Tebbutt. See if you can flesh out your descriptions of your colleagues and if you could give us some contact details for their families? And the plans for the building. If you could fill in positions of cupboards, desks, that sort of thing. As much detail as you can manage.'

Tebbutt got to his feet, grateful to have something to do. Hemmings pulled the list towards him, looking at the notes Alec had made.

'So,' he said. 'We've got one potential miscarriage and a possible heart attack. That's so far. Nice tally.'

Alec nodded. A uniformed officer came and told him that the hostage negotiators had arrived.

'Good. Bring them up.'

'Better be over by the bloody weekend,' Hemmings declared.

'Why? Is there a match on?'

'Too right.'

Alec smiled. 'I'll be sure the negotiators mention that when they call,' he said.

Five

The bank phones had begun to ring a number of times in the past hour and the older man, who seemed to be in charge, had finally ordered they be taken off the hook. It was therefore a shock when a ring tone, piercing in the near silence, sounded from the small office off to the side of the main reception area. The manager's phone, Naomi guessed. He probably had a direct line.

The reaction was immediate.

'What the hell?' she heard the leader shout. 'I thought I told you . . .'

'We did, we saw to the phones. We musta just missed that one.'

The silence, which had been dense before, thickened palpably.

The ringing stopped and the answerphone cut in, the message cheerful and friendly. 'I'm away from my desk just now, but if you'd leave your name and number, I'll get right back to you.'

The tone signalled the caller to begin and a woman's voice came on the line. 'My name is Sarah and I'm an incident manager for the Pinsent and Area Constabulary. I'd like to talk to someone in charge, see if we can't sort this out?' There was a pause, a brief silence, then the voice again. 'Hello, can you hear me in there?'

'Incident manager?' Patrick whispered.

Naomi smiled, wryly. 'It apparently sounds less threatening than negotiator.'

'Who says?'

'Probably some bright spark of a sociologist,' Harry grumbled.

Naomi smiled. 'Hush,' she warned.

The message ended, the phone hanging up as the tape ran out. Almost immediately it began to ring again, this time the caller hanging up as soon as the message cut in and redialling so that its piercing jangle sounded yet again. The fifth time got a response.

Naomi could hear the sound of the wire being ripped from its connection and the phone hurled to the floor.

'Oh,' Patrick breathed. 'That's bad, isn't it? That's very bad.'

Naomi nodded. Right from the start, she had sensed that this man was dangerously unstable; so far he had done nothing for her to revise that view. It seemed his associates also thought this was a move too far.

'Oh, very clever,' someone said. 'Now what're we going to do?'

'We don't need nothing from them, so shut your face.'

'Don't we? We need to get out of here, for starters. How we going to talk our way out when you've smashed up the last phone?'

'Thought you told me you didn't know about that one.'

'I was being sensible. Keeping our options open. Some of us round here actually have half a fucking brain!'

There was a scuffling sound as the older man turned and then a yelp and a thud. A collective indrawn breath.

'What happened?' Naomi demanded.

'Big guy in charge hit skinny guy,' Patrick told her. 'I think he broke his nose.'

One of the children had begun to cry and her mother tried to quiet her. Her sobs alerted the baby, who, so far, had slept through the entire incident. It now began to wail, its yells insistent and hungry.

'For goodness' sake, feed the poor little mite!' The woman who had spoken up before, Naomi thought.

'Mummy, I want a pee,' this from the other little girl.

'Hush, baby, you'll have to wait a minute.'

'I can't wait, mummy. I need to go now.'

'You can't, baby,' the mother's voice edging on hysterical.

'But mummy . . .'

24

'Oh, for goodness' sake!' Naomi heard someone get to their feet. 'I'll take you, sweetheart. Come along.'

'And what the fuck do you think you're doing?'

'The child needs the toilet. Do you want her to wet herself?'

'You are asking for it, old woman.'

'Right now, all I am asking for is for a shred of decency. I'm sure even you can manage that.'

The mother had stepped over the edge into full-blown hysteria now. 'Give me my daughter back. Give her back!'

'Oh, do be quiet, dear. You're frightening the child. Now. Are you going to allow me to take these children to the lavatory or not?'

'I thought it was just this one,' the man sneered.

'You clearly know nothing about children,' she told him tartly. 'They'll declare on oath they don't need to go, then wait until you get back to decide otherwise.'

Patrick laughed, then turned it into a diplomatic cough. 'She's cool,' he said.

'She's bloody dangerous too,' Naomi breathed. She could only guess at what the stand-off looked like. This woman, holding the wriggling, pleading child by the hand while the mother reached for her, too scared to do more than whimper and sob uncontrollably.

'Take them, then,' the man said. Heavy footsteps and then a shriek told her that he must have grabbed the second child from her mother's reach and handed her over to the woman.

'Thank you,' she said, seemingly oblivious to the hysterical wailing of the mother. 'What are your names, sweethearts? I'm Dorothy. Just like in the Wizard of Oz. Have you seen that film? No? Oh, you must get your mummy to show it to you when you get home. I'm sure it's available on video.'

'We've got a DVD.'

'Have you now? My son has one of those.'

'Don't waste time, old woman. You. Go with them. And you, stop that bloody noise, and you,' this apparently to the one he'd hit. 'Get yourself cleaned up and next time I tell you to do something, you fucking do it!'

Naomi listened to the receding footsteps of Dorothy and the two little girls. Her footfalls firm and steady, the little feet

25

pattering alongside. The injured man stumbling to his feet and trailing after them with another gunman in tow. Beside her, Napoleon whined pathetically, upset by the raised voices and the atmosphere of conflict. He was too well trained to react overmuch, but she knew he hated it. Napoleon was a friendly soul and liked the peaceful life. She stroked his head and fondled his ears to calm him, thinking that kids weren't the only people who'd find it hard waiting.

She was aware that the big man, as Patrick had called him, was speaking once again. That the baby's yells had ceased and the girls' mother's subsided into despairing little chokes that wrenched at the emotions and frayed the nerves.

'That's better,' the man said. 'Now let's all keep the noise down. Shut up unless you're spoken to, do as you're told and we'll all get on just fine.'

She could hear the forced control in his tone. That extra effort to seem reasonable, when the underlying note told her that, beneath the facade, he was neither reasonable nor controlled.

Six

'Is that normal behaviour?' Alec wanted to know.

Hemmings barked a laugh. 'You're supposing armed robbers are capable of such.'

'It's not entirely unusual,' Sam Hargreaves said. He was the more senior of the two negotiators, both in terms of rank and experience. 'Question is, have they left themselves with a fall-back position.'

'How so?' Alec queried.

'Well, most hostage-takers will go through a separation phase. A period of time during which they want nothing to do with authority. Refuse all overtures. Then they think it over and realize that they have to talk in order to get concessions. That, in one sense, they are as much prisoners of their situation as their hostages are. It's not unusual, for example, for them to temporarily disable the telephones, but nine times out of ten they'll keep their options open. We have to hope that all they've done is unplug the other phones. The manager's line is now well and truly dead.'

Alec considered. 'Mobiles?' he asked.

'Could be extremely risky. It directs attention at particular individuals. We don't want to do that at this stage. We could offer the gang a mobile phone later on and, of course, we can then monitor any other calls they make. You'd have to authorize the equipment, of course.'

Alec nodded. 'I'll get straight on to it. So, our next move is?'

'We wait them out. We're only, what, two hours in. Meantime,' he added, turning to Bill Priestly, the commander of the armed response unit, 'ensure your people are kept back from the sightlines and keep the streets clear.'

'Already done,' Priestly told him. 'We could do with more

uniform on the cordons though. We've got the usual mix of rubbernecks and journalists. Only a handful of them at the moment, but news will travel.'

'We'll see what we can do. Do you recommend moving the cordon back?'

Priestly considered, then shook his head. 'Moving back at the Blackberry Lane end would interfere with traffic flow. We'd be spilling out on to the main road come rush hour, and the other end, Colbert Street takes a sharp right-hand bend just at that point. There's that nasty staggered junction. Last thing we want is an RTA. Plus, we'd then be forced to cover the side road, that little alleyway that backs on to the industrial estate . . .?'

'The Cut,' Alec provided. It was short and single-track but frequently used as a rat run. There'd been campaigns to make it a pedestrian zone for as long as Alec could remember.

'The Cut, yes. That would, potentially, add to our crowd-control problems.'

'So,' Alec paused thoughtfully. 'We're back to trying to second guess their next move.'

Sarah crossed to another table and collected the plans that George Tebbutt, the undermanager, had been helping to construct. They were essentially copies of the blueprints, with additions made in multicoloured pen, showing the position of desks and phones. 'I've been looking these over,' she said. 'We don't know how many hostages they have, but Sam and I are reckoning on between ten and fifteen.'

'Why?' Alec wanted to know. He'd not met Sarah Milton before. At first sight, she looked too young to be taking on such a role. He was used to Sam Hargreaves, having worked with him before, and Sam's partners had usually looked like him. Sam's blond hair was now fading to grey and thinning on top and he was somewhat portly about the midriff, while the rest of his body seemed to have been thinned out and consumed by nervous energy. Sarah Milton was perhaps thirty at most, with a slender figure and black skin that glowed with health. She looked like an ad for a local gym, but Alec had noted the way Sam Hargreaves deferred on several occasions to his far younger colleague and figured there was a great deal

28

more going on in Sarah Milton's head than the exterior might advertise.

'We know how many staff were on duty, so that gives us a count of four, one having been released. Mr Tebbutt was able to give us a rough figure for the normal customer ratio on a Monday morning, so our estimate is a low of four, assuming the bank was empty, and an upper limit of around fifteen, given the usual Monday-morning trade.'

She paused and pointed at the plan. 'There are, we believe, four gunmen?' she glanced at Alec for confirmation. 'Sergeant Priestly and I had a chat earlier and we decided it's likely they'd keep one watching the back of the bank and another keeping an eye on the street. That leaves two to guard the hostages. Now, even given that the building is not large, that's still stretching their resources if they keep the hostages in the main reception area. To watch the rear of the building, you'd need someone here, in the manager's office, so, physically separated from the other three. A second would need to be here.' She pointed to what showed on the map as a small alcove next to the main door. According to Mr Tebbutt, that gives the only clear view out into the street. All other windows are obscure glass, but this one was broken a while back and there's been a delay getting a match for the glass, so, the top pane is clear. Mr Tebbutt reckons you need to stand on something to see out, but you do get a clear view.'

'Of how much of the street?'

Priestly responded. They'd already tried to work this out. 'You can certainly see the greengrocer's, so, any comings and goings from now on should be through the back way. The two shops on either side are also in clear view, and maybe a little further at a pinch.'

'But not the cordon?'

'No. To get a better view you'd need to get up on to the roof and I doubt they'd do that. No cover to speak of, save a bloody great air vent, for the heating system. If you look out of the window, you can see that.'

'What about the windows on the second storey?' Hemmings wanted to know.

29

'I doubt they'd want to split the team,' Sarah commented, 'but according to Mr Tebbutt the upstairs has been used as a storage area for years and the windows were panelled on the inside for security reasons. If they decide to remove the panels, we'll see them.'

Alec nodded. 'So,' he said, prompting Sarah. 'Control of the hostages is going to be a priority.'

She nodded. 'Here, look, there's a storeroom, on the ground floor, just off the main reception. It's used for stationery, second photocopier, unused chairs, that sort of thing. But, at about ten foot square, you could confine fifteen hostages inside and there's only the one exit. No windows, no other door.'

'Ten by ten is small,' Hemmings said doubtfully.

'I don't think they'd be too worried about the comfort of their prisoners,' Sam Hargreaves put in. 'The gang, if we're reading them right, have found themselves in an unwelcome situation, having saddled themselves with, maybe, fifteen unwanted bodies. At this stage, the hostages will still be depersonalized. Worse than that, they'll be seen as liabilities. This isn't like a kidnapping, where the live victim is your key to getting what you want. These unfortunates will have a nuisance value at best.' He paused. 'You tried to photograph the gunman on the street? I've not had a chance to look yet.'

Alec pulled his mobile from his pocket. 'Sorry,' he apologized. He'd shown Priestly, but then forgotten to bring Sam up to speed on that aspect. 'The images aren't good, but . . .'

Silently, Sam Hargreaves and Sarah Milton scanned through the five shaky, grainy images. They exchanged a look that Alec could not quite interpret.

'Seeing the level of threat exhibited just confirms what we've said.' Sam was sombre.

'But he did let her go,' Hemmings objected.

'In such a fashion as to leave you in no doubt of his intent. He didn't shoot her, no, and that's encouraging. But he did fire his weapon and the shot was random. He gave little thought to where it might go or whom it might hit.'

'Storming the building's a non-starter then.' Hemmings tried to leaven the mood. 'No SAS available, I suppose.'

30

Priestly grinned. 'Nothing big enough for them to abseil off,' he said. 'No, we have to focus on opening some sort of negotiation, getting the most vulnerable out first, like your lady with angina. So, what are your recommendations?' This to Sam and Sarah.

'We have no option but to wait,' Sarah told him. 'As Sam pointed out, it's early days yet, but my guess is they'll try to confine the hostages, make them more manageable a package.'

'I'd concur with that,' Sam agreed. 'The storeroom is the place I'd choose, in their position. It isn't air-conditioned and it's going to be hellishly cramped, which is going to add to both the physical and emotional stress, so we need to persuade them to make a partial release as soon as possible. My feeling is, once they do start talking to us, they'll be open to that. It cuts down the size of their problem. Meantime, the CCTV footage of the earlier robberies would be helpful. Anything that might give us a handle on how to reopen our conversation. Until they decide to do that, our hands are tied.'

Seven

Naomi listened, trying to make out what was going on. They had been ordered to be silent and even Dorothy seemed to have taken this to heart this time. The only sounds were the grunts and heavy breathing of the four hostages assigned to shift furniture and stationery from the storeroom. Naomi had gathered this much from the commands given and the whispered commentary Patrick had managed before the big man, as he called him, roared his orders for silence in such a manner none of them could be blinded to the implied threat.

The only other sound in the room was the sound of smashing metal and plastic as, with an almost ritualistic fervour, he systematically battered mobile phones taken from the hostages with the butt of his gun.

'It's done,' someone said.

'About time.'

Naomi heard the heavy steps go past and then pause as he inspected the job done.

'Right,' he said. 'Search them and get them all inside.'

'In there?' Dorothy again, but her protest sounded weaker than before. She was genuinely shocked, Naomi realized.

'Search them? You've already taken their stuff.'

'Do it. Don't bloody argue.'

Harry helped Naomi to her feet and she stood close to him, listening as her fellow prisoners were searched. When it came to her turn, she realized, to her surprise, that the searches were actually quite cursory and that the man who patted her down was very ill at ease.

'What the hell do you think I could hide under this?' she demanded in a fierce whisper. The fitted summer dress left

32

little room for anything but her. To her surprise she got a whispered apology.

'Look, I'm sorry,' he said. 'It wasn't meant to be like this, OK?'

Naomi did not reply, but she made a mental note to listen for that voice and maybe strike up a conversation with its owner. She wondered if they'd removed their masks yet. Even with the now too chill air conditioning, they must be very hot and uncomfortable if not.

Her thoughts were punctuated by the sound of systematic destruction as the main man continued to take out his frustration on their personal effects, and there was something else niggling at her mind as she tried to recall what she had read about the earlier robberies. The big man's voice. It sounded a familiar note somewhere in her memory. As yet, she'd not been able to access what it was. It came from long ago, from a time, she was sure, in her early days as a serving police officer, long before the accident which had taken her sight and ended her career.

Her thoughts were drawn back to the present by the consciousness of Napoleon pressing against her side, his fat tail thumping against her leg as he convinced himself they could now leave this place and do something more fun. God, she thought, it's been hours for him.

'Please,' she said to the man searching her. 'My dog. He really needs to go out.'

'What? What d'you expect me to do about it?' He had a slight accent, Naomi noticed. It reminded her of her friends the Emmetts', the slight Barbadian lilt.

'Please,' she repeated. 'It's not his fault.'

'Oh God,' he breathed, clearly worried about being over-heard. 'Look, I'll see what I can do.' He passed on to Harry. 'Arms up.' Naomi heard a jingle as Harry's keys fell to the floor followed by a handful of coins.

'You OK?' Patrick breathed. He sounded tense.

'I'm fine. You?'

'Yeah.'

Something in his tone caused Naomi to incline her head towards him. 'What?' she whispered.

'Tell you later. They're moving us inside. God, I hate small spaces.'

'You'll be all right.' She took his hand, Napoleon's harness grasped tight in the other. The man who'd searched her came back.

'Give me the dog,' he said. 'I'll give him some water too, yeah?'

Reluctantly, Naomi relinquished her hold on the harness. 'Thanks,' she said, genuinely grateful. 'Look, he's—'

'Quiet, over there. If you're going to see to that bloody dog, do it now. You don't need a conference over it.'

'I like dogs. I'll look out for him,' the man whispered. He took the harness. 'Come on, fella.'

'You can't force us all in there,' Dorothy declared, breaking into their muted conversation. 'It's inhuman.'

'Inhuman, is it? You want to give a good reason why I should care?' He slammed the butt of his gun hard on to the table, the sound of it loud enough to cause them all to jump in renewed shock.

Loud footsteps again and the sharp crack of flesh impacting upon flesh.

'You can't do that!' This from the usually passive Harry.

'Boss, that is well out of order. She's an old woman. We don't beat up on old ladies.'

'She should think herself lucky I used me frigging hand and not the bloody gun,' he retorted angrily.

'Is she all right?' Naomi demanded. She could hear quiet sobbing now, shuffling feet as though people were moving, nervously, to help, and Dorothy's voice, thick and slightly slurred, assuring someone that she would be all right.

'Inside. Now. Anyone else want to argue?'

Napoleon whimpered, not understanding what was going on. Biting her lip in agitation, Naomi reluctantly allowed herself to be ushered with the others into their effective prison cell.

Eight

'I suppose, since we're here, we ought to introduce ourselves.' Surprisingly, it was Harry who spoke up first. 'I'm Harry Jones and this is my son Patrick.'

'Er, hi,' Patrick said.

'Um, Naomi Blake,' Naomi said at Harry's prompting. The bit of her mind that always misbehaved in situations of crisis wondered if there was some sort of etiquette available for hostage introductions.

'Dorothy Peel,' the familiar voice said.

'We know who you are.' This from the mother of the two little girls. 'You're a mad woman.'

'Possibly,' Dorothy accepted with equanimity. 'But, my dear, I've never in my life allowed anyone to intimidate me and I don't feel ready to do so now.'

'We really shouldn't argue amongst ourselves,' Naomi said. 'We're in this together and, whatever our personal opinions might be, we've really all got to pull together.'

'Well said, dear,' Dorothy applauded and Naomi immediately wished the woman had held her tongue. She was thankful when Harry stepped in.

'I overheard your little girls' names,' he said. 'Holly and Clare, isn't it? But I didn't quite catch yours.'

'Sally,' she said. 'Sally Harding. Do you think we're going to get out of here?'

'Of course we are,' Harry soothed. 'The police will have negotiators talking to those men very soon, and we'll all be home tonight. I'm sure of it.'

Naomi wished she could be anything like as certain.

'I'm Fliss Maybury, and this is Alice,' the woman with the

35

baby introduced herself. 'And look, I'm really sorry about this, but she's going to need changing.'

'Did they leave your stuff with you?' Naomi was surprised.

'They took my handbag, and searched the baby bag. The young black man threw the bag in after us. He's the one who took your dog away . . .?' The questioning tone told Naomi that Fliss wasn't sure this was a good thing or not.

'I asked him to look after Napoleon,' she explained. 'He needed to go out and the man said he'd give him some water.'

'We could all do with some water.' Another voice this time.

Naomi turned her head expectantly.

'Paul Hebden. Brigadier. Retired.'

He sounded tired, Naomi thought, and not the least Brigadier-like.

'Mary Parker,' a woman said next, her voice tremulous. She sounded as though she had been crying. 'This is my husband, George.'

'Pleased to meet you, I'm sure,' George Parker said. 'I just wish the circumstances . . .'

'I'm sure we all wish the circumstances were different,' Naomi said gently. 'Is that everyone?'

'Um, no, there's us,' a man told her. 'Brian Machin. I'm the manager here and I just want to say how sorry I am—'

'It's hardly your fault,' Dorothy informed him, making it, Naomi thought, somehow, sound as though it was.

'Right.' He seemed to hesitate as though thinking the same as Naomi, then continued. 'And my staff. There's Audrey Shields, one of our long-servers. Been with us since long before I came on board. And Megan James, one of our younger customer advisors.'

'Good girl, Megan.'

Naomi recognized the voice of the Brigadier.

'And Tim Barron, of course. Our other lady . . . well, we hope she was released earlier.'

The screaming woman, Naomi thought. She recalled the sound of the bank doors opening and then slamming shut and then the sound of a gunshot and the screaming had ceased. 'Do we know what happened to her? Did anyone manage to see anything?' she asked and immediately

36

regretted it. Asking the question forced the others to face the possibility that . . .

'We hope she was released unharmed,' Brian Machin said firmly.

'I really do need to change Alice,' Fliss Maybury interrupted fretfully.

'Well, do it then,' Dorothy told her. 'I'm sure it won't be the first time we've seen a baby changed.'

'Great,' Patrick muttered and Naomi couldn't help but smile. He wasn't big on babies, left the room when her sister's newest arrival had a dirty nappy, but by the time Fliss Maybury had done and the confined space was filled with the smell of soiled baby, lilac-perfumed lotion and the sickly sweetness of the deodorizing nappy bag which, in the confined space, was almost the most nauseating thing, Naomi felt she had some sympathy with his view.

By the time she'd done, the baby was wailing again.

'Hungry?' Dorothy asked.

'Constantly. Um, look, I'm sorry about this. I'll try –' she giggled, embarrassed – 'I'll try not to let anything hang out, so to speak.'

There was a rumble of combined amusement and discomfort from the others.

'I think, my dear, that catching a glimpse of breast, at this precise moment, is the least of our worries,' Dorothy told her, and, for once, Naomi was forced to agree with her.

In the main waiting area of the bank the four men removed their masks. 'Christ, that's a relief,' Alan Harper muttered.

His father glared at him, then turned his attention to Danny Mayo. 'You going to sort that dog out, or what?'

'I'm just thinking the best thing to do. He ought to go out in the yard, but . . .'

'Oh, for God's sake. Improvise.'

Danny shrugged and went off to do as he was bid. He took Napoleon into the toilets first and filled one of the wash bowls with water, finally getting the big black dog to accept a drink, thirst overcoming training that told him this was not the thing to do.

The three remaining men stood looking at each other trying to figure out what came next.

'Is that phone still working?' Ash Dutta asked, nodding towards the handset behind the cashier's desk.

Alan listened to it. 'Yeah.' He made to plug it in.

'Leave the bloody thing alone.'

'Dad, we've got to talk to them. The police will be out there, waiting. They've tried to make contact once, they don't care how long they have to wait. We're the ones stuck in here.'

'You questioning me?'

'Yeah. I am.'

Ted Harper pointed at the bruising that was spreading across the younger man's face from the injured nose. 'You know what happened last time you questioned me.'

'Oh, come off it, Dad. What you going to do, kill me?'

'If I have to. I ain't going back to prison, boy, I'm telling you that for nothing, and I should never have brought you today. Knew you didn't have the stomach for it. Soft, that's what you are, just like your mam.'

Alan looked about to smart-mouth back, but Ash shook his head, the movement almost imperceptible but Alan took note. Reluctantly, he laid the receiver back on the counter. 'What are we going to do with them?' he asked, jerking his head towards the storeroom, then wincing as the pain shot through his head from his broken nose. His voice sounded thick and his nose began to bleed again.

Harper senior gave no answer.

'Ash, drag that table over there and take a gander out of the window. You, boy, give him a hand.'

Alan grimaced. He wiped the blood from his face with the back of his hand and then smeared it on his jeans before coming back round the counter and lifting one end of the heavy table that Ted had been using as an anvil. They tipped what was left of the mobiles and assorted other objects to the floor, then carried it over to the main door, wedging it into the alcove.

'Don't wind him up,' Ash warned. 'He's been off on one since the last job. We both told him, enough was enough, take the money and run. Clear off to Spain or somewhere, like, but

38

he wouldn't have it. It was all, "one more job and Alan's coming in with us on this one". We told him to leave you out of it.'

'Wish he fucking had. He's right, Ashwin, I'm not cut out for this. Bloody near shit myself when he fired that gun.'

Ash frowned. 'He's not done that before,' he agreed. 'He's been getting worse. To start off with, it was a bit of a laugh, like, with a good pot at the end of it. Danny and me, we just wanted some cash to get out of here. Go somewhere. We didn't reckon on all this.'

He climbed on to the table and peered out of the clear pane above the frosted window. 'You reckon they can see me?' he asked anxiously.

Alan thought about it. 'No, wouldn't think so, you're not backlit or nothing. It's all shadow in here.'

'You see owt?' Ted Harper demanded.

'Nothing. Empty street. I can just about see three, four shops opposite, but that's about it.'

'Police?'

'Told you, I don't see anyone. There's not a fly moving out there. Looks like it's another hot one though,' he added. 'You know, Ted, we ought to give them some water. There's no air conditioning in that little room and that old cashier, she didn't look too good. We don't want her dying on us.'

'You think I give a fuck?'

Ash jumped down off the table and strode across to where Ted Harper stood. 'You should,' he told him. 'Ted, we want all our chips intact if we're going to get out of here. Look, we make our demands. We tell 'em we want to keep the money, get a fast car to the airport. Police escort and a pilot to fly us wherever we want to go. We release a couple of the hostages, maybe that old woman or the kids or summat. Just to show willing, like, and then we take others with us, release them when we're safe. I saw this film once . . .'

'God, you talk some bollix,' Ted Harper told him.

'No. I don't. I'm talking sense and you bloody know it.' He reached out and made to shake Ted Harper by the shoulders, then thought better of it and backed away. 'Just you think about it, Ted. You'll see I'm right.'

The tension was interrupted, though not broken by the

39

return of Danny with Napoleon. The dog looked happier, his tail wafting side to side and his muzzle wet from the water Danny had given him.

'Great dog, this,' Danny enthused. 'You know, he's that well trained . . .' He paused, scrutinizing the tableau. Alan standing uneasily by the door, Harper senior and Ash Dutta facing one another, bodies tense and building for a fight. 'Hey,' he said softly. 'Fighting between ourselves ain't going to do any good. We got to sit down and talk about this one. See what our options are, not start beating seven shades . . .'

Ash glared at him, then nodded and backed off. Ted Harper strode away in the direction of the toilets.

'Not looking good,' Danny commented, bending his six-foot frame to fondle Napoleon's ears. He glanced in the direction of the front entrance, then at the closed inner door leading to the lavatory. 'We could walk out now, take our chances . . .'

'They'll have armed police out there,' Alan protested, but he sounded ready to be convinced.

'And leave him in here with them?' Ash objected. 'We'd have a bloody massacre on our hands, way he's acting just now. Anyway, if there's a chance of us getting out of here with something, I want to take it. We need to negotiate, that's all. We've got the money from this job, and the other cash already stashed. Cut four ways, it's still a fair haul.' He paused and glanced uneasily in the direction Ted Harper had taken. 'Cut three ways, be even better,' he suggested.

'You'd try to cut him out? Man, you got to be mad. He'd find us, no matter how far we run.'

'He could have a little accident,' Ash suggested. 'Way he's been waving that gun about, anything could happen.'

'That's my dad you're talking about.' Alan had drawn closer to the other two and was listening, an expression caught somewhere between hope and pure terror frozen on his face.

'Come off it, Al,' Ash Dutta laughed. 'You hate his guts,' he said.

Inside the storeroom, conversation of sorts had resumed. There was nothing else to do and, Naomi thought, you can only behave like a rabbit frozen in the headlights for so long before

40

the brain takes over and forces the body to resume some kind of normal functioning. She sat listening, her head resting against the wall, as the conversations split between the various groups. The two mothers talked about their kids – Fliss's first. The Parkers told anyone that might listen, how they thought everyone should just do as they were told and not antagonize. Their main audience seemed to be the young cashier, Megan James. Her voice, gentle and sympathetic, filtered into Naomi's consciousness without her really listening to the words.

Dorothy Peel had found a kindred spirit in the ageing Brigadier. They seemed to be exchanging war stories. Dorothy had, apparently, been a refugee. And absurdly, given the circumstances, the bank manager, Brian Machin, and his two other cashiers were discussing the production of the next quarterly report.

Well, Naomi supposed. Whatever helped you to cope.

Her own mind was busy with the dilemma of the man's voice. She knew that voice. It had been important to her once upon a time, albeit for a brief while. The memory was archived in her brain. The question was which particular file had she put it in?

'You OK, Naomi?'

Patrick had said little until now.

'I'm OK. You?'

He laughed. 'Bored. Can you believe that? I've been taken hostage and shut in a cupboard and the only thing I can think of is how boring it is.'

'I think boring is probably the best scenario,' Harry told him. 'We could always play a game.'

'I spy, or something,' Patrick teased.

'Yes, well . . .'

'No, Dad, I think it's a good idea. You know any games apart from I spy?'

'I think I know him,' Naomi said. 'Big guy, as you called him.'

'What?' Harry almost squeaked with shock. 'I mean how? Where from?'

'That's the trouble.' Naomi lowered her voice. 'From before. You know.'

'Ah. Well, I suppose that would make sense. But you can't remember more than that?'

41

Naomi shook her head. 'Not yet, but it's in there.'

'Then you'll find it,' Harry told her, squeezing her hand. 'Pity we can't let anyone know when you do. It might be of help.'

'Maybe we can,' Patrick breathed. He shifted position, drawing his knees close up to his chest and taking Naomi's free hand and sliding it just beneath the hem of his baggy skater jeans.

'What?' She could feel the small, squarish bulge beneath his sock. 'Patrick. Bloody hell.'

She pulled her hand away and raised her voice, suddenly anxious that their whispered conversation might have drawn attention. 'Anyone know any games?' she asked.

'Apart from I spy,' Patrick added.

His comment earned him a laugh.

There was a pause in conversation, followed by a string of rather half-hearted suggestions.

Naomi used the rise in noise level to shift around and move closer to Harry.

'Patrick kept his mobile,' she whispered.

'What?'

'Hush,' she smiled. 'It might be very useful, Harry.'

'I knew he shouldn't have had it early.'

Good job he did, Naomi thought. The tiny Panasonic phone, the smallest available, had been a sixteenth-birthday present. Harry, in a moment of weakness, had given in to Patrick's pleading and allowed him to have it a week or so early.

'He took a terrible risk,' Harry whispered. Then 'Charades?' he questioned, in response to a general query. 'Do you think we've room in here for charades? And what about Naomi?'

Beside her, Patrick groaned. Party games were his idea of hell. 'Oh, I can still act out,' she said. 'I'll let Harry and Patrick do my guessing for me.'

Charades, she thought. Lord, but could you get much more absurd? A group of assorted people held captive in a cupboard, playing a party game she heartily detested.

'Alec's never going to believe this,' she said.

'Not sure I believe it myself,' Harry replied. 'I'll go first, shall I? Now, you have to guess, book or film.'

Nine

By three in the afternoon the tapes of the other robberies and preliminary reports had been faxed through. More intelligence was promised, but, as all investigations were still active, files would need to be copied before being released and that could take time.

Alec counted luck on his side that the past two of the five robberies had been on Hemmings' patch and he'd been lead officer in the investigation. Time he had already taken to review everything available, was time Alec could initially save.

The predicted media interest had developed and Alec had assigned extra officers to man the cordons. He had also, in view of the intolerable heat – hottest day yet that summer – sent an officer out to buy up cool boxes, ice and bottled water, small tokens gratefully received by those on the barriers, and even more by the black-clad rifle officers slowly baking on the roof opposite the bank.

Alec wasn't exactly praying for rain, but the odd cloud or two would be handy, he thought, gazing from the window into an intense blue sky.

He tried not to think of the discomfort of the hostages, if Sarah's proposition were correct and they had been confined in that cramped little room.

Behind him, in the incident room, Hemmings called out that he had changed the tape and Alec returned for the next viewing.

Fortunately, the relevant sections had already been lifted from the CCTV tapes, together with the time codes. Some had been worked on, the images cleaned up and digitally enhanced and showed, frame by frame, the robbers entering the bank, each phase of the robbery. Three masked men, blue hold-all, weapons similar to those Andrews had described.

Nothing new.

'The leader is definitely a white male.' Sam Hargreaves was thinking aloud. 'Witness reports suggest at least one, possibly two black males.'

'They said dark-skinned,' Sarah interrupted.

Alec frowned, wondering if this comment had a point or was just an expression of political correctness.

Sarah elaborated. 'It's important because one or both could be Asian. We start assuming a gang of four, two of whom are black, we could be ignoring other options.'

Alec took the point.

'As it happens,' DI Hemmings said heavily, we've looked at both those options and all possible permutations between. Our list of known Asian Armed Robbers, it has to be said, is short.'

'And black armed robbers?'

'A little longer, but not significantly so. They're scarce creatures round here whatever colour they come in. Summer, we get a drugs problem. Comes in with the holidaymakers, diminishes when the season closes. Doesn't go away, of course, but activity reverts to the sixth-form college, the nightclubs and the university, as they call it now.'

Sarah looked puzzled.

'Used to be the polytechnic,' Alec explained.

Hemmings snorted. In his view it had been a second-rate poly and calling it a university had done nothing to improve its status.

'We get the usual run of stolen vehicles, and Alec here had a rash of ram raids about eighteen months ago. Shoplifters we do in the usual sort of quantity you'd expect per capita of population, and we've had a couple of high-profile murders in the area, past year or so. Armed robbery – in fact, firearms offences in general – don't register much on either Pinsent's or Ingham's equivalent of an earthquake monitor.

'I checked. Last armed incident was a fellow with a shotgun, killed himself after his wife left him. That was eight months ago and before that some fool took it into his head to knock off a couple of post offices with a sawn-off, three, four years back. Brought the ceiling down in the second place, panicked so much he shot himself in the foot. And this place' – refer-

44

ring to Ingham – 'is even more virginal. I'm told the ARV crew had to look it up on the map.'

'Count yourselves lucky,' Sam Hargreaves commented. 'Our local unit averages three calls a day.'

Hemmings shook his head. 'I'm being flippant,' he admitted. 'We get our fair share of violence – most of it domestics. Like most places, seventy-odd per cent of our call-outs would be better off dealt with by a social worker.' He shrugged. 'What I'm saying, and I'm sure Alec will agree with me here, is this is not so much unusual as bloody unique, and that factor led us to speculate about outsiders moving in.'

Sarah was shaking her head. 'Not sure that fits with the geographic profile,' she said. She pointed at the screen; the freeze-frame of a big man in ski mask and long-sleeved rugby shirt. 'He knows this area. It's home ground to him. Oh, I'm not saying he hasn't been away, maybe he's not been active here for quite some time, but he's local. All incidents have been in a rough, thirty-mile radius.'

Hemmings produced a Manila folder and riffled through it.

'Ex-residents, convicted for armed robbery, released in the past two years,' he said. He produced a second list. 'Aggravated assault and GBH. Locals released past two years – we're aware of the theory of escalation too, you know, and we've looked at the geographical data.'

Sarah, not in the least bit fazed by Hemmings' tone, scanned the list. 'These are all currently local residents?'

Hemmings nodded. 'We're working through a second list of those who might still have family links, and we've run down the usual suspects who were arrested but not charged. So far, nada.'

Alec's mobile began to ring; the landline, as though taking its cue, pealed out also. Hemmings picked it up and listened. 'I'll be right down.'

Alec was still speaking. Hemmings waited until he'd finished.

'Maria Childs, you know, the woman released this morning? She's feeling well enough to talk. I'm going over.'

'Hold off on that, I need you here.'

'Oh?'

'That was Andrews, they've contacted the families of all those we know to have been inside, got them over at the station.'

'Right you are,' Hemmings nodded. 'I'll put the Childs lady on hold or send someone.'

'Did you ask about the baby?'

'They told me. It's going to be fine. You'd better get off then. I don't envy you this one.'

He turned back to Sarah Milton with an expansive grin. 'Now, young lady, you have any more bright ideas about my robbers, then?'

Alec exchanged a look with Sam Hargreaves, who shrugged. Alec gained the impression that he was quite enjoying the show. Sarah, he noted, was practically bristling. All in all, Alec felt quite glad to be getting away.

There were six people assembled in the interview room, chairs positioned awkwardly about a table that was too small to accommodate them – six, plus an extra one for Constable Andrews and a spare for Alec. The collection of cups testified to them having been there for a while; or to Andrews' attempt to keep them occupied. Alec took a moment to observe through the wired glass panel in the door.

There was an older man he guessed might be husband to Audrey Shields. He held a plastic cup between his hands and stared stoically into its depths. Two couples, parents, he guessed, of the two younger tellers. One of the women was in jeans and an old shirt. It was paint-splattered, as though she'd been decorating and had spared no time to change.

Would you change? Alec asked himself. Would you even think about it?

The man holding her hand wore grey trousers and a white rugby shirt emblazoned with a company logo Alec could not quite make out. Both were dark-haired, faces pale with strain.

The other couple had their backs to him. They sat side by side, but not touching. Together, but apart and careful to keep a good space of air between them even in this most emotional of times.

Divorced? Alec wondered.

The woman had neat, fair hair, dyed, but skilfully so. He was balding. He wore a suit despite the heat.

The final woman sat alone facing the door. Her red hair, pulled back from a white face, looked natural, wayward and wavy. Alec could just make out freckles standing in relief against the pallid skin. She looked too young to be Brian Machin's wife. Machin was pushing fifty. He doubted this woman was more than twenty-five. She saw him looking, fixed him with a stare, the sudden, increased rigidity of her slender frame alerting the others, who, as one, turned towards the door.

Alec opened it and stepped inside.

He was greeted by a wall of questions. 'Any news, what's going on, they've told us almost nothing. How could you let this happen?'

Alec raised his hands in surrender, then waved them into silence. 'I'll tell you everything I know,' he said, 'but you have to be prepared to listen. Questions after?' He glanced around the table from face to tense, expectant face until he had a nod of acknowledgement from each. 'Good,' he said quietly. 'My name is Detective Inspector Alec Friedman and I'm the officer in charge. At just after eleven o'clock this morning there was a raid on the bank on High Street. Four armed men entered. Constable Andrews spotted them going in. He alerted headquarters and what should have happened next was that our people arrived quietly and discreetly to arrest the men as they emerged.'

'So, what went wrong?' The red-haired woman stared at him.

'And you are?' he asked gently.

'Emily Machin. My father is the manager. Why didn't it happen the way it was meant to do?'

'Because,' Alec sighed. He'd thought of many ways to wrap this up, to disguise the truth, knowing what fools it would make them appear when it got out. 'Because a young officer with far more enthusiasm than experience got the call and raced to the scene, sirens blaring and lights flashing. The robbers were alerted, took hostages and shut themselves up inside.'

'You've sacked him, I hope?' This from the suited man.

'Oh, Roger, for goodness' sake, that's not going to help.'

'Incompetence,' he exploded. 'That's what it is. I expect—'

'Please,' the dark-haired man in the logo'd shirt leaned across the table. 'Surely all of that can wait. What's done is done and we need to know what we can do to get our kids out. Your dad too,' he added.

'And my wife,' the lone man spoke.

'Sorry,' the dark man apologized. 'I sort of assumed you were another father.'

'Your wife must be Audrey Shields,' Alec confirmed.

'Yes. I'm Jack. She's not well, you know, this could . . . kill her.' He swallowed hard and then went back to staring into the depths of his cup.

'I know,' Alec told him. 'We've spoken with George Tebbutt, the undermanager. He told us about your wife's condition. We're doing everything we can to bring this to a swift resolution.'

'Which means what, exactly?'

Alec turned his attention back to the suited man. 'Mr . . .?'

'Barron. My son, Timothy, is in that bank.'

My son, Alec noted, not *ours*. 'Mr Barron. I can't reveal our method of operations, I'm sure you understand that. But I will tell you we've got two skilled and experienced negotiators on site and everything is progressing as we'd expect at this stage.' The fact that the hostage-takers were refusing to communicate with anyone, including the negotiators, was something he didn't think they needed to know.

'How can we help?' the other father asked. 'I'm . . . we're Megan's parents. Megan James.'

'What about Maria?' his wife asked. 'Haven't you been able to get hold of her husband? I thought he'd be here. He'll be worried sick when he hears.'

'Maria Childs was released very early on,' Alec told them. She's in hospital, being checked over, but apart from being terribly shocked, she's going to be fine. The baby too,' he added. He saw relief in the woman's eyes. 'Were she and Megan close?'

'Good friends, yes. We were so thrilled when we heard about the baby . . .'

'Has she been able to tell you anything?' Emily Machin wanted to know.

'I've got an officer with her,' Alec side-stepped.

'Then no,' Emily concluded. 'She could tell you nothing.'

'I didn't say that, Miss Machin.'

She scowled, then subsided into stony silence.

He took a deep breath and released it slowly. It was hot in the interview room. Everyone, with the exception of Emily

Machin, looked ready to melt. His collar was damp and rivulets of perspiration ran down his back with embarrassing regularity. He dare not lean back in his chair for fear of leaving a moist imprint on the plastic.

He thought, briefly, of his people manning the cordon. They'd be cursing him despite the provision of ice and water. He'd insisted on them wearing stab vests at all times when they might be exposed. The paramedics they had on standby were more likely to be treating heatstroke than anything related to the raid.

'I know,' he said carefully, 'that working in a bank requires a high level of confidentiality, but we all make reference to work at home, even if only in passing. What we're trying to establish is how many people might have been in the building this morning. Did any of your relatives ever talk about regular customers, for example, or if Monday mornings were particularly busy times?'

There was a silence. These strangers eyed one another as though reluctant to disclose anything lest it made their loved one out to be less than discreet. Megan's mother was the first to break.

'Meg used to talk about an elderly gentleman who came in. He'd been in the army, she said. Always tried to come to her counter. He used to flirt with her, she said.'

'Not in any bad way,' Megan's father added hastily. 'She wasn't worried by it or nothing. Said he was a nice old gent. Lonely, she thought. He never seemed to have anyone with him and she always tried to have a few words.'

'Can you recall a name?'

They looked at one another as though dredging a collective memory.

'Hebden,' the father said finally. 'Like in Hebden Bridge?'

His wife nodded confirmation. 'I'm sure that was it, and I think he was a Brigadier. Yes, he was, because Megan wasn't certain what one of them was.'

'Was it common to have customers who favoured certain cashiers?'

'Customer advisors,' Mr Barron corrected him. 'They do more than count cash, these days.'

'Quite.'

'Audrey did,' her husband said. His voice choked, thick

with tears he tried hard to keep in check. 'She'd been there so long, she'd watched some of their children grow up and open their own accounts. She had a lot of favourites. You couldn't walk down the street without someone talking to her.' He sounded half irritated, half proud of this fact.

'Dorothy Peel,' Emily announced. With a suddenness that focussed everyone's attention. 'She was a regular, Monday morning. Dad used to hide in his office until after she had gone.'

'Did he say why?'

'Audrey got on fine with her,' Mr Shields informed them. 'Said she was a tough old bird, but fine provided you were firm and gave as good as she did.'

Emily smiled wryly. 'Dad's always said he was a manager not a diplomat,' she said. 'He always reckoned he kept Audrey available for that.'

Mr Shields smiled back, a brief moment of lightness passing between them that Alec was reluctant to interrupt. Then the smile faded and Mr Shields moved to look at him.

'You will get her out, won't you?'

'Our aim is to get everyone out, safe and sound,' Alec told him. He looked up as PC Andrews returned with yet more coffee. 'Constable Andrews here will be your point of contact. He'll be asking me for regular updates until this is over. We'll do all we can to keep you in touch with developments.'

Alec left them then after a few more questions. As he closed the door, he could hear Andrews, calm and placating, rock-steady, soothing the rattled nerves and the frayed tempers and suggesting that, at a time like this, they should be a support for one another.

Some hopes of that, Alec thought, seeing the disparate personalities present in that room, though, if anyone could convince them otherwise, it would be Andrews. An outstanding community policeman with absolutely no ambition to be anything else, he had found his niche and filled it to capacity. Alec pitied anyone foolish enough ever to try and prise him out.

Two names then, and neither of them Smith or Jones or anything else as commonplace, so traceable, he hoped. It put the hostage count up to six, so far.

Alec wondered how many more.

Ten

When Alec returned to the incident room above the green-grocer's shop, it was to find Hemmings and Sarah Milton plotting points on a large map that had arrived in his absence.

Blue pins for the robberies, Sarah told him. Red for the location each car had been stolen from, and yellow for the places the cars had been found, burned out.

He could see what they meant about the tight radius. 'All the cars were dumped in rural areas,' he commented. 'Middle of nowhere. Look, two on the edge of Morton Park and the rest in small side roads.'

'Which implies,' Hemmings added, 'that they had someone waiting for them with a second car.'

'Also backs up the idea of local knowledge.'

Alec nodded and pointed at the map. 'I know this place,' he said, indicating the site at which the car had been left after the second robbery. 'It's a single-track lane leading to a hamlet. Even the locals don't use it much. Last time I was out there, it had grass growing through the tarmac.'

'We're pretty sure the driver never entered the bank,' Hemmings said. 'So, either the second car was left some time before, which is risky – it would only take one concerned member of the public to report it and they'd lose their second vehicle—'

Alec shrugged. 'I'd still think it a relatively safe bet,' he contradicted. 'Joe Public is, frankly, pretty unconcerned by anything that doesn't get up and hit them in the face.'

Hemmings grinned. 'My, but we're cynical. Been doing this job a bit too long, Alec? But no, point taken. My bet, though, is that they had a second car *and* a second driver and that, maybe, that second driver is our fifth man in this little caper.'

51

'Why bring in someone else, anyway?' Sam Hargreaves asked. 'I mean, this was no bigger job than the others, was it?'

Hemmings shook his head. 'Quite the opposite, in fact.' He glanced at his watch. 'Quarter to five,' he said, 'and not a move from inside. Sam, surely this isn't healthy?'

'It's within normal parameters,' he said, 'but I'll admit it's bordering on the unusual and the lack of communication, together with the potential violence we've seen both today and on the tapes, does give me cause for concern.'

'So, what's our next move? I'm reluctant to let you stand in the street with a bullhorn, but if that's what it takes, we can kit you up with a vest.' He glanced at Alec as though just recalling that Alec was the boss here.

Alec nodded. They'd discussed this earlier, but Sam had been reluctant. Loudhailers distorted the voice and the message, no matter how hard you tried to avoid that. They were inherently aggressive in both tone and volume. Sam had suggested they wait, fully expecting some first move from the raiders. They had, periodically, tried the phones again, but to no avail. Now it seemed there were few options open. 'If that's what you advise, Sam. To a large extent, we're in your hands here.'

Sam Hargreaves shook his head. 'Wish that were true,' he said, 'but the truth is, we're most definitely in theirs.'

Five o'clock saw Sam Hargreaves fitted with a vest and officers on roof and cordon put on high alert. Sam, equipped with loudhailer, stood alone in the middle of the road. Alec winced as the horn squeaked as soon as he began to speak. He saw him pause and make some adjustment before trying again.

'My name is Sam. You spoke briefly to my associate earlier on today. I'd like to have a chat to whoever's in charge in there. See if we can't sort this out.'

Sam was right, Alec thought. It's very hard to sound calm and reasonable through something that distorts your voice and makes it sound as though you're yelling at the moon – though, all in all, he was doing a reasonable job.

Sam paused, then tried again. 'No one wants this situation. Not you, not us, not the people you're holding in there. There are families who'll be suffering too. Yours and theirs. If you open the door and come out, we'll sit down and talk and see what's best to be done.'

Silence. Not a move in the breathless air. Alec, standing in the shadowed shelter of the grocer's awning, glanced down the street towards the cordons. Quite a crowd had gathered either end. The air was so still that, in the silence that followed Sam's announcement, Alec could hear the sound of camera shutters.

Sam lifted the horn to try again. Then paused. There was movement behind the tiny, clear-glass window on the right-hand side of the door.

Sam tensed, jerked his chin upward just a fraction. Alec looked to where he had indicated. He raised the horn again. 'My name is Sam,' he repeated. 'I'm hoping to speak to—' He was interrupted by the sound of smashing glass. The little window shattered by a hard blow from the inside, fragments of glass spraying outwards, some landing close to the negotiator's feet. Sam Hargreaves took a step back but otherwise stood his ground. Beside him, Alec felt Sarah Milton's increased tension and heard her swiftly indrawn breath.

'We want to talk.' A voice from inside the bank.

'Good,' Sam said approvingly. He took a few steps closer. Far too close, Alec thought. The loudhailer hanging at his side now. 'You can hear me OK?'

'Yeah, I can hear you. We want to strike a deal. We want—'

'Like fuck!' A second voice.

Sam glanced over his shoulder at Alec, then turned his attention back towards the window.

'I don't like this,' Sarah whispered.

'No more do I,' Alec agreed with her. 'Sam!'

Sounds of a scuffle and a crash sounded from inside the bank. They were faint and indistinct, but a moment later the second voice returned. 'I'm giving you three seconds to get your arse off the street before I shoot. One, two . . .'

Sam dived for cover just before he got to three. Alec reached and pulled him into the shadows. Pieces of tarmac and glass followed him as the bullet hit the ground inches from where he had been standing.

'You get my meaning?' the voice shouted.

'We get you,' Alec shouted back.

'Good. Any of you make a move I don't like, I'll shoot again, and next time I won't miss – and let me tell you this, Sam, or whatever your frigging name is, think of storming the building and I'll take it out on the hostages. Remember, Mr Policeman, they're not so lucky as you are. They don't have the option of running away.'

Eleven

S am seemed remarkably relaxed for someone who'd just
been shot at, Alec thought. They had returned to the
upstairs incident room and Alec stood looking down into
the street. From his vantage point, he could see the front
doors of the bank and both cordons, but no one in the bank
could see him from their one little window. Had he had any
doubts about that, he'd have chosen his lookout a little more
carefully.

Hemmings came over and handed him tea. The British
panacea.

'They'll have had nothing to eat since morning,' Hemmings
observed. 'There'll be water available, but there's no guarantee they'll have given the hostages any.'

Alec nodded. He was watching the cordons. There'd been
a flurry of activity following the shot. Reports swiftly made.
Two television vans had arrived during the afternoon, so no
doubt this would be breaking news on a cable channel somewhere.

There'd been a smattering of phone calls, so Andrews had
told him, from relatives who'd heard about the robbery and
thought family members might possibly have been inside the
bank. Since then, follow-up calls had ensured that most of
these missing persons were safe and well and somewhere else.
No doubt there'd be far more such calls as the evening wore
on and people didn't come home, and as news broke that
another shot had been fired.

The phone rang. It was Andrews. He'd located the son and
daughter-in-law of Dorothy Peel and was calling from their
home. They confirmed their mother's habit of sorting out her
banking on a Monday.

Alec introduced himself and explained the situation, confirming what Andrews had already told them.

'Do you want us to come over?' Ian Peel asked. 'Is there anything we can do?'

'I'd rather you didn't,' Alec told him. 'And until we confirm that your mother is definitely in the bank . . .'

'No, quite. I *do* see. PC Andrews said that some of the other relatives have got together. We could, perhaps, be useful?'

He sounded calm and very collected, Alec thought, though he could hear the underlying anxiety. 'Talk to PC Andrews about that,' Alec told him. 'He's in a much better position to judge. Tell me, Mr Peel, how is your mother likely to react in a situation like this?'

To his surprise, Ian Peel laughed. 'Politely but firmly, I would think, Inspector. Just as she's reacted to everything else in her life so far. Myself included.'

'I see,' Alec replied carefully.

Ian Peel took a deep, calming breath. 'Inspector, my mother is a remarkable woman. You needn't worry about her falling apart or getting hysterical. I've never known a moment in her life that she didn't take control of. Neither have I known her be intimidated or back down, whatever the circumstances.' He paused again and said more seriously, 'I don't suppose that's quite what you wanted to hear, is it?'

Silently, Alec agreed. Aloud, he replied, 'At least she won't panic. That's good news. Panic can be a dangerous thing in itself.'

A few further questions were asked and comments exchanged and then Alec rang off.

'Well?' Hemmings demanded.

'According to her son, Dorothy Peel is close kin to Margaret Thatcher in one of her more stubborn moods.'

'Just what we need.' Hemmings groaned.

'Could go one of two ways then.' Sam was more thoughtful. 'The gunman might respect her nerve. See her as an authority figure. Someone he can deal with on equal terms. He might well despise those he intimidates.'

'Might well do so,' Sarah agreed, 'but that doesn't mean he knows how to handle an equal. He could see her as a major threat.'

Sam nodded. 'That was my other possibility,' he said.

Inside the storeroom the heat was unbearable and no one wanted to talk much any more. They'd been taken to the toilet in the mid-afternoon, escorted by the armed men, taken in twos and threes, and they'd been given water. Naomi had heard Napoleon yip happily when he caught sight of her, but had not been allowed near him. The young man who'd spoken to her before had told her not to worry. That he'd keep him safe and, somehow, Naomi had trusted him on this. Since then her mind had been working furiously as to how she could take advantage of his consideration. Then, there'd been that sudden crash and the sound of shouting. They had all speculated as to what it might presage, but silence had been restored in the other room and they had been able to reach no further conclusion.

That had been two hours ago and Naomi's mouth was dry again.

'Mummy, I'm thirsty. I want to go home.'

'We all do, darling. We will soon, I'm sure.'

She sounded anything but sure, Naomi thought. The child fell silent and Naomi knew she wasn't fooled either.

'I wonder if anyone will water the allotment for me,' Harry mused. His allotment, a recent acquisition, was a major source of pleasure.

'I'm sure Billy'll do it for you,' Patrick reassured him. 'You do his when he can't get there.'

Naomi smiled. She sometimes found it hard to believe that Harry and Patrick were father and son, they seemed so opposite, but they were devoted and considerate of each other's peculiarities. Patrick had originally lived with his mother after the divorce. She had remarried a man with two other boys and gone back with him to live in Florida. It hadn't suited Patrick, though he was actually close to his stepfather and half-brothers. It was his mother he couldn't handle.

Naomi had known Harry since childhood. He'd been big brother to her best friend, Helen, and was now somewhere between big brother and alternative romance for her. Much as Patrick liked Alec, she knew he wished that Naomi would dump him in favour of his dad. Regardless of how she might feel about Harry – and Naomi was never totally sure how far her affections might go in the future – the thought of playing stepmum to Patrick was one that Naomi couldn't handle with any seriousness. She saw Patrick pretty much as an equal, despite the difference in age and experience. The two of them had been good friends since they first met some eighteen months before, when the investigation into Helen's death had been so abruptly reopened. Helen, Naomi's best friend, had been murdered nearly twenty years before.

'Was Mari expecting you to call?' Naomi asked. Mari was Harry's mother.

'Yes, but not till later. She knew we were going to Morton Park. She'll see this on the news. I wonder if . . .'

'My husband will realize I was here,' Alice's mother spoke up. 'I had a meeting with Mr Machin here this morning. I was early, as usual. He'll know I'd have been early.'

'My son will put two and two together, eventually,' Dorothy Peel added. 'I'm here nearly every Monday.'

'Our families will be worried sick,' Megan James said. 'You think Maria's OK?'

'I'm sure she is,' Brian Machin told her, his voice full of overly hearty conviction. 'Emily, that's my daughter, she's just come back to live at home. Came back a week ago. Not much of a homecoming, is it?'

'How old is she?' someone asked.

'Twenty-four. It's only until she gets somewhere of her own. She was offered a job here, you see. I've been glad of the company though,' he laughed uncomfortably.

'Divorced or widowed?' Dorothy again. Naomi winced at her lack of tact.

'Oh, widowed. Last year.'

'Same for me,' Dorothy told him. 'Five years now. Never thought anywhere could feel so empty as the house did that day after the funeral. Everyone went home, and there I was. Nothing but a big empty space and the freedom to do whatever I wanted without consulting anyone else.' She snorted angrily. 'Fat lot of use that is to anyone.'

'I'm divorced.' The slightly tremulous voice of Holly and Clare's mother.

'How long ago?' Naomi asked, not because she was really interested, but it was something to say.

'Nearly four years. He's remarried, got another baby, pays child support as and when he feels like it.'

'I thought they had some organization that chased errant fathers,' Dorothy queried.

'We had an agreement before. I thought it would be better for the children if we could be amicable, but he just took me for a ride, so, yes, I've had to get my solicitor and the CSA involved now, all of that.'

Dorothy made what might have been sympathetic noises. Their earlier fight about Dorothy taking her children to the lavatory seemed temporarily suspended.

Naomi tuned them out. Others had joined the conversation, swapping stories about divorce settlements and the rights and wrongs of the Child Support Agency, taking refuge in the ordinary, everyday scandals that were worlds away from this.

'I've got Alec's number programmed,' Patrick whispered. 'I could try and text him.'

'No,' Naomi told him firmly. 'Later, maybe, when people have gone off to sleep.' The thought that someone might give him away and Patrick be punished had made her very cautious about using this link to the outside.

Patrick had hoped an opportunity might arise when they had been taken to the bathroom, but the men guarding them had told them to leave doors half open and hurried everyone up. There had been no chance.

'Audrey, are you feeling all right?'

Audrey Shields had been complaining on and off all afternoon that she felt unwell.

'It's the heat. It's so close in here.'

'Do you have your pills with you?'

'I told you earlier, Brian, they were in my bag. They took my bag away.'

'Oh yes. I forgot. I'm sorry.'

'We should tell them you feel unwell,' Harry said. 'They have to let you have your pills at the very least.'

'I asked that younger man, the black one, earlier. He said that everything had been smashed to smithereens. He thought my pills had gone the same way.'

'Oh,' Harry said. 'It's worth asking though. Isn't it?'

Naomi recalled the description Harry and Patrick had relayed to her. Mobile phones and anything else that could be broken, crushed beneath the hammer blows delivered by the big man with the temper, as Naomi had come to think of him.

'I'll be all right,' Audrey tried to reassure him, but she sounded weak and sick.

'I'm going to bang on the door again,' Dorothy informed them.

'Oh no, please don't, not on my account.'

'I really don't think you should.' This last from the nervous Mrs Parker. She and her husband had contributed little to the conversation up until now, and their agitation, obvious each time they did get the courage to speak, set Naomi's own nerves on edge.

'It's important,' Dorothy declared. 'Angina isn't something to be ignored, you know.'

'I didn't mean to suggest that it was.' Mary Parker sounded aggrieved. 'But *they* might think so. *They* might think we're just being troublesome.'

Naomi heard Dorothy start to her feet.

'Let me try,' Naomi intervened.

'Oh, very well, if you think that's best.'

Naomi put her hand against the wall and eased herself to her feet. She felt numb and stiff from sitting on the hard floor. Her back and legs were sticky from the heat and her hair felt as though it had melted to her scalp.

Harry, ever the gentleman, helped her to the door. She could hear the shifting of limbs and shuffling of bums as people eased out of her way, conscious that she couldn't see where to put her feet. Firmly, but feeling horribly conspicuous and wishing she had left this to Dorothy, Naomi rapped her knuckles three times against the inside of the door.

For some time, nothing happened. Twice more, Naomi tried to summon those outside, and twice more was ignored. It was on the fourth attempt, when Dorothy was about to give in to frustration and insist she take over, that the door swung wide.

'What the hell do you want now?'

Naomi flinched. The man was close enough for her to feel the heat pouring off his body and the spray of spittle on her cheek when he shouted. She forced herself not to raise a hand to wipe it away. 'One of the ladies is ill,' she said quietly. 'She has a heart condition and the heat and stress are making her feel really sick. If she could have her tablets—?'

'What bloody tablets?'

'They were in her bag. You took her bag.'

There was no reply. Naomi sensed him turn away from her to examine Audrey.

'It . . . it was a blue bag,' Audrey faltered. 'Leather, with a chrome clasp.'

'And I should care?'

'You want her to die?' Dorothy demanded.

'Really, Dorothy, I don't think . . .' Harry began, outraged, once again, by her lack of empathy.

'I'm simply stating what worries us all,' Dorothy told him tartly. 'And if this man has an ounce of decency, he'll take that under advisement and find the tablets.'

'You see' – this time the voice was beside Naomi – 'that's the mistake you're making, lady. You thinking that I even care.' He gave Naomi a shove that would have sent her flying back into the room had Harry not caught her arm, then slammed the door closed once again.

'I told you. I told you.' Mary Parker began to cry.

'Oh, pull yourself together.' Dorothy had no time for such a performance.

'She's scared, that's all.' This from Alice's mother.

'We're all scared,' Dorothy informed her. 'That doesn't mean we have to give in to such funk.'

'Really, my dear, you do need to show a little more consideration,' the Brigadier told her. 'Not everyone has your nerve, you know.'

'Well . . .' Dorothy sounded slightly mollified by his complimentary tone. 'All right, I'm sorry if I was short with you, but there's no sense acting like a baby. That'll get us nowhere.'

Harry had been helping Naomi back to her seat. He made

sure that she was settled and then turned his attention back to Audrey. 'Give him a little while to cool down,' he said firmly, 'and then we'll try again. You never know, we might get one of the others next time.'

Audrey thanked him, wearily, and Naomi could hear Brian Machin trying the best he could to reassure.

Naomi reached for Harry's hand and squeezed it. 'Did you see anything while the door was open?'

'Yes,' Harry told her in an undertone. 'A window has been smashed next to the big door and one of the men was standing on a table looking out. He was keeping to the side, as though he was worried about being seen. And the place was a mess. I mean, even more than before. Stuff strewn all over the floor. Personal things and also papers from the filing cabinets, by the look of it.'

'And,' Naomi prompted, sensing there was more.

'There was blood,' Harry said. 'On the wall and the door and trailed right across the floor.'

Twelve

Time passing. Patrick was right, boredom *was* the worst part, Naomi thought. Boredom and a sort of numbing anxiety that infected her thoughts no matter how she tried to distract herself.

That and the remaining niggle somewhere at the back of her mind, that she knew this man.

Naomi closed her eyes, the better to concentrate. Silly, she knew, but old habits, as they say, and this was one developed in childhood and therefore unlikely to shift now.

She'd always found it easier to focus her thoughts without outside stimulus and, growing up in a rather small, rather crowded terraced house with no central heating until she was about thirteen, meant you found your way to privacy the best way you could. She and her sister crowded into the living room with their parents and often a relative or two, trying to get on with their homework on a winter evening – nowhere else in the house being warm enough. It was either that, or putting the gas stove on in the kitchen and leaving the door ajar. It had led them both to develop strategies for shutting the world out.

Naomi's sister had bought herself a personal stereo out of her paper-round money. Naomi had found a dark and empty space behind closed eyes.

There was something familiar, both in the way the man sounded and in the way he had stood so close to her in the doorway, invading her personal space. The heat of his body so close to hers. It wasn't a sexual thing; more to do with dominance, and it reminded her of . . .

She shook her head, giving up for the moment. There were a great many things it could be reminding her of. Being in a position where something or someone felt threatening or tried to dominate was part and parcel of her former profession. She'd been a serving officer since her nineteenth year, never having considered anything else. The impact of the police investigation that followed Helen's death, changing her perspective forever and steering her in that particular direction almost as a matter of course. Her career, successful and fulfilling, had ended with the car accident that had taken her sight. She had a feeling, though, that this particular memory was a very old one.

Briefly, she had the sense that it was there, hiding only just out of reach. Something about another bank, a different robbery . . . no, not a bank. That wasn't it. Naomi had been involved in the investigation of two other bank jobs during her career, this man had nothing to do with either. Of that, she was certain. No, this was . . . 'Security van,' she said, then realized belatedly that she had spoken out loud.

'What's that, dear?' Dorothy asked her.

'Oh, sorry, nothing,' Naomi said.

'You were talking in your sleep,' Dorothy informed her. 'You must have been having a bad dream. Hardly surprising under the circumstances.'

Naomi managed a weak laugh. 'No, I guess it's not,' she agreed. She tried hard to stay calm, but inside she was seething with a mix of excitement and, now she had the memory pinned, a very real fear.

She knew this man. Knew who and what he was, and the knowledge did nothing to reassure.

Dorothy's comment had sparked the conversation again, the talk turning to dreams and children's nightmares. Naomi waited until their voices were raised enough for her to hide her own, and then she leaned in close to Harry.

'He meant what he said,' she told him, her voice barely more than a breath. 'He doesn't care. He doesn't give a damn for anyone or anything.'

Harry tensed. 'You've remembered who he is?'

'Oh yes,' Naomi whispered. 'I know exactly who Ted Harper is.'

*   *   *

'How's he doing?' Alan Harper peered round the office door and jerked his chin towards the prone figure of Ash Dutta.

'Shouldn't you be on watch? Where's the old man?'

'Toilet.' Alan glanced nervously over his shoulder. 'Will he be all right?'

Danny shook his head. 'Man, but I thought the bleeding would never stop. I got it all over me, look.'

'But you stopped it?'

'I think so. No telling what's happening on the inside though. He could bleed out and we'd not know till he stopped breathing.'

'He asleep?'

'Yeah. Least, I hope that's all it is. Al, your dad's really lost it. How do we get out of this one?'

'We could do like we said before. Just walk out. We could do it now.'

In the corner of the room the big black dog whined miserably. Danny went over to him and scratched his head. Napoleon nuzzled at his hand. A sound from the outer room had Alan racing back to his post by the broken window.

'Don't know what we're going to do, big fella,' Danny told Napoleon. 'But don't you fret, I'll get you outta here.'

Ted Harper appeared in the doorway. 'Stupid mutt,' he said, then, glancing at Ash, 'Well, is he dead yet?'

'Not yet. No thanks to you. What the fuck were you thinking, man?'

'You want the same?'

'Oh, very clever that'd be. You stab me in the guts, like you did Ash, that leaves just you and the kid to look out for things? Fat chance you'd have.'

Ted Harper eyed him with disdain. 'You think I need any of you?'

'You brought us along for the ride, I suppose. You'd have pulled those jobs single-handed, I suppose.'

Ted Harper said nothing. He crossed the room to where Ash was lying on the office floor. The blue carpet was heavily stained with his blood. It had pooled around him and crept outward, soaking the blue, blackening it as it congealed. His breathing was shallow and irregular.

65

Ted Harper leaned in closer and sniffed suspiciously. 'Booze?' he said.

Danny sighed. 'There was whisky in the filing cabinet. It'll probably help him on his way, but it's put him to sleep for now. It's the best I could do.'

Ted Harper's eyes narrowed. 'Wasted on him,' he announced. He drew back his booted foot and kicked Ash hard in the ribs.

Naomi had little opportunity to tell Harry what she'd discovered. Instinct warned her that she should not talk about her career with the other hostages. She knew Ted Harper's attitude to the police and had no wish for anyone to let slip that she was former DS Naomi Blake. Harper might or might not recall the name – after all, her part in his arrest had been small, for all that it had seemed dramatic at the time.

She'd been a serving officer for only eighteen months and was pulling an overtime stint in plain clothes, on surveillance. That night had been boring too, she recalled. Hours of sitting in the bedroom of a house opposite Ted Harper's with an experienced but taciturn sergeant, whose name she could not recall off-hand. The nervous householder dodged her head around the door every few minutes to offer tea.

Just after midnight, the sergeant had been relieved by a young woman called Polly Thompson, newly transferred into CID. Not much older than Naomi and a lot more talkative, the two had been deep in conversation when Ted Harper made his move. So involved, in fact, that they damn near missed him.

Polly had been first to the door, Naomi left to call ahead for assistance. Up until that moment, Naomi had been convinced that this was a waste of time. That Harper was long gone. He was a wanted man. Why risk going home?

She'd been wrong. Harper was not a man for whom logic or expected action held much appeal. Ted Harper believed his wife had sold him out and now he wanted revenge.

By the time Naomi reached the front door, Polly was nowhere to be seen. Naomi, realizing that she'd gone ahead of her into the house, had no option but to follow. She called in this new development as she ran. 'Polly's gone inside. I'm following.'

'You stay put. Stay put, you hear. Back-up is on its way.'

She remembered the running footsteps, dark figures entering the alleyway that ran along the back of the gardens. Satisfied that she would not long be alone, and terribly anxious for her colleague, Naomi ran through the open gate and into the Harper house. Polly Thompson was standing astride a woman's body. Nan Harper lay in a crumpled heap on the kitchen floor, covered in blood. Ted, wielding a knife so large it looked like some prop from a B movie, was circling the pair of them while Polly defended like a lion-tamer, with a broken chair.

Naomi remembered that, for an instant, she froze, then she grabbed the nearest thing to hand and threw it at Ted Harper's head. It missed, but it didn't matter. Her badly aimed missile, or perhaps her sudden entrance, had been enough to distract him and the next instant armed officers had entered the kitchen and assumed control. It was only afterward that she realized she'd tried to hit him with a bottle of tomato sauce.

Polly was reprimanded for not waiting for back-up, as was Naomi, but it was widely acknowledged it was Polly Thompson's early intervention that had saved Nan Harper's life. The commendation followed hot on the heels of the reprimand.

Naomi had given evidence at his trial and Ted Harper had been sent down. Thinking about it, she could not remember for how long. She hadn't really thought of him again.

She'd been on the stand for maybe ten minutes in total, speaking only to confirm what other officers, more senior than her, had said. Would Ted Harper recall her from way back then?

The thought gave Naomi real pause. OK, so she'd been much younger then, had longer hair . . . hadn't been blind, but *she'd* remembered *him* from just his voice, and, now she'd spoken directly to him, would that same trigger apply? His voice and the sudden recollection of that one moment in the police station after his arrest, when he'd passed her in a corridor, arms held tight by two officers. He was still struggling and they had a hard time keeping him in check. He'd

67

paused as Naomi went by. Stared at her and then, abruptly, lurched forward to block her way.

Next second, her colleagues had dragged him on towards the custody suite. The confrontation had lasted for no more than a heartbeat, but Naomi remembered that it had left her shaking uncontrollably.

Funny, she thought, she'd not given Ted Harper a moment's thought for years. Now she had revived the memory, it flooded back with surreal clarity.

Naomi leaned back wearily against the wall, wishing she could talk to Harry about it, but knowing such a long explanation would be overheard. Wishing she could tell Alec. He'd understand that odd mix of instinct and long memory and collected experience that meant you stored all sorts of flotsam and jetsam and kept it fresh until it might be needed. The Harper incident, though dramatic, had been just one incident in her professional life, overshadowed by many more. It had receded into the past, but for Ted Harper it was likely to have more significance, she thought. Far, far more.

Thirteen

Danny had made coffee for himself and his companions in the staff kitchen. He took it through to the main room. 'There's a water cooler,' he said. 'I've got the spare bottle and a load of cups, I'm going to give it to that lot in there.'

'Like hell . . .' Ted Harper began.

'Ted, it's one thing to kill Ash, but you let *them* suffer and we'll all be going down till it's pension time. Think of it as self-preservation, OK?'

Ted Harper glared at him. Alan was staring too, taking in the implication of what he'd just said.

'Ash is dead?'

Danny nodded. 'He just stopped breathing about five minutes ago. I tried to revive him, but . . . Reckon he'd been bleeding into the abdominal cavity. Nothing I could do about that.' He shrugged. 'I've seen it happen before.'

Alan came down off the table and took his coffee. 'How come you know so much about wounds and that?'

''Cos he was in the frigging army,' Ted growled. 'Dishonourable discharge, wasn't it, Danny?'

Danny scowled at him and walked away. Minutes later, he came through with the water container and a plastic bag full of plastic cups.

'Alan, open the door for me.'

'Let him do it himself. And put your frigging mask back on.'

Danny ignored him. He opened the storeroom door and dragged the water bottle inside. Ted Harper glowered, his face reddening with anger at Danny's disobedience. Alan fully expected an explosion and braced himself for it, but none came. Ted Harper stamped off into the manager's office and could be heard clattering around as though looking for something. Snatches of conversation could be heard from inside the storeroom and a few minutes later, Danny emerged again, locking the door behind him.

'I've told them they can go to the toilet in a few minutes. I'll need help with that. Not one word about Ash. Understand?'

Alan nodded, then asked, 'Why?'

'Because,' Danny said heavily, 'first off, we don't want them to know we're a man down and, second, they're edgy enough as it is. We don't want panic. People get unpredictable when they panic and we've got enough of a task trying to second guess your old man.'

Alan glanced towards the office. 'You seem to be doing a good enough job.' He sounded envious.

Danny shook his head. 'Don't bet on it,' he said. 'The only reason Ted gives me leeway is he figures we're cut from the same cloth and he can't be sure how far to push before I let rip. You and Ash, well, he figured he'd got the measure of the pair of you.'

'You mean, he doesn't rate either of us,' Al said bitterly. '*Didn't*, I mean.'

Danny put a large hand on the younger man's shoulder and shook him gently. 'The way your old man measures these things, you don't want to come very high on his scale, believe me. Now, come on and help me with this lot. We'll take them two at a time and no talking. Got that?'

Alan nodded. 'Who's going to watch the window?'

'Ted can do that. Least we know where he is then. When we're done, we got to have a little talk, convince him to let some of these people go.'

'Why?' Alan asked again.

'Because, like I said, we're a man down. They get an idea in their heads to rush the door when one of us opens it, there's a chance they'd get lucky. Like I say, people get unpredictable. It makes no difference if we got five hostages or twenty-five, they're still insurance, but a smaller number puts us back in control and we need all the advantages we can get if we're going to talk our way out.'

'You think we can? Talk our way out? Get away? You think Ash was right and we should ask for a car and a plane

70

and . . .' He trailed off and stared hard at Danny. 'You think the police will storm the building?'

'Not yet, they know we're armed, they'll want to talk us out, negotiate.'

'Dad says he won't negotiate,' Alan said miserably.

Danny patted him on the arm. 'Then we'll just have to convince him otherwise,' he said. 'Trick is to make him think it was all his idea.'

'What . . . what do we do with Ash? We can't just leave him lying there.' He shifted uncomfortably. 'I've never seen anyone dead.'

'Later, we'll find something to wrap him in,' Danny told him. 'Just be thankful we've got air conditioning and hope to hell the police don't decide to cut the power.'

'I'm hungry, mummy.' Holly had slept for a while but this had been her refrain since waking up. Both little girls were fractious and miserable and everyone, Dorothy included, seemed to have passed beyond the desire or ability to try and cheer them up.

The first response of the hostages had been fear; then, when they'd been locked inside the little room, an odd kind of relief. They were together, all in the same boat and out of sight of the guns. It felt almost safe.

As the afternoon had worn on, their mood had been sustained by a grim determination to make the best of a lousy situation. The police would do something. The robbers would give themselves up. Everything would get back to normal . . . it had to be like that . . . didn't it? But as afternoon had become evening and the only break in the routine of sitting still and entering into sporadic bouts of conversation had been the three toilet breaks and the delivery of the water, reality had begun to sink in. They were trapped, in a small room, with four armed men outside the all-too-thin door. Violent men and – to add to their anxiety – so far, there was no sign of anyone doing anything. Mary Parker was now insistently asking why.

'The police will wait it out, see what the robbers do, I suppose,' Harry told her. 'They won't want to come in mob-handed, knowing there are other people inside.'

'But do they even know we're here?' Mary's voice rose petulantly.

71

'Hush, my dear.' Her husband tried to soothe her. 'It will be all right.'

'They'll know which staff were on,' Megan tried to reassure. 'And they'll know there must have been some customers inside. Harry's right, they'll try to talk to the thieves and persuade them to let us go, and to give themselves up.'

'And how long will that take?'

'I don't know, Mrs Parker.' Megan was sounding just a little impatient. 'But it will happen. We just have to manage the best we can until then.'

'You don't have a choice,' Dorothy told her tartly. 'We're all stuck in here until someone on the outside takes action – and, as Harry says, they'll be doing their best to put us in as little danger as possible.'

'But what if they don't?' Mary Parker's voice cracked with the emotional strain. 'We've been locked in for hours now. What if our air runs out? We could die in here.'

'It's not pressurized, Mrs Parker,' Naomi told her with as much patience as she could muster. She was well aware that the irritation she and the others felt with Mary Parker's outburst came purely from the fact that she was voicing their own inner fears. Somehow, while they kept them hidden away and unspoken, they were manageable. To voice them out loud, and with such an air of panic, was unbearable. 'It's just an ordinary door,' Naomi went on, 'and, if it's anything like most doors, it'll have a gap underneath, where the air can come through. Besides, we've had it open several times and that's let more air in, and there's probably a vent high up in the wall somewhere.'

'There's an air brick,' Brian Machin confirmed.

'With tiny, tiny holes in it. How can that possibly let enough air through for all of us? How?'

'Please calm down, dear,' her husband told her, but he sounded weary and unhopeful that his remonstration would have an effect.

'If you don't shut up,' Dorothy told her, 'I'll come over there and slap you.'

'Dorothy, that's hardly a useful thing to say,' Harry remonstrated.

'If she doesn't, I will,' Patrick muttered. 'She's not the only one who doesn't like being closed in.'

72

Naomi gripped his hand. Patrick was not exactly claustro-phobic, but he didn't exactly enjoy enclosed spaces either.

'Audrey, try to drink some water.'

Naomi heard Brian Machin's voice, quiet but clear in amongst the protests provoked by Dorothy's outburst. She leaned towards the sound of it. 'How are you, Audrey?'

'She's not good,' Brian Machin replied. 'She really does need a doctor. Oh, for God's sake, all of you, be quiet!'

Brian Machin had been nothing but calm and polite all through their ordeal, and the effect of his anger was shocked and instant silence. It didn't last for long.

'I'm sorry, I'm sure,' Mary Parker whined, 'but you heard what that dreadful woman said . . .'

'I can't have my wife spoken to in the way that woman did. Too high-handed by far. She has been, all along, though. Dragging those children from their mother. Provoking—'

'Oh, just shut up! All of you!'

Naomi started, recognizing Patrick's voice.

'You're behaving like a load of little kids. We're in this mess together so we'd better make the best of it and think up ways of getting out. Not arguing amongst ourselves. It should be us and them, shouldn't it? Not them and a few of us and then a few more?'

He lapsed into silence, muttering a vague apology. Naomi felt him shift beside her, drawing up his long legs and huddling miser-ably at her side. She slipped an arm round his shoulders and hugged him. He resisted for a moment, but it was token teenage-boy resistance and he gave in, shuffled closer to her side.

'Sorry,' he muttered. 'Didn't mean to get carried away.'

'Sorry for what?' she contradicted, pitching her voice loud enough for everyone to hear. 'You've behaved impeccably, Patrick. Your dad and I are dead proud of you.'

'Here, here,' Dorothy applauded and, not for the first time, Naomi felt she could do without her approval. She sensed Dorothy was about to say more, but whatever it would have been was interrupted by the sudden opening of the door. Two of the men, the leader and the younger one, burst inside and, from the squeals and gasps of shock, Naomi guessed that they were both armed.

Fourteen

'Sir, something's happening. One of the riflemen just reported that the doors are opening.'

'What?'

. Alec crossed to the window, accompanied by Hemmings and the two negotiators. As they watched, the bank doors opened just enough for a man to pass through. He was supporting a middle-aged woman, dressed in a cashier's uniform. She looked sick; he looked fearful. One arm around the woman, he raised the other as though to signal that he was no threat and unarmed. Hemmings turned and strode towards the door. 'I'll get down there.'

Alec nodded. 'I'm guessing that's the manager and Audrey Shields,' he said. 'Alert the paramedics and bring them in through the back.'

He turned his attention back to the view of the street. Brian Machin was struggling a little, Audrey weak enough to be almost a dead weight. Armed officers emerged to give them escort, a further two with riot shields to give them cover.

'There's more,' Sarah whispered.

The door had opened again and this time an elderly couple struggled through. They practically ran across the road, the woman twittering with panic, her voice rising to them and audible through the part-open window.

'Know who they are?' Sam asked.

Alec shook his head.

Then two women followed. The first carrying a baby in her arms, the second leading two little girls. The second woman had reached the bottom of the steps when she turned as though preparing to go back. She looked terrified. Then the door opened a little further and the youngest child reached out for

74

what next emerged. The large black dog came obediently to her side, allowing her to take his harness, then sat down on the curb waiting. The woman screamed at him. And began to drag her children across the road. 'Leave him, Holly, just let go. Just let go.'

'A guide dog?' Sarah was puzzled. Alec didn't reply, he was already heading for the door. Not quite believing what he'd seen, he ran down the stairs, through the shop and into the street. The black dog, puzzled now and whimpering softly, was still waiting on the kerb. He saw Alec and arfed happily. Then, finally accepting Alec's urgent instructions, ambled across.

'What's going on?' Hemmings demanded. 'You know who he belongs to?'

Alec nodded, not trusting himself to speak. Hemmings frowned, but took his cue. 'I'll get them all upstairs,' he told Alec, 'and I'll get a dog handler in to look after him.'

'No!' Alec hadn't meant to sound so emphatic. 'No, it's all right. I'll see to him.' His hands moved to free Napoleon from his working harness, rubbing the dog's sleek coat, checking, as Naomi always did, for any pressure sores or tiny rubs. Napoleon wriggled happily beside him, whining now as though to ask what was going on.

'It's all right, boy, it's going to be OK, old man,' Alec told him, hoping that were true.

Arriving upstairs, he found that Hemmings had taken over and was issuing orders, getting the hostages fed and watered, arranging for transport to the hospital to be checked out. Sarah Milton was taking their names and Sam was watching the window for further developments.

'Our friendly neighbourhood journalists are in a feeding frenzy,' he announced. 'How did they manage in the days before mobile phones?'

Alec's pocket began to ring. He fished out his mobile and stared at the name on the screen, hesitating over whether or not to take the call, finally deciding in favour, aware that his indecision had attracted even more attention.

'Friedman.' He tried and failed to sound businesslike.

'Friedman, is it?' Simon said. 'OK then, Friedman, tell me this. That was Naomi's dog, wasn't it?'

75

'I'm not at liberty to—'

'Oh, don't give me that crap. I'd know Napoleon in a roomful of black labradors. Naomi's my friend too, remember.'

'Are you calling as a friend or as a reporter?' Alec questioned.

'Not fair, Alec!' Simon paused. 'Look, they're going nuts out here, everyone's making the call to say that hostages have been released. You making a statement or what? And, don't worry, I'm not so stupid or, contrary to popular belief, so mercenary that I'd risk a friend over a story. I've been there. Done that. Ain't worth it. But just tell me this, is Harry with her?'

Alec hadn't thought about it until that moment. They'd planned to go out together that day, he'd been supposed to meet her that night. He'd assumed, when he'd been unable to reach her, that she'd heard the story on the television and knew he'd be involved in the investigation. Naomi rarely phoned him at work.

'I don't know yet,' he said.

'Mari should be told.'

'I know that,' Alec snapped. He took a deep but only partially calming breath, aware that Hemmings and the two negotiators were watching him. 'I'll call you back,' he said. 'Soon, Simon. I promise.'

'You going to tell us what's going on?' Hemmings wanted to know.

'If explanations can wait,' Sam interrupted, 'then they should, just until we've finished getting names from the released hostages and then sent out for food.'

'Food?' Alec was momentarily at a loss.

'The lines of communication just opened,' Sarah told him. 'We need to keep them open. Food and water and mobile phone. Maybe by morning, we'll have a dialogue going.'

Inside the storeroom there was a little more space in which to move.

'At least,' Dorothy said, 'those released will be able to give the names of those of us left behind. Our families will know where we are and the police will know how many.'

76

'Mum and Dad will know I'm OK,' Megan said. She sounded close to tears at not being chosen.

'What surprises me,' Dorothy mused, 'is why I'm still here. I'd have thought he'd have kept the Parkers – so much easier to intimidate them – and taken the opportunity to get rid of me.'

Naomi was amused. 'Was that the plan?' she asked.

'Lord, no, dear. I'm like this with everyone. I don't see myself changing just because the stupid man had a gun. Well, I think we should be grateful they let the children go.'

There was a general murmur of agreement at that. 'Audrey too,' she added. 'I just hope she's going to be all right.'

Hemmings listened as Alec told him about Naomi.

'Shit! I should relieve you now. You know that?'

Alec nodded. 'Do what you have to do,' he said. 'But I'm staying put, official or not.'

'We'll talk about it later,' Hemmings said. 'Right now, there's a job to do.'

Alec took a deep breath and tried to consider the business in hand. 'I suggest we have a quick chat to the hostages as a group, before they leave. That way we can collect initial impressions of conditions inside the bank and they should be more at ease as a group.'

'Brian Machin and the woman with angina have gone,' Hemmings reminded him. 'I let him go with her, they've got one of my lot in tow. DC Prior, she's a good lass. Sarah's taken the rest through to the back room.'

The room directly behind the shop had been used as a kitchen-diner by the owners and Sarah had them gathered around the table, drinking tea and fizzy pop. She'd conjured up a couple of packs of biscuits from somewhere, and the two little girls were tucking in. The adults looked shell-shocked, but the kids were prattling about the lady who took them to the toilet and the men with guns. Sarah was encouraging them to talk, and Sam, keeping in the background, quietly took notes.

Hemmings joined the hostages at the table. 'We're arranging to get you all ferried to the hospital for a general check,' he

77

said. 'Your families will meet you there and then we'll assign officers to take statements. I'm sorry to have to insist, but we'll need those tonight, as soon as possible. We need to know as much as possible about what's going on in there.'

'She's a mad woman!' The mother of the two little girls could not seem to get her mind off Dorothy Peel. Alec began to wonder if she saw her as a bigger bogeyman than the four with guns. 'She just snatched them from me and marched them off to the toilet. She could have got them shot.'

'I think she was very brave,' Alice's mother contradicted.

'Brave!' Mary Parker had other ideas. 'The woman is insane. She threatened to hit me!'

Alec watched and listened, oddly detached, unable to get Naomi out of his mind for long enough to focus on the others. A small part of his brain told him that they were getting nowhere fast and that to talk collectively to these people was not the good idea it had first seemed. Hemmings seemed to be reaching the same conclusion and, when word came that vehicles had been arranged to take them away, he released them without protest or comment.

Sam came over to Alec and handed him a list. 'Those still left inside,' he said. 'There are seven. Megan James we knew about. Tim Barron, the other cashier. Mrs Dorothy Peel, who seems to have stirred up a certain amount of controversy, and a retired Brigadier, Paul Hebden. I believe you had them both on your original list.'

Alec nodded.

'Then there's a Naomi Blake. The guide dog belongs to her, but I gather, from what's *not* been said, that you know that already. Where is he, by the way?'

'I've got someone getting him fed and watered.' Alec's voice cracked slightly. He coughed and carried on. 'Who else?'

'A father and son, Patrick and Harry Jones. They were with Naomi Blake.'

'Yes, they would have been.'

'Alec, how deeply are you involved with this woman?'

Alec managed a false laugh. 'Oh, not very,' he said. 'I keep asking her to marry me, she keeps telling me maybe. That kind of close.' He shut his eyes. 'Don't even think of telling me I should go,' he said.

Sam shifted uncomfortably. 'Fortunately for me,' he said, '*I* don't have to make that request. It looks as though the food's arrived, we should get the delivery organized.'

'Good.' Alec approved. 'Good, I'll see to that.' The strangest thing, he thought as he left Sam, was this crazy jealous feeling that he couldn't shake even though he knew it made no sense. Harry was in there, going through this with her, when he, Alec, was shut outside.

Fifteen

Three officers with riot shields gave cover as Alec, laden with pizza and soft drinks, made his way across the road. Hemmings had not been happy about him doing this, but Alec didn't feel in the mood to argue.

It was almost dark now, the summer evening finally giving way to night, though yellow streetlights distorted the colour of the sky and hid the first stars.

Alec stood at the foot of the steps, feeling foolish and vulnerable, aware of the eyes watching at either end of the street, eyes from the windows of the incident room and, in all probability, from inside the bank.

'I've brought food,' he announced. 'And drink. For all of you. And a phone in case you want to talk.' He remembered, belatedly, that Sam had advised him not to mention the phone, but simply to leave it and see what transpired. To draw attention to the fact that they wanted to communicate might, Sam had advised, be counter-productive.

Alec bent down and placed food and drink upon the top step. He balanced the phone on the pile of pizza boxes and then took a pace back, wondering if he should wait for a response, or just get the hell out.

'Sir, we should be moving.' One of the armed officers made the decision for him. Alec sighed. His momentary reluctance, he realized, was nothing to do with uncertainty about the response, but had everything to do with the knowledge that Naomi was inside.

'Sir. Now, sir.'

Alec turned and allowed them to escort him back across the street. He stood in the ever-deepening shadows of the shop doorway and waited for what seemed like forever, then, slowly, the bank door opened and a hand reached out and pulled the boxes, then the bottles, inside.

'Good,' a voice announced.

Alec jumped. He'd been so intent on watching the door that he had not even noticed Sarah there.

'You OK?' she asked. 'I mean, as OK as you can be under the circumstances.'

'I think so. Yes. I take it you think that's promising, the fact that they've accepted food.'

'It's a start. Lord knows, we need a start. Tom's been working on a press release. He wants you to look it over, then he'll go and talk to the gathered masses.' She smiled and gestured towards the cordon at the end of the street.

'Tom?' Alec looked stupidly at the woman. 'Oh, you mean Hemmings.'

'You two not on first-name terms?' He could hear the laughter in her voice.

Despite his anxiety, he responded to her tone. 'Never thought of him as anything but Hemmings,' he confessed. 'How long before we get some word from them, do you think? And can we be sure they'll feed the hostages?'

'The answer to the first is, I don't know, and to the second, probably. Why wouldn't they?'

'I don't know.'

'Look, they've got a manageable group now. Four of them can easily control seven, so, chances are they'll be a lot less jumpy – and food is a social thing. It reminds people of their basic needs. Their essential humanity.'

She moved to go back inside. Alec followed reluctantly, hoping he could believe her.

Tom Hemmings' statement was brief.

'About an hour ago, at 11.15 p.m., a number of the hostages were released. We have reason to believe that there are seven remaining, held by four gunmen. Food and drink have just been delivered and taken inside and we have high hopes that this signals a new phase in our negotiations. The families are being kept informed and we have officers on standby to take statements from those released. As a precaution, they'll all

81

have medical checks and then be reunited with their loved ones. We will keep you informed as new developments arise.'

A barrage of questions bounced off Hemmings' broad back as he turned and walked away. In truth, no one had expected more than had been given and, as it became clear that they would get nothing else, the crowd dispersed a little, taking their mobile phones to call in with the latest details.

Simon watched as a woman journalist from one of the cable networks did her piece to camera. Most of the terrestrial groups wouldn't break this until morning, a few of the papers would manage to reset the front page, but by and large it was too late for anything but the twenty-four-hour carriers. The analogue world would hear of the hostage release in the early morning.

Simon stepped away from the others and found Alec's number in his mobile. He'd been shocked to the core to see Napoleon and could only guess at Alec's reaction. He was trying to think of a way of playing this story that would both give him an inside track and not betray a friendship, nor put Naomi and the others in danger. There was no way of knowing if the robbers had access to radio or telephone or other form of outside information – hence the conciseness of Hemmings' statement.

Alec answered on the third ring.

'Well?' Simon asked.

'You heard the statement. I can't tell you any more.'

'Does Mari know?'

Alec hesitated. 'We're in the process of informing the families,' he said.

Simon nodded, then said, 'I'll see you over there. Half an hour. Don't worry, I won't tell her anything until you get there.'

'I thought you claimed to be a friend!'

'I *am* a friend, Alec. Half an hour.'

Simon rang off and switched the phone to silent, guessing Alec would try to ring him back. Professionally, Simon had had a run of bad luck lately, he could do with an exclusive, and if his editor got wind of the fact that he'd got a chance of getting one with this, and that he'd passed it up . . . well, he was already on probation . . . Trouble was, he cared about Naomi and Alec and the rest and, right now, Simon didn't have a clue how he could square these two demands.

'Trouble?' Hemmings asked.

'Maybe. Look, hold the fort here. I'm going to let Mari Jones know about her son and grandson. It'd be better coming from me. Naomi's family are on holiday and I can't for the life of me remember exactly where they've gone. Somewhere in Spain. Dorothy's son and daughter-in-law will need bringing up to speed. Andrews can take care of that. We still don't have anyone for the Brigadier?'

Hemmings shook his head. 'Neighbours reckon he lives alone and has done for years. They're out at work all day, so don't notice if he's there or not half the time, or what visitors he might have.'

'Right, well, try again tomorrow. Meantime, chase up those witness statements. I want them here for when I get back.'

'And that will be?'

'Hour, two tops. Anyone who can be relieved, send them home for a couple of hours sleep. I want them back here for six. Try and make everyone else as comfortable as . . . well, you know.'

'It'd be a shame to wake the super tonight, so I think we'll bring him up to scratch on the Naomi problem after morning prayers,' Hemmings said casually.

'Thanks,' Alec said gratefully. Morning prayers . . . he thought. He'd not heard the daily briefing called that since his probationary days. 'Any developments . . .'

'And you'll be the first to know. Now, go!'

Alec slipped out the back way into empty streets. Earlier that day, a handful of journalists had figured out that the police were using the rear entrance to the shop, and had camped briefly outside the wooden gates that led into the tiny yard. A paramedic crew had been on standby, but other than that, there'd been little to see, and the paramedics, knowing nothing, could only join them in the speculation game. They'd drifted off around tea time. Back to the cordon or to get background in one of the local pubs, Alec supposed. Right now the street was empty. A second crew of paramedics sat in their vehicle with the windows open to the inadequate evening breeze and glanced at him as he passed.

'Any news?'

'Nothing much. We took them food and they've accepted that. Other than that, it's all quiet.'

The man nodded. 'Well, I suppose that's something.'

'Hopefully so,' Alec agreed. He walked on, reflecting that he'd just fuelled a further hour or so of speculation, and a little kudos back at base when they revealed they'd known this before the radio news. He reached his car, fired up the engine, wincing at the growl that echoed through the quiet terraced street. Mari lived a scant half mile away, and he'd thought of walking. Decided against, purely in case something should break and he needed to get back fast. He glanced at the dashboard clock. It was a quarter to one. Nearly thirteen hours.

Simon was waiting for him outside Mari's door, sitting on the low wall separated by a few paving stones from the house. Mari lived alone now. Widowed for several years, though Alec had rarely known her to actually *be* alone when he visited. The Joneses had lived on this little street all their married lives and so, it seemed, had half the other residents. There was a feeling of community here that Alec had rarely met with elsewhere.

Harry and Patrick had moved in briefly when the reinvestigation into Helen's death had brought them back to Ingham, but last winter they'd bought a place of their own on the edge of town. Several nights a week, Patrick would stop off at Naomi's after school and Harry would collect him from there. Otherwise, he'd call at his grandmother's. Patrick was more settled this term, Alec had noticed. He'd even taken to going out with friends from time to time, but he was still something of a loner, preferring adult company to that of his peers and finding it hard to communicate on a normal teenage level. Shy and awkward, upset by the breakdown of his parents' marriage and the shadow cast by Helen's death, he'd had a bit of a rough time of it, Alec knew. It was his birthday soon. Alec prayed he'd be out to celebrate it.

'It's all dark,' Simon commented, bringing him back to the present.

'It's late. OK, let's get this over with. You shouldn't be here. You know that?'

Simon ignored him and rang the bell. Mari emerged a few minutes later rubbing the sleep from her eyes as she peered around the edge of the door. She'd put the chain on, Alec noted with vague approval.

'Alec? Simon?' She shut the door again so she could release the chain, then opened it wide. 'What's wrong? Come inside.'

She ushered them into the little sitting room, pulling her old pink dressing gown around her and tying the belt. 'Tell me,' she demanded. 'It can't be anything good that brings you here at one o'clock in the morning, so tell me now.'

'It's Harry and Patrick,' Alec told her. 'Naomi too. They got caught up in that bank raid this morning. Mari, I'm sorry, but they're still inside.'

She stared at him for a moment, taking this in, then frowned. 'Why didn't you tell me sooner?'

'Because we didn't know. Some hostages were released a little while ago and we got the names of the others from them. Until then, no one knew anything about numbers or identities. I'm sorry, Mari, I couldn't tell you because I didn't know.'

It was typical of Mari, Alec thought, that her first concern thereafter should be for him. 'Oh, you poor love,' she said. 'You must be worried sick. Now tell me everything and let me know what I can do.'

Gratefully, Alec sank into the nearest chair and Mari turned her attention to his companion. 'And what brings you with him?' she asked. 'Business or friendship?'

'Bit of both, to be truthful. I've got to cover the story. Someone has to.'

Mari let it go and turned her attention back to Alec. 'So, what do you know?' she demanded. 'Tell me everything, Alec, I need to know.'

The storeroom stank of unwashed people and sweaty feet – his sweaty feet, Patrick admitted – and now, stale pizza.

It had been a relief to have food, though the sugar in the Coke seemed to have gone straight to his head and he felt slightly giddy. Beside him, Naomi had gone to sleep, curled up with her head on his father's jacket. His dad was lying on his back, snoring slightly. He needed a shave and his prematurely greying hair stuck up at odd angles that Harry, who liked always to be tidy, would never normally allow. He too had kicked off his shoes. His socks were darker across the toes, where his feet had been sweating, and the normally immaculate white shirt was creased and smeared with tomato sauce where it had dripped. Harry normally looked as freshly pressed at the end of a day as he did at its newly ironed beginning, and he never ate pizza with his fingers, always cutting it into neat bites with a knife and fork. It had amused Patrick tonight that he'd fallen upon the messy food with as much enthusiasm as the rest of them, even taking off the bits of pepperoni with his fingers to give to Patrick, something the everyday Harry would not have dreamed of doing.

Patrick smiled, a sudden rush of affection for his slightly uptight dad flooding through him. He wouldn't recommend being taken prisoner as a way of losing your inhibitions, but maybe, once broken down, they might stay that way?

Thinking about it, Patrick wasn't sure this was either a likely or desirable state of affairs. Harry's sense of order, though it sometimes bugged him, also gave Patrick a sense of predictable security that he both liked and needed.

Everyone was sleeping. The two cashiers, Tim and Megan, had curled up together, and Patrick wondered if they were an item. Dorothy had slumped down in the corner and the Brigadier had arranged himself next to her. Funny, he thought, that such a simple thing as food can change your perspective, but it had transformed a room full of very miserable people, sagging from the heat and the disappointment of not being released, into a gathering that generated an almost party atmosphere.

He wondered if they'd still be here on his birthday. Maybe they'd send in a cake. The image of hostages and captors singing happy birthday, and Patrick blowing out his sixteen candles while they all cheered, almost caused him to laugh out loud. He smiled.

'Funny thoughts?' Dorothy asked.

'Oh. I thought you were asleep.'

'I dozed. At my age you don't sleep a lot. Or I don't anyway. She gestured that he should come and sit beside her and, not wanting to be rude, Patrick did as he was told.

'So,' she asked him. Can you use that little phone of yours to call out, or would that be too much of a risk, do you think?'

'What?'

'Yes, dear, I saw you and I read Naomi's reaction. My husband was deaf, you see, I picked up the habit from him, I suppose. He had this habit of listening to music and watching television with the sound turned down.'

Patrick laughed. 'My gran does that, but she has the sub-titles on. I don't know about using the phone. Dad's dead against it. I thought about sending a text message.'

'Is there someone who could help us and who'd have the sense not to try to call you back?'

Patrick nodded. 'Alec. He's Naomi's boyfriend.'

'Oh?' Dorothy was surprised. I thought she and your father . . .'

Patrick shrugged. 'No such luck. They're best friends, but my dad doesn't seem to get his act together enough to ask her out.'

'Well, if she's already got a boyfriend, I suppose that wouldn't be right,' Dorothy commented.

'I suppose.'

'And what's he like, this Alec?'

'Oh.' Patrick hesitated. 'Actually, I like him a lot too, which makes it difficult. If I could hate him, it would be almost easier, you know what I mean?'

'I do indeed.'

Patrick frowned. He had no idea why he should be admit-ting any of this to Dorothy Peel.

'How old are you?' Dorothy asked.

'I'll be sixteen in three days' time.'

'Oh, well, I hope we're in a better place for celebration. It would be a bit grim to be still in here.' She laughed. 'It's a long time since I was sixteen. Does that mean you've been taking exams, or is that next year?'

'No, I took them already. I'm the youngest in my class. At least that means I can retake and not be behind.'

'And will you have to retake? That's not a very hopeful view.'

Patrick shrugged. 'I don't know,' he said. He'd made progress this year but there were still his difficulties with writing and spelling – though, put a pencil in his hand and let him draw, and he'd be happy for hours. He was planning on repeating the year, do a BTEC or GNVQ or something, which he reckoned would bring his results up to an acceptable standard, and which was all project-based.

'And what do you want to do with your life?'

It was such a typical adult question, Patrick thought, and he was used to the rather patronizing reaction his reply generally earned him. He sighed. 'I might become a photographer,' he said. 'I started that this year as a one-year GCSE. I should actually get that one OK. And I want to do an art and design course. Something like that.'

Dorothy nodded. 'I met Lord Lichfield once,' she said. 'I was at a wedding and he was taking photographs.' She smiled. 'It was a very upmarket wedding. That was years ago, of course. Now, are you going to contact this Alec, or not?'

Her change of tack surprised him, but he was glad to have the emphasis lifted from his personal ambitions – which, so far, only Naomi had really taken seriously. Naomi and the photographer he'd met. Tally Palmer. Though he wasn't sure any more that she counted, seeing as she was now in jail for killing someone.

'I ought to ask my dad,' he said.

'If you feel you must.'

'I do.'

'I'm glad to hear it,' Harry told him. He sat up and glared at Dorothy. 'I've been lying here listening to you and, to be frank, I'm not sure I like the way this conversation's going. It's bad enough that Patrick kept the blasted thing. I told him, he should take the opportunity to chuck it out of the toilet window rather than risk being found with it on him. But to use it, that could be really dangerous.'

'Why would it?' Dorothy demanded.

Harry frowned, unable to articulate his reasons.

The others were stirring, voices and tension filtering through into even exhausted sleep.

'What's going on?' the brigadier demanded.

'I'm trying to convince this young man to use his mobile phone.'

'You kept your mobile?' Megan asked. 'Oh, well done. Why didn't you say?'

'Because, with all the coming and going, I thought he should keep it quiet,' Harry told her, irritation clear in his voice.

'And while the others were here, I think that was sensible,' Dorothy concurred. 'The Parkers would have given him away in a heartbeat, but none of us will, I'm sure of that.'

'I thought I could text Alec,' Patrick said. 'What do you think, Naomi?'

'Who's Alec?' Tim Barron asked.

'Apparently, he's this young woman's boyfriend,' Dorothy told him.

'And tell him what?' Tim Barron asked. 'For that matter, we'd all like to contact family.'

'Alec is a police officer,' Naomi said quietly.

'Ah,' Dorothy mused. 'You failed to tell me that, young man.'

Patrick shrugged. He hadn't been sure Naomi would want that given away. He watched anxiously as she considered. She pushed her matted curls back from her face and bit her lip. 'If Alec knew more about those involved,' she said, 'it might well give them the edge in negotiations.'

'What can we tell them that the released hostages can't?' Tim Barron asked.

'That Naomi recognized one man.' Dorothy sounded triumphant.

'What?' Patrick saw Tim Barron turn to stare. 'You're sure? You can identify one. Which one?'

'The leader.' Dorothy was enjoying this.

'You're certain?'

Naomi sighed heavily. 'Before the accident that blinded me, I was a police officer,' she said. 'You can understand I'd rather our captors didn't know that, especially as I was involved in the arrest of Ted Harper.'

'Well, that puts a different complexion on things,' Brigadier Hebden said. 'Look, my dear, we'll keep your secret, and yours, Patrick, but if it can give the police a lead, I don't see that we've any choice.'

Naomi nodded reluctantly. 'OK, she said. Patrick, you've got Alec's number programmed in.'

Patrick nodded. His heart suddenly began to beat that little bit faster. He slid the little phone from where he'd been concealing it inside his sock and opened it up. 'Can I have your jacket, Dad, it chimes when I switch it on, I want to muffle the noise.'

Harry handed the jacket over without a word and Dorothy immediately managed to conjure up a coughing fit. Even so, the tinny, happy, chime that sounded as Patrick powered up the phone seemed terribly loud in the enclosed space. They held their breath and then Patrick began to key in his text.

'Naomi says main man Ted Harper. All OK, don't call back.'

Patrick pressed send then switched off and tucked it firmly back inside his sock. He was only just in time. The storeroom door opened and Ted Harper himself appeared in the doorway.

'You lot shut your mouths or I'll shut them for you,' he announced. His gaze travelled suspiciously across their faces and came finally to rest upon Naomi's. He frowned and in that moment Patrick knew. He'd begun to see something there. Something familiar, and it would only be a matter of time before he remembered what it was.

Alec's phone bleeped at him as Patrick's message arrived. He frowned. Who would be sending him a text?

'What?' Mari questioned.

'My phone.'

'You'd better get it then.'

Alec shrugged and tugged the phone out of his trouser pocket, making a mental note not to keep putting it there. It was ruining the lining. He flipped it open and read. 'What the hell . . .?' He stared at Mari. 'It's from Patrick.'

'Patrick? How?'

'I don't know. According to the other hostages, their phones were taken away and smashed.'

'Harry let him have his new one early,' Mari told him. 'It's a tiny little foldy thing. He must have hidden it somewhere. That is *so* like Patrick. Always far too impulsive.'

'What does it say?' Simon had taken the mobile from his hand before Alec thought to stop him. 'Who the hell's Ted Harper?'

Alec snatched it back 'One word, Simon . . . To anyone.'

'You think I'm stupid? But who is Ted Harper anyway?'

Alec shook his head. 'I don't know,' he told them. 'Look, Mari, I've got to go. You know how to reach me.'

Mari nodded. 'Just you take care,' she said. 'Now go. Find out who this bastard is that's got our family.'

Our family, Alec thought as he headed for the door. Yes, he rather supposed it was.

Sixteen

Alec returned to the incident room. It was past two in the morning and they were running on a skeleton crew. The negotiators had gone to sleep in the back room, the kids' room, Alec guessed, from the jumble of toys and the bright pictures on the walls. Alec made a mental note that he must see the residents in the morning. They'd been put up in a local hotel while their house had been requisitioned. He must check that they had everything they needed. The living room, which they were using as their main control centre, was draped with sleeping bodies. Collapsed constables snoring in chairs or occupying the sofa. One asleep on the floor, his legs beneath the coffee table.

Hemmings sat at the table at the other end of the room, eating what smelt like Chinese takeaway. Alec wondered where he'd managed to get that this time of the morning, and if there was any left. Then he frowned in puzzlement, noting the identity of the second person at the table.

'Mr Machin? What are you doing here?'

Brian Machin held out a hand and shook Alec's. 'I got the liaison officer to bring me back,' he said. 'Audrey and I put a sketch together of the one who showed his face. Audrey is a very skilful artist. She does portraits of people's kids from photos and such. We thought it might be helpful.'

Alec looked at the picture lying on the table. 'Is it a good likeness?' he asked.

'I would say so, yes.'

Hemmings had seen him looking at the food. He produced a plate from the sideboard cupboard and began to scoop noodles and chicken with cashew nuts on to it. 'Eat,' he said. 'I've got someone making fresh tea. That is, if he's not fallen asleep on the way. You pass any unconscious constables on the stairs?

92

'Not on the stairs, no,' Alec told him. He was ravenous, he realized as he started to shovel food. 'How is Mrs Shields?' he managed between mouthfuls.

'Oh, much better. She'll be kept in tonight and maybe tomorrow, but she's already chafing about going home. She's tough, thankfully, though there were moments when I thought . . .'

'I'm sure. Have you seen your daughter?'

'Yes. She was at the hospital. Emily was a bit cross that I wanted to come back here instead of going home, but she understood in the end.' He smiled. 'She's like her mother, likes to make a fuss.'

Alec didn't feel able to comment on that. Instead, he found his mobile phone and called up the message, handed it to Hemmings. 'Did Naomi Blake say anything about recognizing one of the men?' he asked.

'Naomi? The blind lady? Not to me, but . . .' He frowned. 'I got the impression she was uneasy about something.' He laughed. 'I mean, over and above the obvious. And the boy, Patrick, I'm sure he'd managed to keep his phone. I was just praying he wouldn't let the Parkers see. It was crowded in that storeroom. Hard to keep things hidden. I noticed she talked to Harry when the rest of us were making noise, as though she wanted advice but didn't want the rest of us to hear.'

Alec nodded. Far as it went, this was mere speculation, on Brian Machin's part, but his was the kind of job that encouraged you to take notice of people, and Alec was prepared to accept that he was a better than casual observer.

'Patrick kept his phone,' he confirmed, 'but, Mr Machin, I don't want that to go any further than this room.'

Brian Machin frowned. 'Of course not,' he said, then nodded towards Alec's mobile. 'He got a message out?'

'Yes,' Alec said, but gave no further details. 'What were your impressions of the four men?'

Brian Machin had obviously been giving this a lot of thought. 'The leader seemed unstable. Unpredictable. Constantly angry, even when we were all doing as we were told. Then there was a much younger man. At least, that was the impression I got. I didn't see his face. He seemed nervous. Overawed by everything. I got the feeling he was almost as scared as we were.'

'And the other two?'

'One, I can't tell you much about. I think he was in my office watching the back, not that he'd have seen very much. You get a nice view of the dustbins if the blinds are open, and a brick wall with a row of rather decorative ironwork on top. I think it must predate the bank, because it runs along the back of the building next door as well. He had dark skin, from what we saw of his hands and legs.'

'Legs?'

'He wore shorts. Red. They stopped at the knees and his calves were bare. Asian, I'd have said, unlike the other man, who was definitely black.' He indicated the drawing. 'He brought us water, made sure we had opportunity to go to the lavatory and I think he was probably responsible for getting some of us released.'

'And his relationship with the main man?'

'I got the impression that he was the only one the older man took any notice of. The others were . . . makeweights, I guess you might say. He was a calming influence, but I wouldn't like to guess how long he might be able to maintain that calm. When they let us go, he was the one organizing it, but the other man, you could almost hear him grinding his teeth.'

'Would you say there was general friction within the group?' Hemmings questioned.

'Yes, I'd say so. They weren't prepared for what happened. I don't think they'd even considered it as a possibility, and suddenly things went very much astray.'

Brian Machin was obviously tiring now, his reserves of adrenalin finally letting him down. Alec suggested they arrange a lift home. When he'd gone, Hemmings picked up Alec's mobile and read the message once again. 'Tell me about this Patrick.'

'Hard to know where to start. He's almost sixteen. Shy, doesn't make friends easily, but he's intensely loyal to those he cares about. I cause him a few worries.'

'Oh, how's that?'

'I'm in the way.' Alec smiled. 'Patrick and I get on very well, but his dad, Harry, fancies Naomi as much as I do. I was there first and I think Patrick often wishes I wasn't. He's a sensible kid, but a bit impulsive. I'm not surprised he managed to hang on to his phone. I'm more surprised that Harry let him use it. That concerns me.'

'Any idea who this Ted Harper is?'

Alec shook his head. 'But the fact that they've told us means they think we should be able to find out easily enough. If Naomi recognized him, it's likely to be someone she ran across at work.'

'Someone she arrested?'

'Maybe, or was involved in investigating.'

Hemmings thought about it. 'No one on any of our lists by that name,' he said, referring to the checks they'd made on criminals whose MO fitted with these robberies.

'So, someone from some time ago,' Alec concluded. 'Andrews is our man here, memory like an elephant. I'll have him consult with the collator first thing and get someone down to records.'

'We should have had Sam and Sarah sitting in on our talk with Brian Machin,' Hemmings said.

Alec shook his head. 'They need some rest,' he said. 'We can bring them up to speed.' He yawned and buried his face in his hands. 'Those other statements come in?'

'You should get some sleep too.'

'Later. Mind's going nineteen to the dozen.'

Hemmings nodded. He reached across the table and dragged a Manila folder into the middle, pushing the remnants of their meal to one side. 'Help yourself,' he said. 'My betting is, the only useful statement to come out will be Machin's.'

Alec woke to find the room stirring around him and hazy dawn faltering through the open curtains. He glanced at his watch. Five thirty. He couldn't recall having fallen asleep. One of the witness statements lay crumpled beneath his hand and he was embarrassed to find that he'd dribbled on another while he slept. Across the table, Hemmings slumbered in a similar undignified, exhausted state. Alec left him where he was and went off to find somewhere to wash his face. He'd have to get home at some point, to find a clean shirt; his stank of sweat and stale food. He found the bathroom, bathed his face with cold water and found a spray antiperspirant on the shelf. After a moment's hesitation, he borrowed a couple of squirts, spraying it up under his shirt, not sure whether it improved the situation or merely added to the discordant cacophony of smells. He thought of Naomi again. She hated to be without her shower and her clean clothes, and it would be driving Harry mad. Harry being Mr Neat. Patrick, well, apart from the fact that Patrick usually smelt OK – if you ignored the feet – it was hard to tell how often he changed his clothes. They were almost always black, though Alec had noticed that the long-sleeved T-shirts he favoured did have slightly different logos. Patrick had grown rapidly over the past few months. Now, just taller than Naomi, he had about him that gangly, untidy look that teenage boys seem to catch once they start with the growth spurt. He was still small for his age, though, and stick-thin despite the fact that he was always eating.

Alec looked at himself in the mirror. He looked old and grey, his skin ageing overnight, and he was gaining lines around his eyes that he was sure had been absent before.

'Gov. Your phone.' Someone was banging on the door. Alec opened it. The officer held his mobile out to him and Alec remembered that he'd left it on the table. 'I answered it,' the officer told him. 'Someone called Simon.'

Alec thanked him. 'What?' he said.

'I know who he is.'

'Who?'

'Don't be thick, Alec. Ted Harper. I went to the morgue last night.'

'Morgue?' Alec wasn't with it yet.

'Newspaper archive. Wake up, Alec! The night porter knows I research out of hours, so he let me in. I've been at it since I left you, but I found him. Ted Harper was arrested thirteen years ago come November, armed robbery and assault. The last assault was on his wife. He was convinced she'd grassed him up. Naomi was one of the arresting officers. She gave evidence at his trial.'

Seventeen

Day two, eight in the morning, though no one had any way of knowing that, their watches also having been confiscated by Ted Harper. Patrick had suggested turning on his phone, both to see what the time was and in case Alec had responded to his message. Harry had vetoed it, saying that use of the phone should be kept to the absolute minimum, and Naomi reminded him that he'd told Alec not to respond. She thought that Alec would be likely to take that instruction seriously.

Breakfast arrived and Danny brought it in. The younger man, still masked in their presence, stood guard at the door.

'You want to wash up and such before you eat?' Danny asked.

Wash up, Naomi thought. She'd noticed the odd Americanism slipping into the man's speech before, but it could mean nothing. Maybe he just watched a lot of films.

'I think that would be a very good idea,' Dorothy approved. 'I dread to think what I look like.'

Naomi couldn't help but smile.

'You look fine.' The man's voice was soft, as though he didn't want to be overheard. Fine, Naomi noted. The Emmetts said 'fine' in that same approving way that meant more than just OK. She shrugged and shook herself to get the tension from her shoulders, wondering if she was making far too much of someone's linguistic peculiarities.

The men in the group were escorted in twos and the three women allowed to go together, something Naomi was grateful for. She used the toilet and then opened the door, and took a few hesitant steps towards the line of basins. She was becoming familiar with the layout now, but it was still disconcerting, finding her way around a new environment, especially without Napoleon to guide her so carefully around the obstacles.

'It's bright sunlight again,' Megan commented, taking Naomi's hand and guiding her the rest of the way. 'I am so sick of seeing just four walls. Now I understand what they mean by cabin fever.' She hesitated and then added, 'No offence, I mean . . .'

Naomi laughed. 'I don't feel any less hemmed in just because I can't see the walls doing the hemming,' she said. 'And it's lovely to feel the sunlight – and actually, it's bright enough for me to get just a glimmer of red.'

'Really? I didn't know that.'

Naomi felt she would have asked more, but Dorothy breezed over and began to run the tap. 'Lord, but I look dreadful,' she announced loudly, then added in a whisper, 'The catch is broken in that last window, did you know that?'

'No,' Megan told her. 'But it's tiny, anyway.'

'The boy could get through,' Dorothy informed her.

'So?' Megan queried.

'Well, he could get away.'

Naomi washed her face, half glad she couldn't see the way she looked. She ran damp hands through her hair in an effort to untangle it and unstick it from her scalp. 'Apart from the fact that neither Harry nor I would allow it, what good would it do?'

'Well –' Dorothy sounded faintly offended – 'It's the duty of all prisoners to try to escape!'

'This isn't Colditz,' Naomi told her, 'and we're hostages, not prisoners of war. I think there might be a subtle difference.'

'You lot in there, hurry it up.' It was the friendly man's voice. Naomi had noticed that he only raised it when Ted Harper was hovering. Dorothy had made the same observation.

'Old big mouth must be on the prowl,' Dorothy remarked.

'We'd better go.'

'Keep the bugger waiting,' Dorothy announced. 'What can he do?'

'Dorothy, I don't think we want to find out,' Naomi told

her. She began to move towards the door, hand outstretched. Megan took her arm, leaving Dorothy to bring up the rear.

'You know,' Megan said quietly as they crossed the reception area of the bank. 'I'm not sure if I'm more scared of what *he* might do, or of Dorothy.'

Naomi squeezed her arm, but said nothing. Two totally unpredictable souls in the one place and on opposite sides. No, it didn't exactly make for a sense of security.

Danny shut the door on the hostages and crossed back to where Ted and Alan were standing. Ted leaning against the wall and Alan at his post by the window.

Danny perched beside him on the table.

'We need to talk.'

'Talk? What about?'

'About how we propose to get out of here. You've got to open communications, Ted. We let some of the hostages go, they gave us food, now it's our turn again.'

Ted scowled at him.

'They won't wait forever,' Danny told him, 'and they'll know by now where we're keeping the others, and the layout of this place. It's only a matter of time before they give up on us and come in mob-handed.'

'Then we split the buggers up and, if the filth try anything, we shoot somebody. That old woman for a start.'

'Why didn't you let her go?' Alan asked.

Ted shrugged. 'What's it matter to you?'

'Ted, this is getting us nowhere. Use the phone they sent in. Tell them we'll release the others if they guarantee us safe passage. Let a couple go, once we have transport, just to show good faith, and the others when we reach our destination.'

'Where would we go?' Alan asked.

'Somewhere with no extradition treaty. Brazil, maybe, even Spain for starters.'

'With no money.'

'We'll ask for money.'

'I don't ask for nothing.'

'Demand it then. Ted, it's either that or we wait until they

99

bust in here, and the only place you'll be going after that is back to jail, and it'll be Cat. A all the way through this time. Not some soft option of an open prison, like you've had the past few years.'

'I don't want to go to jail,' Alan said plaintively. 'I—'

'Oh, shut your mouth. You're a bloody wuss. Just like your mam.'

'Mam used to say I was just like you,' Alan retorted. It didn't sound as though the accusation had given him any pleasure.

'There's another thing,' Danny added, changing tack and raising his voice to stop the incipient father–son argument. 'What to do with Ash.'

'Leave him where he is.'

'They won't let us out if they know he's dead, will they?' Alan asked miserably. 'I mean, robbery – even robbery with shooters – is one thing, but killing someone . . . That's something else.'

'Which is exactly why we treat the hostages right,' Danny said. That'll count in our favour. The ones we let out will tell the police we treated them OK, looked after them.'

'You think that'll make any difference, you're more stupid than you look.'

Danny sighed. 'OK, leave that for the minute,' he said. 'What do we do with Ashwin? We can't just leave him there.'

'Why not?' Alan sounded as though he didn't really want to know.

'Because he'll start to stink. And the flies have already moved in. This time tomorrow there'll be maggots.'

'Flies? How did they get in?' Alan gazed through round eyes as though Danny had scared him with a tale of monsters.

'Through the window,' Danny explained patiently. 'The flies arrive minutes after someone dies. They smell it – and there's something else, either of you noticed it's getting warmer in here?'

Ted looked sharply at him then glanced upward at the lights. They'd been left on all night and no one had bothered to switch them off again. 'They've cut the bloody power,' he announced.

Danny nodded.

'When?' Alan sounded even more panicked.

'I don't know for sure. I noticed the hand dryers weren't working earlier, so I tried the lights. We can't leave Ash inside. The temperature will go up rapidly now, and he's going to rot.'

Alan turned away. He looked sick. Ted Harper shrugged.

'We'll manage,' he announced. 'Those buggers in there are going to suffer too. They'll switch the power back on soon enough.'

'I don't think they will. They know who's in there now . . .'

'And whose bloody fault is that?'

'They'll know that they're all able-bodied and capable of coping with a little more discomfort. Ted, my guess is, we don't start talking soon, they'll wait until it's dark and come and get us anyway.'

'Then we'll be waiting for them, won't we?' Ted Harper said.

Alec glanced once more through the press clipping Simon had delivered to him. They would be joined soon by the official files – now Simon had told them what exactly they were looking for; and Alec had to reluctantly admit that had saved them some time.

The story the clipping told was a worrying one. Ted Harper was a local man, but thirteen years ago he'd also shown signs of sense. He'd committed three armed robberies, but the closest one had been a good hundred miles away, which was why Hemmings hadn't picked him up on the initial collection of evidence. Local records would have focussed on the assault on his wife and his subsequent arrest. The likelihood was that it would have been filed as a domestic. He had been tried in the area where he'd committed his third robbery and, although it had made a bit of a splash in the local papers, coverage had not been nearly as active as it might have been had he gone through the local courts.

Although, now, it would have been perfectly possible to cross-reference data on Ted Harper through computer records of other forces, records from a dozen years before were still on paper file and not easily available.

101

The reports mentioned Naomi as a minor player. She'd been part of a surveillance team on the night of his arrest, but the hero of the moment was her partner that night, a young woman by the name of DC Polly Thompson, who'd entered the building without waiting for back-up and so probably saved Nan Harper's life.

Alec had a vague memory of Polly Thompson. She'd transferred to the Met a few years before and was now, if he remembered right, a fully fledged inspector. Definitely someone worth talking to, he thought, if this went on much longer. According to the reports, Harper had demonstrated excessive levels of violence in the robberies – carried out with an accomplice who had never been caught – and his battery of his wife had been brutal in the extreme. He believed that his wife had tipped off the police. Something she had, apparently, continued to deny.

'I'm still not happy about us cutting power,' Alec said. He looked across at Sam. 'I'll go with your recommendation, of course, but I don't like the idea—'

'Of making the hostages more uncomfortable? I know. But we have to show we're in control. This is a bargaining chip, Alec. They start to cooperate, we put the power back on. Maybe. Or we send in more food.'

'You'd recommend withholding food?'

'Maybe. Not water, of course, though supplies of that won't be affected with what we've done so far. But food is another bargaining chip. It can be provided or withheld. We'll allow them to consider for a while, then we'll use the phone later. Unless, of course, they contact us first.'

'If the phone's still in one piece,' Hemmings commented.

'I tried a half hour ago. There's a signal,' Sarah told him. 'We can test without it ringing.'

'Couldn't we have fitted it with a bug or something?' Hemmings asked, a plaintive note in his voice.

'Well, in theory, yes,' Sam told him. 'Getting the right technical back-up and the expertise at short notice isn't that easy. And it costs. Someone would have to decide whose budget it was coming out of.'

Hemmings snorted. 'So,' he said. 'We're waiting again?'

'We are,' Sam agreed. But knowing what we do about Ted Harper adds a certain urgency to the situation. Naomi remembered him. It's entirely possible that Harper will realize who she is, and the longer this goes on, the more time he has to think about it.'

It was not, Alec thought, a comforting analysis. He glanced at the clock. Nine thirty. He had a press conference scheduled for ten followed by a meeting with the relatives. 'Has anyone found family for the Brigadier yet?' he asked.

'Not so far as I know. So far we've not found anyone that cares if the poor old bugger's alive or dead.'

'I'd better be off,' Alec said.

'Right you are, but before you go. We took a guess at your size, so, if it doesn't fit, blame me.'

'What?'

Hemmings nodded at someone behind Alec and he turned to find a young officer holding out a still wrapped shirt. 'Don't worry, Alec, he's one of mine, I'll mark his shopping trip down as admin. Have a wash before you put it on.'

Alec took the shirt gratefully and headed for the bathroom.

'My father was a soldier and his father before that. It seemed like the only thing to do,' Paul Hebden said.

'Were you in a war?' Patrick asked.

'I missed out on the second war by three or four years, but I saw action, yes. In the Far East mainly, and I was in India in '47.'

'Partition,' Harry said.

'Yes, that's right. Messy time. Bloody messy time. I've been back since. It's a beautiful country, it really is.'

'Partition?' Patrick didn't get the reference.

'India and Pakistan,' Harry explained. 'When the British pulled out, the country was divided along roughly religious lines and Pakistan was born.'

'Pity the fool that drew the line on the map didn't actually take a look at the ground first,' Paul Hebden commented. 'There were a lot of people caught on the wrong side when the borders closed, and a great many died because of it.'

'Naomi says that's what happened in Africa,' Patrick

103

commented. 'That people just drew lines on a map and divided the country up. That's why there are so many straight lines.'

'It happened all over,' the Brigadier told him. 'Have you ever seen any pictures of Simla?'

'No, I don't think so.'

'If you *do* become a photographer, you should take a trip there,' he recommended. 'It was the place that all the bigwigs in the raj escaped to when the summer got too hot. They camped out in the mountains where the air was, well, not cool exactly, but at least bearable. Simla is . . . well, it's as though someone took an old English town and planted it up there in the foothills. A little train winds its way up the hillside there, through the tea plantations, it takes an age. You can almost walk faster. If you go there, you should walk up and take your pictures on the way. You'll think you're walking out of India and into . . . Stratford upon Avon. Somewhere like that.'

'It sounds cool,' Patrick said. 'There's lots of places I'd like to go.'

'You've not mentioned family,' Dorothy said. She'd been quiet for a while, listening to Paul Hebden talk. It was the first time he'd really opened up.

'Oh, family. I've a brother somewhere, unless he's dead. He was older than me. But I never married and I was always on the move. I always thought there'd be time for that later, but you know, suddenly you find that it is later and you never noticed until you were there.'

There seemed no easy way of following that and for a few minutes silence reigned. Typically, it was Dorothy who broke through the reverie. 'Did anyone notice that little window in the lavatory?' she said. 'The catch is broken and I bet that Patrick could get through.'

Naomi sighed.

'I noticed it,' Patrick said. 'But I wouldn't leave my dad or Naomi.'

Naomi could have hugged him.

'I noticed something else as well,' he added before Dorothy could get another word in. 'I think the electric must have gone off.'

'Oh?' Naomi was intrigued. 'Why?'

''Cos the hand dryers wouldn't work and the black man, the nice one, he noticed and he tried the light switch. Nothing happened. I started to ask him about it but he shook his head, so I didn't. The big guy was standing just behind him and I think he didn't want him to realize right then. Do you think the police had the power cut, Nomi?'

'It's possible. If they did, then they're trying to put the pressure on. Speed things up.'

'Well, I'm in favour of that,' Dorothy applauded. 'Anything that gets us out of here sooner.'

'It means it'll be very dark tonight,' Megan commented.

'Scared of the bogeyman, Megs?' Tim asked her, poking her playfully in the ribs.

She squeaked. 'Fool!'

'Seriously though,' Tim continued, 'do you think that means they plan to do something tonight, storm the building or something when it's dark?'

Naomi frowned. 'I don't know,' she said. 'It could just be a bargaining ploy. They want more cooperation from the thieves, I suppose.'

'So, what do we do, if that does happen?' Megan asked.

Funny, Naomi thought. Since they had found out what she had once been, she was suddenly the expert on everything. 'Stay calm and stay down,' she said. 'Flat on the floor and wait. If they do come in, there's a chance they'll use stun grenades first. You'll hear a very loud bang and there'll be a lot of smoke.'

'Hopefully,' Harry said, 'the police will simply be able to talk the thieves out before it comes to that.'

Eighteen

Simon went home for long enough to change, then drove across town to Trigo Place, where Ted Harper had been arrested.

The layout of the road was an odd one. A square of houses facing on to a green, houses in the corners set at right angles to one another and a cut through between those gardens leading through to the next street. He parked his car and wandered down between the houses at the second corner. Looking up to his left he could see the bedroom window from which Naomi and Polly Thompson must have kept watch, and a little further on his right, the back gate to the Harper property, as it had been then. The gate was slatted and he could see into the garden. Children's toys were scattered across the lawn and two children played on a swing set. He could just glimpse a woman, their mother presumably, as she moved from the window across to the open back door. She looked quite young. He knew from his check of the electoral role that the residents were called Williams. He wondered if Nan Harper had stayed for long after her husband's arrest and if these people knew about the violent past their house had observed.

He returned to Trigo Place and knocked on the door of number twenty-seven, the house next to the Harpers'. He had noticed the neat, well-established front garden and the old but immaculately kept car on the hard standing just in front of the front door. By contrast, number twenty-five, the Harpers' old place, looked slightly overgrown. Not untidy, not exactly uncared for, just the sort of garden owned by a woman with small children and a man who worked all hours. Their gardening tasks were confined to odd hours at weekends. Unlike the house next door.

106

Older people lived here, Simon guessed. Probably retired. Possibly long resident.

He walked up to the red front door and rang the bell.

At first he thought he'd been wrong in his guess. The girl who answered the door looked no more than twenty. She looked askance at him.

'Whatever you're selling, we don't want any.'

Simon smiled. 'I'm not selling,' he said. 'I'm looking for someone, but you'd be far too young to remember them.'

The girl frowned, then smiled as though unable to decide how to take that statement. She half turned – careful to keep one eye fixed on Simon – and shouted over her shoulder. 'Nan, it's someone for you.'

For a moment, Simon was utterly confused. Had he got the wrong house? Was Nan Harper living next door? 'Nan?' he asked.

She looked at him as though he were stupid. 'My gran,' she said. 'Look, what is it you want?'

Simon almost laughed aloud. Nan. Of course. His own grandparents were always referred to as Gran and Grandpa, his mum holding the opinion that 'Nan' was 'common', but Patrick usually talked about Mari that way. 'I told you, I'm looking for someone,' he repeated. 'Her name's Nan. For a moment, I thought . . .'

'Oh,' she said, then laughed. 'Oh, I see. I didn't think Nan was a name . . .'

'You must be after Nan Harper,' a woman said.

The girl stepped back from the doorway, allowing her grandmother to see the visitor. She stood guard though, and Simon could still see the suspicion in her eyes despite the brief laughter. *

'That's right,' he said. 'I know she's not here any more. I wonder if you knew where she'd gone to.'

The older woman studied him carefully, a frown creasing between her eyes. 'What would you want with Nan Harper?' she wanted to know. 'She moved out nine, ten years ago.'

So, not straight after Ted Harper's arrest, Simon thought. That was one question answered. 'Do you know where she went to?'

The woman shrugged. 'Moved to Pinsent, I think. That lad of hers was taken into care and she shifted herself fast enough after that. A bad lot, the whole family. We were glad to see the back of them. Now, what do you want with her?'

Pinsent, that was good. A simple check of the electoral roll and, hopefully, she'd still be there. 'Her son?'

'Yes, her son. Look, who the devil are you?'

Simon smiled. 'Thanks,' he said. 'You've been very helpful.' He turned and strode back to his car.

'I've a good mind to call the police round,' the woman shouted at him.

Simon, sitting in his car now, with the engine humming, waved at her. No need, he thought. A police car could be seen rounding the corner of Trigo Place, no doubt coming to make the same inquiry he was making. Careful not to draw attention, he drove away. A quarter of a mile down the road, he pulled in for long enough to use his phone.

'I need an address,' he told Millie, the older of the two archivists. She had a soft spot for Simon and he traded on it. Quickly, he told her what he wanted, then set the phone in its cradle and groped in the glove compartment for his headset. With luck, she'd get him the information he wanted before he got to Pinsent. And hopefully, too, before the police headed the same way.

Alec had a dislike of press conferences, which came from his having to front far too many. Both Superintendent Blick and Alec's immediate boss, DCI Travers, pushed him into the role as often as they could. Travers said he reckoned Alec's accent added class to the proceedings, but Alec figured he was only winding him up. Alec, it had to be admitted, was generally pretty good at managing such events. Not easily rattled, and at ease with awkward questions that others stumbled over, he had been his own worst enemy in the avoidance game.

Today was different, though. Today was personal and he was going to find things doubly hard.

He was uncomfortably aware that his shirt was still creased from the packing. He wore his jacket, despite the heat, partly to convey a more formal air, partly to hide the square creases

108

that decorated him, front and back. He hoped that they would drop out with wear and body heat.

They had borrowed a function room at a nearby hotel. It was being used by some of the visiting journalists and others were rumoured to have spent most of the night in the bar. It made a convenient location. Across the room, he spotted Dick Travers. He nodded acknowledgement. Alec knew he'd have to talk to him afterwards. He'd avoided two calls from Travers that morning, allowing Hemmings to field them for him. He knew what they'd been about. Travers would have seen the list of remaining hostages. He would have recognized Naomi's name.

Alec took his place at the table. Travers came to sit beside him and Andrews, as chief liaison for the families, joined them. It had been agreed, Alec would make a brief statement and they would allow a few questions. After that, they'd then leave, pleading operational confidentiality as reason for not saying more.

Andrews gave him a brief smile. He looked tense and tired and Alec wondered if he'd managed any sleep.

'Good morning,' Alec began. 'As you are all aware, we have a hostage situation that developed from a failed armed robbery yesterday morning. A number of those held, including three children, were released unharmed late last night and all indications are that they were treated well by their captors. Negotiations to facilitate the release of the others are ongoing and will continue for as long as necessary. Our main, in fact our only, concern here is to get everyone safely out of the building and back with their families.'

'Does that include the hostage-takers?'

'It includes everyone. We've no wish to see anyone hurt.'

'Clement Fry. *Pinsent Herald*. Do you know how many hostages are still inside?'

'There are seven,' Dick Travers replied. 'Their families have been informed and are being given counselling and support.'

'How dangerous are these men?' someone else asked. She was from a cable news channel, but Alec didn't catch which one.

'Anyone armed with a gun has to be perceived as dangerous,' he said. 'We are striving to keep the situation as calm and controlled as possible.'

'You understand, I'm sure, that, for reasons of operational security, we can't give details,' Travers added.

'You're making use of hostage negotiators?'

'We have a team of experienced negotiators at our disposal, yes.'

'And when do you expect this to end? What's the cost going to be to tax payers? Do any of the families want to make a statement? Are there terrorist links?'

The questions had begun to blur, but that last one caught Alec's attention. It hadn't occurred to him that such a notion might be raised.

'These are common or garden criminals,' Dick Travers said heavily. 'There's no reason at all to believe there's anything more than greed here as a motive, or they intended this situation to escalate in the way it has.'

'And why did it escalate? How did it get to *be* a hostage situation?' Alec glanced around, recognizing the voice. 'As I understand it, the police arrived, sirens blaring and tyres screeching, and alerted the robbers to what was going on. Surely, Inspector, if they'd arrived quietly, you could have nabbed the beggars as they came out?'

'Mr, er . . . Tyso, isn't it?' Dick Travers asked, though Alec knew he had no difficulty recalling the name. Tyso was a pain in the proverbial. 'Still freelancing, are we?'

Tyso just smiled. 'Once in a while we freelancers get lucky,' he said. 'I suggest you keep your eye on the evening news, Inspector.'

Travers frowned and Alec noted Constable Andrews shifting uncomfortably at his side. 'Tell you after,' Andrews whispered. 'I only just found out.'

'We will, of course, be examining the operational side of this and carrying out a complete analysis once we have brought events to a satisfactory resolution,' Alec said. He was operating on automatic now, resorting to bland report-speak.

Travers rose to leave and Alec took his cue. 'If that's all, ladies and gentlemen, we'll give you an update later on today.'

Numbly, he followed Travers out of the hall.

*   *   *

110

Travers led him out to his car and motioned him inside. Andrews hopped in beside the driver.

'Two questions. Why haven't you stood down and what the hell was Tyso talking about?'

'I can tell you the answer to the second,' Andrews said, buying Alec some thinking time. 'I found out this morning. The Parkers, husband and wife, released last night, they've agreed to be interviewed by Tyso. It's going out live on the six o'clock.'

Travers groaned. 'Who was their liaison officer? Why didn't they try to put a stop to it or at least give us some warning?'

'The Parkers didn't want anyone. Refused point-blank. Said they'd handle things their own way. I took their statement and passed it on with the rest. How Tyso got wind, I don't know, but they were making enough noise at the hospital last night for anyone to have heard. I only found out this morning because Brian Machin had given them a call to see how they were, and they told him about it. He got straight on to me, but by that time . . .'

'Right load of wallies we're going to look,' Travers said heavily. 'What have you done with the gung-ho idiots who made all the noise?'

'I'll suspend them when we can do without,' Alec said heavily. 'I've got them standing the cordon. Full uniform. Compulsory stab vests.'

Travers made a dismissive sound and Alec knew it was his turn now. He got in first. 'I told Hemmings yesterday, about Naomi. We both agreed there was a job to be done and we'd do better to get it done. If you replace me now, after what Tyso said in there, it'll look like a vote of no confidence and, frankly, I resent that.'

'This isn't about you saving face, Alec. It's about personal involvement.'

'Half the team know or knew Naomi,' Alec returned. 'You going to pull them off the case?'

'It's hardly the same thing,' Travers replied angrily. 'Look, Alec, I've got a meeting with Superintendent Blick in –' he glanced at his watch – 'twenty minutes. I can't keep this from him, but I'll recommend that you remain as SIO, for now.

111

However, I'm telling you this as a friend as well as your boss: the first time you show yourself less than up to the job, you are out. Got that?'

Alec nodded. 'I'd expect no less,' he replied with as much dignity as he could muster. 'Drop me here, I'll walk back to the incident room.'

Travers gave instructions to his driver and Alec left. He watched the car drive off and felt suddenly terribly bereft and very much alone. He was left wondering if he'd done the right thing.

'Be all right, Naomi. You've just got to be all right.' He didn't think he could live with the alternative.

The sound of a telephone shocked them all. Naomi had been dozing and it dragged her rudely back into the waking world.

'I thought he'd smashed them all,' Megan whispered.

'They must have sent a mobile in with the food,' Naomi guessed.

'You think they'll answer it, or just smash that one to bits too?'

Naomi didn't reply, she strained her ears to hear through the storeroom door. The ring was silenced, but there had been no crash, no sounds of breaking. 'Sounds as though someone answered it,' she said. She shuffled towards the door and the others crowded round her, ears pressed to its surface. A murmur of voices filtered through the thickness of wood and insulation, but hard as they tried, they could hear no more.

Danny had picked up the phone. Ted stared at him, his eyes cold and his jaw working, clenching and bunching the muscles, but he said nothing and did not intervene.

'Yes?' Danny said. Then listened. 'Look, Sarah, or whatever your name is, we want to get out of here and we want the power put back on.'

He listened again. 'Well, talk about stating the bloody obvious. Yes, it's getting hot. Yes, we're all frigging uncomfortable. So, what's our next move? And don't give me that "it's up to you" crap.'

Ted moved impatiently and Danny shifted further from his reach, keeping an eye on him as he did so. 'Look, we've got demands and we've got seven people in here who would rather be just about anywhere else, so I suggest you listen.' He frowned then and shook the phone. 'Hello. Hello.' He stared at Ted Harper. 'She bloody hung up on me.'

'Was that wise?' Hemmings asked.

'He'll ring me back. The number's on fast dial, like I just told him.'

'What if he doesn't?'

'He will,' Sam reassured. 'It might take a little while, but he will.'

They had been listening on the speakerphone and Alec was looking far from happy. 'That's not Ted Harper,' he said. 'Sounds too young.'

'No, I'm guessing that's the man in Brian Machin's picture,' Sarah suggested. 'Slight trace of accent, not local, not strongly anything.'

'Reasonably well educated, I'd have said,' Sam added.

'Shouldn't you have listened to their demands?'

'We will,' Sarah reassured Hemmings. 'When he calls back.'

Danny paced the length of the bank reception. Ted had said nothing, just growled something under his breath, as though letting Danny know this was exactly what he had expected. Alan was twittering with anxiety, but Danny wasn't listening to him.

'I'm going to try again,' Danny said to no one in particular. 'Call them, tell them what we want.'

'You know what we want, do you?' Ted Harper mocked. 'What's that then? A helicopter loaded with cash to land on the roof and fly us over the rainbow?'

'Why not?' Alan wanted to know. 'We've got them in there. We could make them give us anything we want.'

Danny's look was pitying. 'It won't be that easy,' he said. 'Alan, our main concern here is to stay out of jail, remember. Anything else is a bonus. Right, the lady said to press one if we wanted a little chat, so . . .' He held the phone at arm's length and pressed a button, then hesitated for a moment before lifting it to his ear.

Sarah let the phone ring. Twice, three times, four. Alec's nerve was breaking when she finally, casually, reached to pick it up. 'Good afternoon, this is Sarah.'

'Right, hang up on me again and I'll make sure someone suffers for it.'

'I don't think you will. I think you've got more sense. More compassion, for that matter.'

'You're assuming a hell of a lot, lady.'

'I'm making my assumptions based on sound evidence. You got yourself into this by following the wrong man into the wrong situation, now your main concern is to get yourself out with as little of the shitty stuff clinging to you as possible. Stop me if I'm reading you wrong.'

'No. Maybe. I don't know. Look, we want the power back on. We released those people last night . . .'

'And we rewarded you with food, drink and a phone. Same again this morning. Now, what do you have to offer us?'

'The lives of seven people, that's what.' His tone had changed and Sarah was quick to recognize it.

'Your boss listening to you, is he?' she asked softly. 'Now, hear me. You can salvage this. So far, no one's been hurt and you've gone out of your way to make sure people have been taken care of. That's in your favour. Apart from trying to rob the place in the first instance, you've got everything right so far, so don't screw up now. He's not worth it.'

'How would you know?'

'No one is. Not this. No one. Nothing. What amount of money would make this right?'

The man on the phone took a deep breath and released it slowly. 'We want a car. No, we need a minibus. Take us and the hostages to the nearest airfield. Then, we want a plane. When we're free and clear, we let the rest go.'

'And where would you want to fly to?'

'Spain. Yeah, you'll fly us to Spain.' His confidence seemed to be growing now she'd not denied him out of hand. Sarah was silent for all of thirty seconds before she spoke again.

114

'I have people to talk to,' she said. '*I* can't authorize anything, you understand that?'

'Yeah.' He sounded slightly deflated. 'Well, you talk to those people and you make sure we get what we want.'

He hung up that time.

'Well, what do you think?' Alec said.

'About what? It'll be bloody tough to get authorization for that lot. It's against policy, you know that, Alec.'

'We give them time,' Sam said quietly. 'Time to consider what they've asked for and to make them think we're taking their requests seriously. And, Sarah, next time, remind him that these are *requests*. He's in no position to be making demands.'

Sarah nodded. 'Right you are. You taking the next call?'

'Yes. I think that might be best.'

Hemmings was puzzled. 'I thought the idea was for you to build a rapport? Wouldn't it be better for them just to bond with the same person?'

'We have to play it by ear,' Sam told him. 'If this was a suicide, then yes, you allow that rapport to be built and you keep consistency right the way through. In a case like this, you want to keep your subject on the edge of their comfort zone, gradually guide them to where you have the control.'

'You make it sound like a game,' Alec said harshly.

Sam regarded him thoughtfully for several seconds before replying. 'I don't play games with people's lives,' he said.

Two in the afternoon and Simon was lost in the middle of Pinsent. The roads that led back from the seafront narrowed dramatically and suddenly once you got away from the promenade and larger residences converted to bed-and-breakfast accommodation. Beyond that, a network of terraced streets and old factories told the story of the town's industrial past. There had been complaints a few years before of commuters using these streets as rat runs to get to the new industrial estate built on the outskirts, and the local council had made many of them one-way. The result was, you could see the street you wanted; it just took a bit of working out how to get to it. In the end, Simon parked his car and walked.

He was trying to get to Alexandra Road. The streets either side were named for other members of the royal family – the Victorian royal family. Albert and Edward and Victoria herself, plus her cousins and many offspring. Alexandra had a shabby, run-down look to it. The houses were flat-fronted and opened from the pavement directly into the living room. The front steps were grimy and the doors that hadn't been replaced by UPVC mostly needed a coat of paint. A few stood out from the rest because they'd been far more carefully maintained. Three in a row had cascading hanging baskets suspended between front door and living-room window. They were a little garish for Simon's taste, but a welcome splash of red and blue in a street of dull brick and grey net curtains. He was surprised to find that one of these decorated abodes was home to Nan Harper.

The door was white plastic and the bell next to it bore a sticky label that told him to ring three times. Simon did as he was told. He wondered if he'd find anyone at home that time of day, but he was in luck. The woman who opened the door and asked him what he wanted was a faded blonde. A scar ran from the side of her nose and marred the corner of her mouth, and another, faded but still visible, pulled at the corner of her eye. He wondered if she'd ever tried to do anything about them, then wondered if they'd show as much if her skin was less tanned. 'Nan Harper?' he asked. 'Ex-wife of Ted Harper?'

She started, stared at him in something close to horror, and then she slammed the door.

Simon had expected many reactions, but not that one. He rang the bell again.

'Piss off, or I'll call the police.'

'I half expected you to change your name,' Simon told her. 'Go back to your maiden name, or something. He leaned back against the corner of the wall and the doorpost and crossed his arms comfortably. 'I wondered if you'd seen him lately, Mrs Harper. If you knew what he'd been up to.'

'I don't know and I don't care. Anyway, he's still in prison.' He heard the doubt in her voice and a moment later the door opened a crack. Simon pushed away from the wall and turned to face her. 'Isn't he?' she asked.

'No, he's most definitely not. But don't fret; if he'd been after you, I think you'd have had a visit by now, he's been out near on eighteen months.'

Nan Harper stared at him. 'The probation service was supposed to let me know,' she said. 'They gave their word they'd tell victim support.' She lifted a shaking finger to touch her face. 'He damn near killed me . . . if it hadn't been for that girl.'

'I know,' Simon told her. 'I found the old reports in the papers.'

She was puzzled. 'What the hell made you look for *them*? You'd have been a kid at school when Ted Harper made the news.' She frowned, peering more closely at him. 'Who are you, anyway?'

Simon had thought of many excuses to give Nan Harper – a long-dead relative; a survey from the British Crime Institute, a double-glazing salesman with a distinct absence of samples and an odd curiosity concerning the wives of armed robbers. He'd finally settled on the truth, or something close to it. 'I'm a journalist,' he said. He found that the word journalist had more kudos than reporter did. The likes of Kate Adie and Jon Snow were journalists. Reporters were, somehow, a cheaper lot. 'I'm doing a series of articles on the rehabilitation of criminals, particularly those involved in violent crime. I'm interested in the victims' point of view as well. Do you believe that rehabilitation can ever work? What would you want to say to the . . .'

'What would I want to say to Ted Harper? You wouldn't be able to print it. I live with what he did to me and I wake up at night scared to death in case he comes back.' She was retreating again, about to close the door. Simon thought about putting his foot in the way, but he'd done that once before and ended up with a broken toe. Instead he used a more metaphorical wedge.

'What effect did it have on your son, Ted going to prison? Did he know what his father had done to you?'

Nan Harper recoiled as though he'd slapped her.

'Alan was like his dad,' she said bitterly. 'Never thought. Just did what he wanted. I couldn't cope with him before his dad went, and after – afterwards he were even worse. His gran took him for a while, then my sister. I was in and out of hospital. Neither of them could understand him or control him. He ran wild, didn't want to talk, didn't play like other kids. He just went quiet and withdrew like no one in the world was worth talking to.'

'The night Ted assaulted you for the last time, was Alan there? Did he see?'

Her expression was contemptuous. 'You're all alike,' she said. 'Talking about Alan like he were the victim. Yes, he saw. He saw what his dad did to me time and time again, and you know what he said? Dad didn't mean it. Dad told me he didn't mean it. Don't make him go away. Ted trained him like that. Trained him to take his side. Well, I couldn't cope with him any more, no more than I could cope with his dad. He got taken into care when he was nine, and I signed the papers. Maybe I was an unfit mother, I don't know, but he was sure as hell an unfit son.'

Her gaze flickered past him and Simon turned. A police car had parked a little way down the street and two uniformed officers approached. They were staring at Simon and Nan Harper.

'What the hell do they want?'

'Probably to ask if you've seen Ted,' Simon told her. 'Thanks, Mrs Harper, you've been very helpful.'

Nan Harper looked from him to the officers and then stepped back and shut the door.

'Doing a survey,' Simon said to the approaching officers. 'I don't think she's buying today.'

He decided not to push his luck any further and was glad that he hadn't given his name. Word would get back to Alec, he supposed, and Alec would put two and two together. Afro-Caribbean men asking difficult questions about a certain armed robber were likely to be thin on the ground.

He sobered, thinking about Naomi and the others. They'd been good friends to him when he'd really needed them. What was happening back there?

The reports in the newspapers had made no mention of the boy, Alan. Was he still using his father's name? People did, more often than not. Changing your identity in the normal run of things, without access to big money and false passports, could be a major pain, especially if you still lived in the same area and – he acknowledged this might be the snob in him coming out – he didn't see any of the Harper clan going through the legal complications of deed poll. That seemed too sophisticated by half.

So. Back to the electoral roll? Look for Alan Harper. Or back to the cordon, see if anything had changed in his absence. He decided on the latter option, then he'd go back to finding Alan Harper, see if he'd seen his father since his release, could guess at the names of his associates.

Unless, of course, Alan Harper knew exactly where his father was because he was with him inside the bank.

Nineteen

In the middle of the afternoon, Danny used the mobile again. Sam answered.

'Where's Sarah?'

'She's taking a break right now.'

'A break.' Danny was silent for a moment. 'Nice for some. Maybe I'll call back later.'

Sam caught the ironic note, but ignored it. 'If you'd prefer that,' he said. 'Or you could talk to me. The choice is yours.'

'I wanted answers,' Danny told him. 'She told you what our demands were?'

'Sarah relayed your *requests*, yes.'

There was another hesitation. 'Well?'

'They're being considered.'

'Considered! You've had long enough to *consider*. You're playing games with us, man. I know it.'

'I'm not playing games,' Sam told him. 'Look, I'd feel a lot more comfortable if I knew what to call you. You have a name I can use?'

'Why should I give you my name?'

'I didn't suggest that. I said any name. Just something I can use. Make things a little more comfortable.'

'Danny. Call me Danny.' Then, as though catching himself and pulling back, 'Look, I don't bloody care what makes you comfortable. I want answers, and if you can't give them to me, I want to talk to someone who can.'

'OK, Danny, I'll get on to it,' Sam told him. He frowned, there seemed to be some kind of altercation going on in the background and Danny could be heard remonstrating. Then a second voice came over the speakerphone.

'Enough bloody stalling. You'll get us what we asked for

120

and you'll do it now. You've got an hour, then I start hurting people.'

'You hurt anyone,' Sam warned, 'and you'll get nothing.'

'So, no change then? That supposed to be persuasive, is it? Way I see it, we hold all the cards, all seven of them. They'd be any less valuable, would they, if we reduced that to six? Five maybe? Think about it, copper. An hour.'

He hung up and left Sam staring thoughtfully at the phone.

'That how you intended it to go?' Hemmings asked.

'It's what I half expected,' Sam told him.

'Do you think he'll carry out his threat?' Alec was anxious.

'We need to stall him,' Sarah said. 'Make him think there's some chance of him getting what he wants. That the threat is working, but also that if he carries it out, we'd act, regardless of the hostages.'

'We wouldn't though,' Alec said. 'Not unless the situation got desperate. Ted Harper may not realize that, but this Danny certainly would. What are the odds on it being his real name?'

'I'd say pretty high,' was Sarah's opinion. 'There was no thinking time. He came up with the name very quickly.'

'Danny wants out of there.' Sam sounded certain. 'I think Danny's getting to the point when he doesn't even much care about the consequences. He knows they're in a no-win situation and he's making the best he can of it.'

'We should let them know we're aware of Harper's identity.' Hemmings had put this view before. A decision had been held over.

'Maybe,' Sam was still hedging. 'The wife's still refusing to come and talk to him?'

Alec nodded. 'I've had two teams of officers talk to her. The first lot didn't even get a response and the second had to argue through a closed door.'

'We should have pulled your reporter friend.' Hemmings was severely narked at what he saw as Simon's interference.

'He did nothing illegal, and probably did nothing to alter Nan Harper's decision,' Alec reminded him. 'And it's highly unlikely she could have got through to Ted anyway.'

'Might have shocked him into some kind of response.'

'The wrong kind, possibly,' Sam reminded him. He'd been

121

against Nan's involvement, feeling she'd be the wrong kind of trigger. 'Nothing on the son either?'

'He's not at his home address. He has a record for minor offences. Nothing violent. He stole a couple of cars, was caught third time out, but the neighbours reckoned someone matching Harper senior's description visited several times over the past few weeks, which gives us probable cause. I've got Dick Travers arranging a warrant.'

'You think he's in there with his father?' Sarah asked. She shrugged. 'It would fit with what we know.'

'Wouldn't surprise me. So, we wait a while and then call back, tell them what? That we're making progress? Think they'll buy that? How long does it take to obtain a minibus?' Hemmings was as impatient as Harper in his own way.

'We tell them the plane will take more organizing,' Alec advised. 'He might not buy it, but he'll want to. It puts the ball back in his court. He can believe we're dancing to his tune for a while and that buys us valuable time. Then we try to get Danny back on the phone. Danny's our fifth columnist.'

'Divide and conquer,' Hemmings said, but he didn't look happy. 'It could go the other way, you know that. Nothing more dangerous than a cornered animal, and if Harper decides he's being manipulated . . .'

'The alternative is to do nothing,' Sam reminded him. He pushed the dull blond hair back off his face and stretched. He looked as crumpled and tired as Alec felt. Sarah, by contrast, in her short denim skirt and fuchsia top, looked cool and neat. Her braided hair, caught back in a band, lay prettily around her shoulders. Some people, Alec had noticed, seem to have that knack of always looking good.

Alec thought about Naomi. She'd let her hair grow over the past months, after years of keeping it short. It curled now it was longer, slightly wiry, unruly waves that resisted her efforts at control. A little imagination and he could feel it, twining about his fingers.

'Alec?'

He realized belatedly that Hemmings had been talking to him. 'Sorry. What?'

122

'Reports just in, they've found the car, the Granada the thieves used yesterday. It's been burned out in a lane about a mile from Morton Park. A local farmer called the fire brigade and they called us, he was worried about his wheat catching. Reckons he saw someone running away across towards the main Pinsent road. It's a long way to walk back to town from there, good chance someone will have picked him up.'

'Do we have the manpower for a roadblock?' Alec wondered.

'Is it worth it? Any car that gave him a lift would be well away by now and might have turned in any of four directions at the next crossroads.'

'No, you're right. We get a checkpoint up tomorrow after-noon, catch any regulars who might have seen someone. Forensics?'

'Have to wait until the car cools down,' Hemmings reminded him. 'But we can always hope.'

Twenty

The hour deadline passed and nothing was heard from inside the bank. At four thirty it was decided that Sarah should call them, tell them that the plane might take a bit longer to organize, and see what reaction came of that. Alec handed charge to Hemmings and left them to it. They'd decided to try again with Nan Harper, now she'd had time to think about her earlier encounters with the police – not to mention a reporter – that day. Alec figured she might be able to shed some light on Ted's associates, though, according to what she'd told the police officers and the information that Simon had relayed to him, she had seen nothing of Ted since his committal and didn't even know he'd been released. Discussion with the probation service confirmed this was probably true. They'd tried to contact her to tell her Ted was out, but she was no longer at Trigo Place and had given no forwarding address. Evidently, no one had thought to use the electoral register, or to ask a neighbour where she might have gone, as Simon had done.

Inside the bank it had become unbearably hot. Alan had given up his watch and slumped against the wall, his legs out straight on the table top, feet pointing at opposite angles as he dozed in the heat.

Danny sat with his back to the wall, close to the main door, watching Ted Harper. He had the phone to hand, intending to be the first to answer should it ring again. He worried about Ted: the man had been pacing that same path across the floor for the past hour. Danny half expected to see a track worn in the heavy-duty carpet and it was evident he had something pressing on his mind. Danny wasn't certain what it was, but he didn't think it had anything to do with the ultimatum. That, he was pretty certain, was Ted-style bluster . . . though you could never be sure with Harper. Nine times out of ten he'd just make a lot of noise about something. It was that tenth time you had to watch for, preferably from a safe distance away.

He wiped a hand across a perspiring forehead and then dried the hand on damp jeans. The hostages, confined in a room with minimal airflow, were suffering. He should take them to the toilet again soon – and add more soap and toilet paper to their demands maybe. Instinct told him that now would not be a good time. Ted's agitated pacing described a trackway between Danny and the storeroom and Danny was not inclined to cross it just yet.

A smell hung on the still air. They'd pulled the manager's door closed, but it seeped out from beneath. Danny had been in to look earlier. Body fluids stained the carpet and the face had begun to bloat, eyes sunken back into the head. Flies crawled and buzzed at the corners of the eyeballs, inside the nostrils, miring themselves in the dried blood on Ash's mouth. In his mind's eye, Danny could see the maggots that would hatch, the corpse revitalized by their creeping, writhing mass.

It had always surprised him just how swiftly decay began. That the smell of death could be there almost from the split second life departed, and how fast nature set about the job of returning what was left back to the earth.

His reverie was broken by the harsh shriek of the phone. He silenced it at once, answering on the second ring, eyes fixed on Ted Harper in case he should try to take it from him again.

It was Sarah. Danny smiled. He liked her voice.

'We've been talking to our superiors, Sarah told him, and they're doing what they can to accede to your requests, but we have to have assurances about—'

'It's all right.' Danny's voice was soft. 'He seems to have forgotten you for the moment. Look, I know the score here. You stall us hoping we'll just give up, but I'm telling you, he won't do it. He don't think like the rest of us. You want to

125

get your people out, you've got to help me out here. Give me something to work with.'

Sarah nodded, glancing meaningfully at Hemmings and Sam.

Like what? Sam wrote on a pad which he pushed towards her.

'Like what?' Sarah asked. 'Tell me what you want, Danny, and I'll do everything I can.'

Danny laughed quietly. 'I'd suggest dinner in a nice restaurant,' he said. 'That would help me a lot, but I don't suppose it's on?'

'I guess not,' Sarah confirmed. 'Come on, Danny, what do we do to resolve this?'

He started to reply, then, 'Hold it. Look, I'll get right back.' He broke the connection, leaving them staring at the speakerphone.

'Try and get him back,' Hemmings demanded.

'No, wait,' Sam told her. 'Let him make the call. Something must have been happening to make him ring off. We don't want to aggravate it.'

Hemmings was angry and disturbed. 'You heard the way he sounded.'

'All the more reason why we shouldn't add to the situation,' Sam told him firmly. Let him deal with it.'

'And if he can't?'

Sam didn't answer.

Ted Harper had stopped pacing and crossed to the storeroom door. He seemed to hesitate for a moment before turning the key and flinging it wide.

'Ted!' Danny shouted to him. 'Ted, what's up, man?'

Alan, startled awake, scrambled up to peer out of the window, then, realizing that this wasn't the cause of the alarm, clambered down and began to cross the room in Danny's wake.

'What's wrong with him?'

Danny shook his head. 'I don't know. Hey, Ted, don't get rough with the lady. Ted!'

Ted Harper had his weapon in his left hand and he raised it briefly in Danny's direction. 'You stay out of this.'

'Ted?' Danny halted. Puzzled and scared. Until now Ted had distanced himself from the hostages. This new development was frightening. He had the blind woman, Naomi, his fingers in her hair, dragging her to her feet. He was staring hard into her face.

Satisfied that Danny had halted, Ted swung the gun back and pressed it against her head.

'What's your name?' he demanded. 'No lies. I'll bloody know.'

'It's Naomi, Ted. I could have told you that. You don't need—'

'I didn't ask you!' The weapon swung back again and Danny wondered how good a shot he was with his left. He backed off, deciding he didn't want to be the one to find out.

'Naomi what?'

'Blake. Naomi Blake.'

All things considered, she sounded very calm and controlled, Danny thought. He wasn't sure he'd sound that calm with a gun against his temple. He'd be wetting himself.

'What happened to your eyes?' Ted Harper growled.

Danny was startled. What kind of a question was that?

'I lost my sight in an accident.'

Ted grunted and dropped her. She crumpled and the man called Harry gathered her tightly into his arms. He stared at Ted Harper with an expression of such hatred that Danny was taken aback. He'd figured Harry for a gentle, compliant sort. Ted would have to watch it. The hostages were approaching the stage when they would act regardless of the consequences.

Ted continued to glare for a moment, then he spat at Naomi's hair. 'Maybe there is some bloody justice after all,' he said, then turned on his heel and left, striding back into the main room.

Danny paused to lock the door and then ran after him and grabbed his arm. 'What the hell was all that about?'

'I knew I recognized her.' Ted's eyes were wild. 'I thought I'd got it wrong, but, no. It's her.'

'It's who?'

'The bitch that helped put me away last time.' Ted was

crimson with fury, veins standing out on his forehead and throat.

'Slow it down,' Danny told him. 'God, man, she's a blind woman. You got it wrong.'

'You heard what she said!' Ted Harper was almost screaming with rage now. 'She was blinded in an accident. She's the one. Naomi Blake. There was another woman too, that night. Burst in on me when I was sorting Nan out.' He turned abruptly and grabbed the front of Danny's shirt, his face so close, Danny could smell his breath and was forced to inhale two days' worth of dried-on sweat. 'When this is over, I'm going to find that bitch and finish what I started, and I'll tell you something else for free. That one's not going to be around to stop me this time.'

'OK, OK, whatever you say.' Danny raised his hands, signalling surrender. 'I believe you.'

Ted held on for a moment longer, then let go and strode away into the staff kitchen. Danny heard water running.

He turned to Alan. 'You know about this?'

'I know he nearly killed my mam,' Alan shrugged. 'I was there, hiding behind the cupboard door. I remember seeing someone come in, but that's about all. Mam seemed to blame me for it all.' He shrugged again. 'I'd seen him beat up on her so many times, but that last time, I think he would have killed her and me too if he'd known I was there.'

Danny was at a loss. He glanced at the main doors, tempted to just open them, walk out and leave the rest to chance. Alan followed his gaze.

'We could do it,' he said hopefully. 'I figure prison's going to be better than this anyhow.'

Danny nodded. 'We'd never get the bolts off without him hearing,' he said. 'And he'd kill them in there, you know that?'

'Not our problem,' Alan said, but he didn't sound convinced.

'Alan, don't. Just don't. You're not like your dad yet, so don't make the rest of the trip. OK. You've still got a chance of coming out of this human, so don't screw it up.'

Harper had returned from the kitchen. His hair was wet and so was the front of his shirt, but he looked slightly calmer.

'She's dead,' he told Danny, in a voice that brooked no argument. 'Whatever else happens, she's going to pay.'

Inside the storeroom everyone was silent. They stared at one another through the windowless gloom, too shocked to speak.

Patrick rummaged on the floor and found a soiled napkin from their last meal and used it to clean Naomi's hair. 'I hate him,' he said. His voice shook and Naomi reached for his hand. Patrick took it gratefully, moving close to Naomi and his dad and slipping an arm around her shoulders, his hand touching his dad, the three of them huddling close, bodies stiff with fear and anger.

'Use your phone,' Harry told his son. 'Tell Alec that Harper's recognized Naomi – and,' he added, listening to the argument outside in the main area, 'that he's becoming dangerously uncontrolled.'

'You'll . . . you'll have to tell me how to spell dangerously,' Patrick told him in an attempt at humour. 'I always miss something out.' He paused and fished for his phone, hoping Ted Harper and his people would be too involved in their argument to hear the cheerful sound as he switched it on. He turned away from the door so the screen light wouldn't show beneath it, and began to text.

'Amazes me how young people can do that so quickly,' Dorothy mused. 'Patrick, tell him we need to get out of here,' she added. 'Someone has to do something and do it fast.'

Twenty-One

Alec was driving when he heard the sound of his phone receiving a message, then another a few minutes later. Impatient, but unable to find anywhere to pull over, he waited until he had reached Nan Harper's a few minutes later before reading them.

'Shit!' The content of the messages almost made him turn around and head back to the incident room. Instead, he closed his eyes for a moment and gathered his thoughts, then called Hemmings and relayed the messages.

'Ah,' Hemmings responded. 'That explains something.' He told Alec about the sudden end to their phone conversation with Danny, and the anxiety it had left them with.

'We just have to hope Danny managed to calm things down,' he said, trying to reassure. 'You at Nan Harper's?'

'Yes. Look, it's probably a wild goose chase anyway. I'll come back.'

'You're there now,' Hemmings told him firmly. 'Get the job done that end and let us take care here.'

Alec sighed, knowing that Hemmings was right. He was at least as capable as Alec and it was a relief to know that someone was able to share the load. He knew he wasn't handling this well. He was having trouble keeping all the facts in mind and his thoughts kept drifting to Naomi and Harry and Patrick.

He got out of his car, released Napoleon from the back and clicked his fingers to bring the dog to heel. Obediently, Napoleon trotted at his side to Nan Harper's door, but his tail was down and his head dropped. Even his coat seemed less glossy, though that, Alec reminded himself, was perhaps because no one had found time to brush him; something Naomi took seriously.

130

He rang Nan's bell and fondled the dog's ears. 'I know, old man. I know. Let's see if this lady can help us any.'

The door opened just a crack and Nan Harper peered out past the chain that held it in place.

'What now?' she asked, then frowned, puzzled when she saw the dog.

Alec held out his ID. 'I know,' he said. 'You've had all you can take from us. But I need information.' He took a deep breath. 'We told you we wanted you to talk to Ted.'

'Yeah, and I told you where to go.'

'No one explained why, or where he was?'

'No, just that he was in trouble again. I told that reporter this morning, I didn't even know he was out.'

Alec nodded. 'Nan, he's holed up in a bank in Ingham and he's got seven hostages. One of them owns this old boy here, and she's very special to me, so I'm not asking you as a policeman, I'm asking you as a fellow human being, do you have any idea who his associates might be or where we can find anyone who might have seen him since his release?'

She said nothing, just continued to peer at him through the crack in the door.

'Please, Nan. You may think you know nothing, but . . . right now anything you could tell us would be better than what we've got.'

'You on your own?' she asked. 'I reckoned you lot normally travelled in pairs.' She sighed again. 'God, I suppose if I don't talk, you'll not leave me alone.' She closed the door and released the chain. 'You'd better come in. You'll be getting me a reputation worse than the one I've got.'

Alec and Napoleon followed her through to the second living room. The kitchen door leading from that was open and she went through and filled the kettle. 'Dog want a drink?' she asked.

'Thanks, he'd appreciate that.'

She found a plastic bowl and filled it with water, put it on the floor and called to him. 'Come on then. Don't have any food for you, I'm afraid. You'll have to nag him for that.'

Napoleon looked at Alec to see if it was all right to go. Receiving confirmation, he went to the bowl and drank thirstily.

'Poor old thing,' Nan said. 'He was parched.' She stood, watching him while the kettle boiled, then dumped two tea bags into mugs and poured water on them. 'Milk and sugar?'

'Thanks. Two.'

'You look knackered,' she told him frankly, setting the mugs down on a tiled coffee table of the sort Alec remembered from the seventies. Maybe they were making a comeback, or maybe this was just a relic of times past.

'I don't know anything,' Nan told him. 'He got carted off to prison. I made a new life. I didn't even manage to hang on to my son.'

'What happened to Alan?'

Nan laughed harshly. 'Ted did, I suppose, and I didn't have enough sticking plaster to make it better. When Ted got sent down, it was all I could do to get through the day. If I managed to get dressed before mid-afternoon I was doing well. Depression, they reckoned. I was in and out of hospital having the broken bits fixed up, and Alan was shunted from pillar to post. No one wanted him, not really. He was Ted's son and in some ways he was a lot like him. He'd fly into rages and I couldn't do a thing with him. Got himself suspended from school so often they finally chucked him out. In the end, I had social services take care of him. Nothing I could do any more.'

She told the story in such a flat, emotionless tone that Alec guessed she'd told it many times before. Had it down pat, not because she didn't care, but because she'd been defeated by it. Sticking to the story, keeping in the groove, made it easier to bear.

'We think Alan may be with Ted,' Alec told her softly.

'Oh Christ.' She closed her eyes. 'Stupid little fool.' She blinked rapidly and Alec wondered if she'd start to cry. 'I heard he'd been thieving. Joyriding. Heard he'd got caught too. I thought, best thing for him. Lock him up and teach him a lesson before he gets in any deeper.'

'When did you last see your son?'

'I last saw Alan a couple of years back. He'd called in to see his gran and I was there. We spoke, but we didn't say anything. You know.' She drew a deep breath. 'Alan stopped being my son a lot of years ago.'

Alec fished the tea bag from his tea and, following Nan's example, dumped it in a glass ashtray lying on the table. He stirred the sugar and then lay the spoon on top of the tea bag. 'Most of Ted's associates have moved on. Any you know of that we might have missed?'

'How would I know? It's been years.'

'Years in which Ted hasn't changed. There's no reason to expect his friends will have either.'

She leaned back in the armchair and thought about it. The room was too small for a proper three-piece and, to Alec's mind, was back to front, the dining table being in the front reception, furthest from the kitchen, whereas Nan clearly used this as her main living room. Two chairs from a cottage suite faced the television, and a wooden-armed sofa from the same suite had been set against the wall. They were upholstered in a mock tapestry fabric decorated with small sprigs of flowers and out of keeping with either the coffee table or the large and modern television. The room, though clean and tidy, looked as though it had been furnished with charity-shop finds, bought because they happened to be cheap and available rather than because Nan liked the look. Life, he thought, had not been kind to any of the Harper family.

Nan reeled off a list of names, and Alec noted them down. Most they'd already checked. A depressing number were either in jail or on probation or had absconded from same. Two, however, were new. Ian Hendrickson and Steve McGuire. Nan didn't know exactly where either lived or even if they were still around, though she thought McGuire had family in Ingham.

'Thank you,' Alec told her.

She shrugged. 'Don't think it'll help you.' She frowned. 'My mam said something about one of the McGuire kids. Reckoned he was with Alan when he stole that car. The one he was caught for.'

Alec nodded. That probably meant McGuire senior was still around and, with the rough address she had given him, there'd be something to cross-reference.

He rose to go and Napoleon joined him, leaning against his leg the way he did with Naomi.

'I hope you get them all out,' Nan said.

'So do I.' He hesitated, not sure he should be laying this on an already overburdened woman. 'Naomi was one of the officers who arrested Ted the night he attacked you,' he said.

Nan's hand flew to her face, she touched the scars at the side of her mouth and stared at him in horror. 'He recognizes her, she's a dead woman,' she told Alec in a whisper. 'Ted never forgets and he never forgives.'

Twenty-Two

A lec notified Hemmings of the results of his chat with Nan. And asked for confirmation of the address from the voters' register, Hemmings promised to get it to him before he arrived back in Ingham and Alec connected the hands-free kit.

'Don't forget,' Hemmings reminded him, 'the Parkers are due on the evening news.'

Alec groaned. 'I'll not be back in time anyway,' he said. 'Tape it and fill me in when I get back. Any more from Danny?'

'No,' Hemmings told him. 'Nothing. We're waiting until after the news broadcast, then we're going to try again. You should be here by then?'

'I hope so. Look, arrange some back-up for me from uniform, just in case. Nan reckoned McGuire was a regular driver back then. Could be he's still playing the same game.'

Hemmings told him he'd arrange things and Alec drove off towards Ingham. Nan's final words revolved in his brain and he could not shake the feeling of despair.

Inside the bank, Alan was wondering if and when they'd be sent food and urging Danny to make contact and find out. Danny was paying him little attention, his head still full of other things. He reran the earlier conversations with Sarah over and over, and had come to one conclusion. They knew Ted Harper was the main man.

It had been a tiny slip on Sarah's part and she'd covered it quickly. But she'd said to Danny, 'He's not worth it', as though she knew who 'he' was.

It might be that he was jumping to completely the wrong conclusion, but Danny didn't think so. And when Ted Harper

135

wandered over to check the window, Danny told him so. He could have predicted the response.

'That bitch. She sold me out again.'

'What bitch? Naomi Blake?'

'No, that frigging wife of mine.'

'Nan?' Danny laughed. 'Come off it, Ted, you'd had no contact with her in years. Even supposing she'd heard about the bank raid, why would she suspect it was you?' He thought about it. 'It could have been Naomi,' he mused. 'Told one of the hostages we released and they told the police.'

'We should have kept the lot of them,' Ted stormed at him. 'You and your bloody concessions.'

'Oh, leave off, Ted. What was the good of keeping the kids? They'd have caused us more problems than they were worth. We've got enough with what we've got.'

'Yeah, well, maybe I should reduce the numbers a bit more. By one.'

Danny sighed. 'Ted, I told you, leave over.' He produced the phone. 'Alan reckons he's hungry. Let's get us some food, huh?'

'They might have found Steve,' Alan said. He'd not spoken in a while and the other two turned to look at him. 'Steve McGuire, they might have picked him up. He'd grass us up, no time at all.'

Danny was nodding. 'It's possible,' he agreed. 'Not that it makes much difference,' he added gloomily. 'They'll put it together one way or another and it doesn't help us either way.'

Alec was at the address Nan had given for Steve McGuire when the message came through from Hemmings that she'd been three houses out. 'Hold off, until I've got you some back-up,' he instructed Alec.

In the background to Hemmings' call, Alec could hear the television and Mrs Parker's voice. 'How bad is it?' he asked.

'Bad enough. I've already had Superintendent Blick on the other line. Not a happy bunny.'

Alec was about to retort that he'd never known Blick to be anything but a miserable sod, when a patrol car crept around the corner of the street and parked up behind him. 'Your lot's just arrived,' he said. 'Napoleon. Stay. Good dog.' The black tail beat the car door with only a modicum of enthusiasm and the large dark eyes that peered over the back of the seat were heart-wrenchingly mournful. 'Oh, for God's sake,' Alec told him. 'Don't you start, please. You'll set me off.'

The officers were not local and he guessed they were from Hemmings' division. Right now, he didn't care. He directed them round the back way into the McGuires' place, aware that they were already getting too much attention from the locals. Kids playing football in the street stopped to stare and, across the way, a woman had come to stand on her doorstep to watch. She was soon joined by her neighbour. Alec began to wish he had more than two men. He knocked loudly on the McGuire door.

'You want me dad, he's not here,' a voice shouted from an upstairs window.

'Where is he then? You know that?' Alec looked up at a child who was probably about thirteen, though the amount of make-up made it hard to tell. 'Is your mother home?'

The child shrugged. She ducked her head back inside. 'Mam?' she yelled at the top of her voice. There appeared to be no reply, because when she peered out again it was to inform Alec that, 'She ain't in.'

'Gov, he's doing a runner,' the shout came over the radio, and had Alec bolting for the rear of the property. The child watched with only a modicum of interest. Running down between the houses, he could see a figure scrambling over a rear garden gate and an officer following a second later. The second, keeping commentary, advised that he was cutting down an alleyway and out on to the next street. They didn't know the area, Alec thought. They might lose him yet. He turned left past where the man and the officer had gone, and ran to the end of the row, shouting instructions to the second man as he did so. The garden McGuire had entered was the last in the row. If it kept true to the usual pattern, it would have a short stretch of land running along the side of the house. The only way through. McGuire would know that, the second officer would not and would now be entering the street too far along to be of use.

137

'I'm on him!' The first officer sounded breathless. 'Assistance required, assistance . . .'

Alec reached the end of the next row of four. He tried the gate. Locked. He clambered over, hoping that the rotten-looking structure would support his weight. It creaked and cracked, but was still standing as he landed on the other side.

'Hey, who the hell are you?'

'Police!' Alec shouted back.

'That doesn't give you the right. What the hell . . .?'

Alec didn't stay to find out what it didn't give him the right to do. He could see the officer on the grass verge, struggling with a man twice his size and build. He had one cuff in place and was using it to restrain, pressuring the man's wrist. Alec knew, from a demonstration in prisoner control, just how painful this could be, but it didn't seem to be having an effect on Steven McGuire. Alec dived in and grabbed the second, flailing arm and together they managed to cuff him. Alec shouted a rather breathless caution as the second officer arrived. Together, they hauled their man to his feet and led him back into his street to the waiting car. Alec watched as they got him inside. McGuire wasn't fighting now, but he wasn't doing anything to help. He checked that they could cope and then returned to his own car. The girl he had spoken to was standing there, arms folded, watching her father being bundled into the police car, but he didn't seem to be the thing holding her attention and, as Alec approached, he realized that her interest was focussed on Napoleon.

'You shouldn't leave a dog locked in a car,' she told Alec angrily. 'You should leave a little gap in the window open, especially in this heat.'

Alec opened the door and Napoleon yipped joyfully at him. 'You're dead right,' Alec told her, solemnly. 'You OK, big fella?'

'Is he a police dog?' she wanted to know.

'No, I'm looking after him for a friend.'

She raised an eyebrow and Alec amended his statement. 'I'm trying to look after him. You like dogs?' He stood back so that she could pat Napoleon's head and stroke the warm black fur. 'Yeah,' she said. 'They're better than people.' She stood back and glanced in the direction the police car had driven off in. 'I'll tell me mam,' she said. 'What's he done? Stole another car?'

'Something like that.' Alec nodded. 'What's your name?'

She gave him a suspicious look, as though she thought that giving your name often led to the giving of a whole lot more. Then she shrugged. 'Hayley,' she said. 'And if you want someone to watch him next time, all you got to do is ask.'

Twenty-Three

Simon had been watching the news with Mari, the two of them observing intently as the Parkers gave their live and exclusive interview.

'So, when did you realize,' Tyso asked them, 'that the very people you relied upon to help in times of crisis had put you and the others in such mortal danger?'

'Mortal danger!' Mari almost exploded with contempt. 'No one says that any more. Simon, when you come to write your account of all this, I expect you to use more civilized language.'

'Are you all right?' Simon asked her. 'Mari, if this is too upsetting . . .'

She shook herself angrily. 'No, I'm the one who wanted to watch it, love. I am glad you're here, but I seem to have spent most of the day looking for company and then not wanting it. I don't know what's the matter with me.'

Simon said nothing. He didn't need to. He knew exactly what was the matter with Mari. She'd already lost a daughter to violence. Now she was facing the possibility of losing a son and grandson as well.

Mrs Parker was explaining how they'd heard the shot and all been so scared. How they'd been threatened and forced to lie on the floor and how her husband had whispered not to panic, just to lie still until the robbers went away. And then they'd heard the sirens and the robbers had closed the doors. 'I thought we were all going to die,' a tearful Mary Parker finished. Her husband, who'd contributed little to the interview so far, reached across and patted her hand. 'It's all right. We're safe now.'

'No thanks to the local police,' Tyso finished triumphantly. He turned to camera. 'So far, senior officers are refusing to say if those responsible have been suspended. Our sources

140

suggest that these were inexperienced young men, just out of training, which begs the question, why had they not been placed with more senior and experienced personnel who would have known to use discretion in an incident like this. It also begs the question—'

Mari switched off. 'I can't stand that man,' she stated. 'He used to do this late-night discussion thing. I never used to watch. He'd put my blood pressure straight through the roof. Never give anyone the chance to get a decent word in.' She shook herself again and managed a smile. 'I've tried to get hold of Alec, but he's been so busy, I told them it wasn't urgent.'

'He'd have talked to you, Mari. You only need have given your name.'

'I know that. Truth is, Simon, I don't think I knew what to say to him. I went to a meeting with all the other families today. That Constable Andrews is trying to get us all together to support one another, but I couldn't stay. There they were all sitting and waiting for news. Oh, Simon, I've done all that, sat and waited for that phone call or that knock on the door. When I lost my Helen . . . we hoped and hoped and kept on hoping even when it was stupid to think anything but that Helen was dead. Simon, if any of them . . . I couldn't go on.'

'Oh Mari . . .' Simon sat down beside her on the arm of her chair and hugged her tightly. 'Look, do as I said and pack a bag. Mum and Dad want you there and they know not to ask stupid questions or waste their breath on platitudes. Mum doesn't want you to be on your own and I think she's right. I'll tell Alec where you are.'

Mari nodded. She'd been resisting until then and it worried Simon that she'd given in. He'd never known Mari to give in.

'If I lost any of them, Simon, I couldn't cope. Naomi's become like a daughter to me and having Harry and Patrick so close has been wonderful. We've been a family again after all these years.' She clung to him, dry sobs racking her body.

'They're together,' Simon told her. 'They'll look out for one another. You know they will.'

He felt her nod her head and then she pushed away from him, wiping her eyes with the palms of her hands. 'I'll pack a bag,' she said. 'Simon, I don't want to be alone.'

Twenty-Four

Sarah had Danny on the phone. So far, the call had been tense and somewhat one-sided, Sarah listening while Danny outlined what he wanted and what he feared. He had presaged this by telling her, 'Look, I don't want to be rude, but I've only got a short time before he starts yelling at me to get back in there, so listen.'

'I'm listening,' Sarah told him. 'Talk to me.'

'He thinks you're planning a raid tonight. That's why you've cut the power. He's threatening the hostages, and one in particular; he's got a grudge against her. He's decided she was one of the police that arrested him and he thinks she should pay. Is she? Her name's Naomi. Naomi Blake. She's the blind woman.'

Sarah looked across at Hemmings, who nodded. 'Harper's right,' Sarah told him. 'Naomi was there.'

'Shit!' It was clear Danny had been hoping otherwise and that he'd be able to placate Ted Harper. 'So,' he said. 'You *do* know who he is?'

'We know,' Sarah confirmed. 'We believe his son might be in the bank as well. Is that right, Danny?'

Danny didn't reply directly. 'Look,' he said. 'Put the power back on, send us some food. I'll try to keep the lid on things.' He hesitated. 'You know, I nearly walked out today. There was a moment when I could've done it.'

'Why didn't you, Danny?'

'You don't understand. He's capable of killing. Time you got in here, there'd be no one left to rescue. He'd do it too. Just put the power back on and send some food.'

He broke contact then.

'So.' Hemmings looked grave. 'Things are getting nasty.

142

There was water running in the background, so he must have been in the toilets. Ted Harper probably doesn't know he's contacted us.'

'I suggest we call back, now, tell them we've decided to put the power back on,' Sam said. 'Tell them food will be sent in. See how we get on. That way Harper might think he's making progress and back down a bit.'

'I'll arrange it,' Hemmings said. 'Then I'm going to talk to Superintendent Blick. I'll brief Alec when I get back.'

'With Alec gone, you should stay here. Make the super come to you.'

Hemmings frowned, but nodded. 'You're right, of course. By the time he gets here, Alec might be back and, come to that, we could do with your input. But I'm going to advise that we're caught on the back foot here. We've got to go in and do it soon.'

'You think Alec will agree?'

'I don't know. Ultimately, it's not solely our decision.' Hemmings frowned. 'Sarah, I think you should make that call. Hopefully you'll get our friend Danny and not that other tosser. I'll call Blick and see if I can find out how Alec's getting along.'

Steve McGuire liked to play the hard man but he knew when he was cornered. He'd always been a bit player in the scheme of things. The driver, responsible for getting the rest away and disposing of the car that had been stolen to order the day before. He got his fair cut and was satisfied with that. Always in trouble of one sort or another, his family were used to doing without the services of a husband and father and it was probably apathy rather than affection that meant his family were still there when he came back.

He'd occasionally been known to hold down a proper job.

Alec had no problem getting him to admit to stealing the Granada, but McGuire seemed more reticent when it came to giving names. Ted Harper, it seemed, had an advantage over Alec. Harper scared McGuire; Alec did not.

'I know it's him,' Alec pressed.

'If you know it's him, why keep asking me?'

143

'Because I want to know who else. You know anyone called Danny? Big guy, well built, black. Ring any bells?'

McGuire reacted and Alec knew he'd struck oil.

'So, Danny what? It won't take us long to find out anyway, so you may as well tell us about him.'

'Why should I want to save you time?'

'Because it'll look better for you in court,' Alec told him. 'Your solicitor will tell you that.'

McGuire glanced sideways at his brief. He was the duty officer, not one of McGuire's choosing, but he hadn't asked for anyone else. Alec thought he was past caring. Probably so used to the system that he didn't give a damn.

'It might help.' The solicitor was wary.

'Of course,' Alec qualified, 'it would depend what part your client played in the other robberies. Stealing cars is a long way from firing a gun in a crowded bank and threatening violence.'

'I never did that. Anyone says I did is a bloody liar.'

'So, who provided the weapons?' Alec questioned. 'Harper?' No reaction. 'Danny?' A tiny upward glance. 'Danny then. Got connections, has he?' Again, that momentary twitch. 'So, what sort of connections? They tell me that more guns come in through the channel tunnel in a week these days than were smuggled in the average year a decade ago. Then, of course, there's all these little scams going we hear about. I believe the going rate for a week's hire on an AK47 is about ninety quid. Not that Harper has anything quite that sophisticated, does he? Couple of handguns and a sawn-off, maybe a second shotgun.'

McGuire looked his way again. He was biting the inside of his bottom lip and Alec knew he was scoring more times than not. McGuire was scared and this time some of it was coming Alec's way.

'Or were they souvenirs, I wonder? You hear all these tales of army officers bringing stuff back and selling it on for little or nothing. The Balkans were a good source, apparently. There's all sorts got into the system from that neck of the woods, or so I'm told.'

McGuire shifted uncomfortably.

144

'My client is not in a position to speculate,' his solicitor told Alec, feeling, presumably, that he'd been silent for too long.

Alec ignored him. 'Ex-army, is he, this Danny?'

'Why should I tell you anything?'

'So, ex-army then.' Alec got up and paced slowly around the room. McGuire shifted in his seat. He didn't like it when Alec moved out of his view, Alec decided. He deliberately walked around the back of McGuire and his solicitor, and then back again, before sitting down. Steve McGuire had been craning his head around to watch where Alec was.

'So,' Alec continued. 'We've got Ted Harper and his son Alan and this Danny, the ex-soldier, and you and another man. You know, I bet it really got to you, Steve, when Ted Harper brought someone else on board instead of offering you the opening.'

'I drive. I never wanted anything else.'

'Oh, so you *did* drive on this one, then?'

'I never said.'

'No, but you didn't deny it either and it's a logical assumption, isn't it? You stole the car; you delivered them all to the bank. You have a talent for stealing things, I believe.' He paused and frowned as though something had just occurred to him. 'Maybe I'm barking up the wrong tree about Danny getting the weapons,' he suggested. 'Maybe, with your skills at procuring things, you could have been the one, eh, Steve?'

McGuire glowered. 'I never stole no guns. I had nothing to do with anything like that.'

His solicitor glanced at his watch. 'If I might have a few moments alone with my client,' he said.

'We keeping you from something?' Alec asked. 'Did you have a prior engagement?'

'Alone,' the solicitor said heavily. 'With my client.'

'Of course,' Alec agreed. He spoke into the microphone, making a big deal of it. 'Interview suspended, nine thirteen. That's what I have, everyone satisfied with that? Good. Inspector Friedman and Constable Freer leaving the interview room.'

He didn't keep them waiting for long. Ten minutes later

they were summoned to return. 'My client agrees to name those involved, on the understanding that the weaponry had nothing whatsoever to do with him. My client will insist that he did not even know the men were armed. They requested a driver and a suitable car. My client was in a position to oblige, that's all, his total involvement.'

Alec blinked. Did McGuire really believe a jury could fall for that? He shrugged. 'The names,' he said.

McGuire glowered. 'Danny Mayo,' he said, 'and the other bloke's called Ashwin Dutta, or Datta or summat.'

'Addresses?'

'I don't know. That's for you to find out,' McGuire sneered.

Alec nodded. 'Good enough,' he said. 'I'll leave this officer to help you with your statement, Mr McGuire,' Alec said, indicating Freer. 'And I'm sure your solicitor won't mind holding on here for a few minutes until I get a second officer in here. We have to abide by the regulations after all.'

He left before anyone could object.

Naomi had calmed down after her confrontation with Ted Harper but she was still terribly anxious. The moment the lights came back on was one of profound relief. Danny arrived about ten minutes later with food and drink, but he didn't speak. Just unlocked the door for long enough to deposit their refreshments on the floor and then departed.

'Pizza, again,' Harry moaned in an attempt at levity. 'You'd think someone would have more imagination. It's funny, you know, I've never been afraid of the dark, but I'm so relieved the light is back on, I can't tell you.'

'I think it's a good sign,' Naomi agreed. It was an odd thing, she reflected, but even now, she switched on the bedside lamp if she woke in the night and she always put the lights on in the kitchen when she worked in there, no matter what.

'You know what *is* weird though?' Patrick commented with a mouth half full of pepperoni.

'Don't talk with your mouth full,' Harry chided.

'Sorry. But you know what's strange; we've not seen the fourth man at all, not since that first day. And when they were

146

arguing, you could hear all three of the others. I mean, their voices, even if you couldn't make out the words. But not him.'

'It's a good point,' said Dorothy.

'Surely he can't have escaped?' Megan sounded very doubtful.

'Couldn't he have got out the back way?' The brigadier seemed only mildly curious.

'I wouldn't have thought so,' Megan replied. 'We heard them dragging something, a filing cabinet probably, over the back door. We kept some of the old files in the kitchen,' she explained. 'There wasn't a lot of room anywhere else. You saw how full it was in here.'

'And there's no other way?'

'Well, if he had the key to Brian's window, I suppose. Brian kept one on his ring and there's a spare taped underneath his desk, in case of emergency, but you'd have to know it was there.'

'There's the toilet window,' Dorothy suggested, 'but I doubt anyone but Patrick here would be able to get through that. Even for him it would be a tight squeeze.'

'So, where is he?' Patrick asked.

No one answered.

'There's been an odd smell in the air,' the brigadier observed. 'I don't know if any of you noticed . . .'

'I thought that was just us,' Harry laughed. 'I've never been so long without a bath and a change of clothes.'

'Maybe so.' The brigadier joined the joke and Naomi knew it was because no one wanted to pursue that other possibility. That the reason they'd heard nothing of the fourth man was because he was no longer alive.

Across town four police officers arrived at Ashwin Dutta's house. Strictly speaking, it was his parents' home, a standard semi-detached in a quiet suburb. Ash, being the only unmarried child left, still lived with them.

The situation was explained to shocked parents as the officers stood around in the neat little living room. Ashwin's mother offered tea, asking if they would prefer English or chai, sweet and spiced, made with boiled milk. His father, solemn and anxious, showed them up to his son's room. 'Ashwin would do nothing like this,' he told the officer in charge. 'Nothing like this has happened to my family.'

'I'm sorry, sir. I know how distressing this must be. It would be best if you waited downstairs. Perhaps there's someone you could call, to come and sit with you?'

Rikesh Dutta nodded his head. 'I will call my other sons,' he said. 'But I know you're wrong. My son would never do what you say. He is a dreamer, he spends his spare time watching films.' He gestured, indicating walls that were covered with framed film posters and shelves stacked with videos and DVDs.

'No one ever wants to believe the worst of their children,' the officer told him as gently as he could. 'If you'd please go downstairs, I'm sure your wife needs you.'

The older man turned, shaking his head in disbelief. The officer closed the door and he and his men began to take Ashwin's room apart.

A second team had been dispatched to Danny Mayo's home, but here there was no one to let them in. His flat was on the first floor of a purpose-built block, housing-association owned and with a caretaker on call but not present. It would take a while for the keyholder to be called and to arrive, and the four-man team chose not to wait. Neighbours emerged on hearing the noise of splintering wood and watched in disbelief as four armed policemen broke into the home of a man they'd thought of as a friend.

'What's going on?'

'If you'd go back inside, madam.'

'That's Danny's flat. Is he in there? Do the association know?'

'If you'd knocked on my door, I've got a bloody spare key,' a second woman said. 'Danny is forever locking himself out.'

The officer had the grace to look slightly put out by that piece of information, but his professional face was soon back. 'If you'd go inside please, there's nothing to see.'

'Right,' she said. 'Like this is nothing.'

Danny Mayo's flat didn't have a lot inside. Furniture was

148

sparse to the point of being spartan. Two armchairs, a small table and a dining chair in the living room. A few flat-pack shelves stacked high with books and topped with potted plants. His bedroom held a single bed and a canvas wardrobe. Three storage boxes were pushed beneath the bed.

In the kitchen the fridge was empty of all except a pint of milk and a dozen eggs and cupboards held the minimum requirements of a man living alone.

'I've seen more personalized hotel rooms,' someone commented.

The bathroom, equally tidy, equally bare, spotlessly clean. One toothbrush in the holder. Soap in a wire rack that had been wiped after use.

The officer in charge began to drag out the storage boxes from beneath the bed. He pulled the lid from the first and rummaged inside. 'Army stuff,' he said. 'Photos, documents and stuff. Bag and tag,' he ordered. He uncovered the next. 'Christ! I don't think we have to ask where the weapons came from. What's he plan to do, start a revolution? A second officer peered over his shoulder at the three handguns lying atop a leather case. He reached down and removed the case, opening it with care. 'I suppose we ought to be thankful he didn't take this with him,' he commented, his finger tracing the lines of the telescopic sight and long muzzle of the rifle, neatly broken down and packed in a custom box. The metal gleamed with a faint sheen of oil.

Back in the incident room they listened as the first updates arrived. Superintendent Blick and Dick Travers had heard all options and were considering the best next move.

Nothing of significance at the Dutta house; the finds at Danny's were of a different order.

'How does this change our opinion of him?' Blick asked.

Sam yawned wearily but shook his head. 'I don't think it should,' he said. 'It confirms what we already know. He shows restraint and plays his cards close. If Ted Harper knew more weaponry was available, I'm guessing he would have wanted it. We don't know how many rounds they have on them, of course, but as the team leader in charge of Danny's

149

place just told us, there were upward of two hundred and fifty available in various calibres. That's a lot of bullets. A lot of killing power. If Danny was overtly violent, he'd have behaved differently.'

'I concur,' Sarah told them. 'I think he's just out for Danny. I'm not claiming any particular altruism on his behalf, but he's a survivor and right now he knows his best chance of both survival and leniency is to keep the hostages alive and well cared for. I think he's gone past thinking he can just walk away from this. He knows he faces arrest and jail, so he's making the best of a bad job.'

'Unlike our friend Ted Harper,' Alec said heavily.

'What about this Ashwin Dutta? He has no record, no connection that we can find to any of the others. What's the story on him?'

Hemmings shrugged. 'Too early to tell. A fantasist maybe? Bored with life in suburbia? Who knows? But it's another family torn to bits by this whole escapade.'

'This still doesn't bring us closer to a decision,' Alec pressed.

'We wait,' Blick decided. 'We give them peace tonight and see what the morning brings. You're on the ground, Alec. If you think the situation warrants incursion, you've got my backing. Get a strategy in place with Sergeant Priestly, the armed response commander.' He sighed. 'Alec, I'm still not happy about you even being here. I've agreed with DCI Travers' decision about you remaining, but . . .'

'I know, sir. If I'm found wanting . . .'

Blick nodded. He rose to go, Travers following him. 'Tomorrow will be judgement day, whatever happens,' he promised. 'Beyond the humanitarian concerns, there are budgetary constraints to consider. An operation of this size on top of two major incidents in the past twelve months. Well, it's not what we need. Indeed, it's not what we can cope with.'

Alec, wisely, said nothing.

The night moved into the early hours. Darkness was settled on a scene of quiet. The cordons were still manned, by journalists and news crews, and by police. By now they'd formed a comfortable, comradely association. Bored, but unable to leave 'just in case', they were doing what they could to amuse themselves. Several poker games had started, with the betting getting heavy. A book was being kept on just how many hours the siege would last, and a second on which rifle officer would have to fire first. Another, more macabre perhaps, on how many months suspension he'd serve before internal inquiries cleared him to return to work – standard procedure if someone was shot and killed. The tacit assumption was that this would not end without the letting of blood.

Alec watched from the window as the street settled for the night. Lights burned in the bank, hazily visible through the frosted glass, suddenly brighter where the pane had been broken. Occasionally in the daytime, he'd noted a shadow crossing the glass as though someone stood and watched from inside, but at night, with the light behind him and therefore an easy target, whoever it was kept clear of the line of fire.

'Tomorrow is judgement day.' Alec remembered what Blick had said. He closed his eyes, almost dead on his feet, then slumped into the nearest chair, exhausted beyond thought, even beyond fear. Alec slept.

Twenty-Five

Alec woke and realized with shock that it was eight o'clock. He'd slept for five straight hours. Sam was at the table, eating breakfast and reading through the updated reports from the raids the night before. He bore the wrinkled look of someone who'd slept in most of his clothes, and had the grey skin of someone who'd gone beyond tired. Sarah wandered in, rubbing her eyes, but still managing to look as though she'd slept well and for an adequate time. The denim skirt was crumpled and today it was teamed with a pale-blue top decorated with sprigs of flowers.

'Where's Hemmings?'

'Bathroom,' Sarah told him. 'Someone's left clean clothes for you. They're downstairs next to the shower room. Someone called Mari, I think.'

'Mari was here?'

'Yeah, arrived an hour or so ago. Just handed your clothes over and told the officer on watch not to disturb you. Oh, and she's staying with the Emmetts, apparently.'

'Good.' Alec approved. 'Mari is Harry's mother, Patrick's grandmother.'

'She has a key to your place? Real family affair, this is.' She studied him for a moment. 'How are you holding up?'

He nodded. 'Fine. I'm fine.' He didn't bother to explain that Mari didn't have a key to his house; she just knew where he hid the spare. He didn't think Sarah would approve of his lack of security. He showered quickly and dressed in clean clothes, bundling the ones he'd been wearing for the past two days into a carrier bag before dumping them back into the holdall. He was glad Mari had gone to the Emmetts'. Simon's parents were two of the most sensible and comforting people

152

Alec knew. They possessed that rare quality of knowing when not to talk but just to be there, and Alec had past reason to know how rare and valuable that was. He must call Mari and thank her later, he thought. He didn't think he could face it just yet though, any more than she had been able to face him. There was too much at stake and the unspoken sympathy, Alec knew, would be enough to have him break down.

He found Hemmings at the table when he arrived back upstairs. He pushed buttered toast and a mug of tea in Alec's direction. He'd managed to change his shirt and wash, but he had almost three days' growth of beard blackening his chin. Alec rubbed his own ruefully. He hadn't thought about shaving. Perhaps he should.

Sam grinned and patted his own beardless face. 'Sometimes comes in handy,' he said. 'I still don't need to shave more than twice a week and I only do that to make me feel more manly.'

Alec laughed and then sipped his tea. He couldn't face the toast. 'So,' he said. 'What does this new day bring?'

'Well, we had breakfast sent in an hour ago. All seems quiet. We thought we'd wait until you were here before Sarah tried to talk to them again.'

'I'd hoped that Danny might get back to us.' Sarah sounded anxious. 'We have to assume that the level of tension is still very high, but just hope that a quiet night will have brought it down enough for them to listen. Personally, I think we're getting close to crisis point. Harper is unstable; the son is probably not an influence. Ashwin Dutta is an unknown quantity, but, judging from his background, I can't see Ted Harper taking a fat lot of notice. He's an amateur. Lord knows how he got involved, or why, but I don't factor him in. Not where Harper's concerned.'

'And Danny can't keep the lid on forever,' Sam agreed. 'We've already had some discussion with the ARV commander, I think we need to firm those plans up and, frankly, expect to have to implement them before the end of the day.'

Alec listened and then nodded. It made sense and, much as he regretted it, he had to agree that their reading of the situation was probably accurate. 'Get Bill Priestly up here,' he said. 'Get the contingency plans finalized this morning and everyone in place. Sarah, get on the phone and hope Harper's in a better mood.'

Inside the bank, breakfast was over and Danny, with Alan also on escort, had taken the hostages to the toilet. Danny had not spoken to anyone and a depression seemed to have settled overnight, which kept the hostages from trying to start a conversation.

The phone rang just as Danny was about to lock the door. He turned, cursing beneath his breath. He'd left the phone on the table in the middle of the room and Ted Harper got to it first.

The silence was so profound that Sarah's voice could just be heard.

'Good morning, Mr Harper. Did you sleep well? I thought you'd like to know that Mr Steve McGuire was arrested last night. He's been very helpful. Mr Harper? Can you hear me, Mr Harper? Just give it up and come on out, leave your weapons inside the bank and come out through the front door. No one will fire; no one will be hurt. If you give yourselves up, Mr Harper, it will look much better in court. We can't believe that you want this to continue any more than we—'

'Look, you. Sarah or whatever your frigging name is. We'll come out when I'm good and ready and not before. We'll come out when you agree to our demands. An hour I gave you yesterday, and I decided to let it run much longer than that. But I'm done with messing about and I'm done with you taking me for a frigging fool.' He strode across to where Danny stood and pushed him aside.

'Hey, Ted, what?'

Ted ignored him. Instead, he grabbed Naomi by the hair and dragged her from the storeroom, put the phone to her ear. 'Talk to the lady,' he demanded. 'Tell them who you are.'

Naomi shook her head. Ted yanked hard on her hair and she yelped with pain. 'I'll tell you who she is,' Ted shouted into the phone. 'That's your Naomi Blake. Your ex-police-woman Naomi Blake, and I'll tell you something else for free. You either have that vehicle here within the hour and a plane to fly us out of this dump of a country, or she dies. You got that? And don't kid yourselves that I'm not capable. He released his grip on Naomi, then backhanded her with the fist that held the phone. Unable to see it coming, she took the full force of the blow on the side of her head. She cried out in pain and slumped to the floor.

'Nomi!' Patrick yelled. He lunged past Danny and ran to his friend, totally ignoring the fact that Ted Harper had now retrieved his gun from the far table.

'You bastard, you leave her alone.' Patrick stood guard, his wiry body shaking with fury.

'Or you'll do what?' Ted Harper sneered. 'You think you can stop me, kid?'

'Ted, don't!' Danny had moved forward to intervene and Harry shot past him, going to his son's aid.

'What the hell you playing at?' Danny threw himself at Harry's legs just as Ted fired. Harry went down. The bullet hit the wall at the level of his head.

Patrick was truly incensed now. Placid and quiet in the general run of things, this overt threat to both his father and Naomi had snapped him and released all usual control. He launched himself at Ted Harper as he raised his gun again.

Alan Harper watched, slack-jawed. 'Shoot the bloody kid,' Ted Harper ordered him and Alan fired. The shot went wide, coming closer to hitting his father than Patrick. Harry struggled with Danny, desperation giving him a strength he didn't know he had.

'For God's sake,' Danny whispered urgently. 'Stay down. He'll kill him if you don't let me help.'

Patrick was no match for Harper. The big man had grabbed him and now held him with one hand as Patrick struggled. He lifted him bodily from the floor and stuck the gun beneath his chin.

'Ted! No!'

'Why the hell not? Give me one good reason.'

Patrick kicked out. His boots were in the storeroom and his feet bare but for black socks. He made contact with Ted Harper's shin and Harper laughed at the futility of his efforts.

'Someone help him!' Naomi shouted. She didn't know what was happening; only that Patrick was in trouble.

Patrick kicked again, higher this time, his flailing heel making contact with something soft. Ted Harper grunted, his grip loosened just for a second and Patrick struggled free. As he landed, something blue and chrome and small also hit the floor.

Ted Harper stared at it. If he'd been angry before then that was nothing to how he was now. He bent down and picked up Patrick's little phone. 'I thought you searched them!' His fury was now directed at both Alan and Danny.

'We did,' Alan objected.

Harper swung the gun again, this time aimed directly at Patrick's head. The boy began to back away, hands outstretched as though pleading with Ted Harper not to.

Naomi heard someone cry out in fear. She heard a shuffling of feet and then the shot. 'Patrick. No!' Naomi screamed.

Inside the incident room, time seemed frozen. They had heard the shouting, then what sounded like a shot, then the phone had gone dead. The ARV commander, Bill Priestly, was speaking into his radio. 'Confirm. Was that a shot? Confirm.'

He nodded at Alec.

'We should go in now,' Hemmings told Alec urgently.

'What if . . .?' Alec seemed unable to respond.

'Alec!'

'Yes. You're right. Get your men in position. I don't see what choice we have.'

The commander nodded and spoke rapidly into his radio. Alec stared at him as though he spoke in a foreign tongue.

'Patrick!' Naomi screamed.

'Patrick, run!' Megan shouted. 'Remember the key!'

'Patrick?' Naomi heard running feet, the slamming of a door and the sound of something heavy being dragged across a floor.

Someone took her arm. It was the brigadier.

'Get back.' Alan's voice, quavering and unsure. 'I said, get back in there.'

'Can you get up?' Peter Hebden asked her.

'Yes. What's happening?'

He helped her to her feet and guided her towards the others. She could hear sounds of a struggle off to her left and Ted Harper shouting. Then a grunt and a thud. A momentary lull, into which broke the sound of a man groaning in pain.

'You! Keep that gun pointed at them. Anyone so much as moves, you shoot.'

'Patrick? Harry?'

'Patrick's in the manager's office,' someone said. 'Harry and Danny attacked Ted Harper.' Naomi realized it was Megan speaking. She sounded scared and impressed in about equal measure. 'He shot Danny and he's hit your friend.'

'I've got to go to him.'

'You've got to stay put,' the brigadier told her. 'We've got a very scared-looking boy holding a gun on us. I think we'd better do exactly as he says.'

'Can Patrick get out?' Naomi whispered, trying to remember what Megan had said about the key.

Across the room she could hear Ted Harper trying to force the door.

Patrick was having a hard time thinking straight. He didn't want to leave his dad and Naomi but the last vestiges of common sense left in his head told him he had no choice. He was crying. Tears washing down his cheeks like they hadn't done since he was a little kid. His dad and Danny had bought him time to get away and he had to use it, no matter what was going on in that other room.

The manager's desk was heavy. Patrick grabbed it and dragged it by one edge as far as he could. His wrist was hurting and black bruises were beginning to show. He had an idea it might be broken, but that seemed such a little thing right now. He squeezed round the other side and pushed the desk the rest of the way against the door. The room stank. A heavy sweetish stench that caught in the back of his throat and choked him when he drew breath. They'd noticed it yesterday and then stronger today. He looked over to the corner of the room to where the smell seemed to be coming from and yelped in

157

shock. Ashwin's face was black and bloated and flies moved across its surface in a blue-green swarm. Around him the floor was darkly stained and his bare arm, outstretched towards Patrick, had whitened on its upper surface. The lower surface was red and livid with pooled blood.

He tore his gaze away, aware that someone, Ted Harper presumably, was hammering on the door. The desk moved fractionally, and fired Patrick into renewed action. If he didn't shift soon, he'd be as dead as that man lying there.

What had Megan said? A spare key to the window lock beneath the desk. He dropped to the floor, turning on his back to peer beneath. The door rattled on its hinges and the desk moved again.

He saw it, held in place with a strip of red tape.

'Thank you. Thank you.' He peeled the tape free and wriggled out from beneath the desk.

The door again. It shifted this time, opening a fraction, despite the bulk of desk behind it. A minute more and Harper would be through.

Hands trembling, Patrick inserted the key into the security lock and turned, praying it would work. It did, the lock turned, he pulled the handle down, the window opened just enough for Patrick to slide through. He fell on to the tarmac in the yard, his feet not responding properly to the need to run. Somehow, he regained his footing and stumbled to where the bins stood side by side close to the wall. He was up and on to the wall by the time Ted Harper stormed into the room. Ted fired again, armed with the shotgun this time. The window shattered. Patrick screamed, but he was over. He dropped eight feet to the pavement beyond and rolled. Then, breath burning in his lungs, he ran.

'We're in position,' the ARV commander told Alec. 'Your command. No, wait. Belay that.'

The door had opened and Ted Harper came out on to the steps. In front of him, struggling and fighting, but held close enough to his body to act as a human shield, was Naomi.

Alec gasped and moved toward the window.

'Get back out of the line of fire.' The ARV commander grabbed his arm and dragged him into cover. 'God's sake, man, don't you know anything!'

'That's his fiancée,' Hemmings said quietly.

'What?' Priestly was incredulous.

'Sir, I can get a clear shot.' The radio crackled.

'What's your position?'

'I've got a clear shot from just in front of the cordon. He's wide open on his left side.'

'Alec? Inspector Friedman!'

'Sir, I'm going to lose the shot.'

'Take it!' Hemmings ordered. 'Alec. You're relieved as of now.'

'Sir, it's too late, sir. He's turned.'

'Target of opportunity,' the ARV commander told him. 'The chance comes again, you make it.'

He glowered at Alec. 'Why wasn't I told you had involvement here? My men put their lives on the line, I don't expect to have to deal with increased risk because someone bloody freezes up.'

'He's going back inside. He's taken the female hostage with him. The doors are closed.'

'Sir!' Another shout on the radio. 'We've just picked up a boy. We think he came out of the bank but he's not making much sense. He says his name's Patrick and he's looking for Inspector Friedman.'

Twenty-Six

The hostages had been lined up with their backs to the wall in the main room. No one spoke but the fear was a tangible thing. Harry held Naomi's hand, trying to reassure her by sense of touch alone that he was all right.

Had Patrick got out? They had to believe he had, the alternative could not even be thought about.

Danny lay bleeding on the floor.

Ted had his son cover them while he cut the phone cords and used them to tie Danny's hands and feet. Naomi heard him moan in pain as Ted dragged him across to sit by the wall. She felt his weight as he slumped beside her unable to support himself.

'Get in there,' Ted ordered Alan. 'Cut the pull cords on the blinds and anything else you can find. I want them tied up.'

'In there?' Alan sounded twitchy. 'But . . . I can't go in there. *He's* in there.'

'And you'll be with him if you don't do as you're bloody told.'

Alan left and, a little later, Naomi could hear him going down the row, binding hands and feet. By the time he reached her it was obvious that he'd almost run out of rope. He tied her wrists, but his hands were shaking so much, she almost felt she should ask if he wanted her to put her finger on the knot so he could pull it tight.

'What about the feet?' Ted Harper demanded.

'No more rope,' Alan told him. 'I'm sorry, Dad, I did look everywhere.'

Harper muttered something under his breath.

'What do we do now, Dad?'

'Got yourself in a right mess, haven't you?' Danny's speech was slurred. 'You're down to just the two of you.'

160

'Shut up, or I'll finish you off now.'

'Now or later. What's the difference?'

The mobile phone began to ring. Naomi flinched. It sounded unbearably loud and painfully harsh.

'You going to get that or what?' Danny asked.

Ted picked it up and weighed it in his hand. Then he flung it against the wall. Naomi heard the crash, and the collective gasp as though the last link with the outside world had been destroyed.

'He still has Patrick's phone,' Harry whispered.

'Shame he doesn't have the intelligence to use it,' Danny taunted. Naomi felt Harry flinch as Danny's comment drew attention back to him. She tightened her hold on his hand.

Patrick was distressed and didn't know where to begin. A paramedic examined his wrist but was of the opinion it needed an x-ray to tell if anything was broken. He thought not. Patrick refused to be moved. The thought of being taken further away from the people he loved was just too much. Hemmings had given him some painkillers and a cup of hot tea and Alec sat beside him on the couch. Napoleon, unable to decide which of his people needed most comfort, wedged his head between them and whined.

'Take it slow,' Sam told him. 'That last phone call sparked this off?'

Patrick nodded. He cradled his mug tightly between his hands, pressing them together against the glazed surface to stop them shaking. 'He just lost it. Danny had brought us back and was about to lock the door. The phone rang and Ted Harper answered it. He just went off on one.'

He stared down into his mug.

'Drink your tea,' Sarah told him gently. 'It's all right, Patrick. Just take your time.'

Patrick swallowed convulsively and almost choked.

'He grabbed Naomi,' he continued with the story, 'he was hurting her. I don't know, I just wanted him to stop, so I ran out past Danny and I . . . he hit her and she was on the floor. I just wanted to protect her.'

'So you faced off against a man with a gun?' Hemmings sounded impressed.

161

'You could have been killed.' Alec was furious.

'I know that. But I didn't then. I mean, I wasn't thinking.' He closed his eyes as though to picture everything. 'It gets a bit mixed up after that, but Ted Harper grabbed me. He's really strong. Dad had tried to help me, Danny had him on the floor, then . . .' He opened his eyes again as the image behind the lids became far too intense. 'He was holding me with one hand and I kicked him. He had the gun here.' He let go of the mug with one hand, nearly spilling the contents. Sam reached out and cupped his own hand over the boy's. 'He pointed the gun at my throat and I kicked him in the balls. Danny came up from somewhere . . . or maybe that was after. Yes, it was, he dropped me and my phone fell on the floor. Ted Harper saw it and then he really lost it big time.'

Patrick relived the moment when he'd been backing away with the gun pointed at his head. He stumbled over the words, the emotional impact of it really hitting home. Alec remembered how he had felt that first day when the barrel had swivelled in his direction. This was so much worse.

'Then Danny and my dad just threw themselves at him and someone shouted at me to run and I knew if I didn't, Ted Harper would still get me, no matter what they tried to do, so I ran into the manager's office and I pushed the desk against the door.'

He paused for breath. His face was very pale, even the lips were blue and he had begun to shake with cold despite the heat of the room and the bright sunlight streaming in through the window.

He's going into shock, Alec thought. 'He should be in the hospital.'

'No!' Patrick's response was unequivocal. 'I can't, I have to be here. Then I looked for the key.'

'Key?'

'To the window lock. The windows are double-glazed, that makes them difficult to smash. Megan said Brian kept a spare taped under his desk in case there was a fire or something. I'd pushed the desk against the door. It was heavy, but Ted Harper was breaking through. The desk kept moving. Then I found the key and opened the window and as I climbed over

162

the wall he shot it out. I heard the glass shatter and then I fell off the wall and I was on the floor and someone shouted, 'Armed police!' Naomi said if you came to get us we should all get on the floor and spread our arms so you could see we weren't armed. So that's what I did.'

'You did right,' Alec told him. 'You did well.'

Napoleon whined and put a paw on Patrick's lap. He looked as though he wanted to climb on to the sofa, but knew that wasn't allowed. Patrick slid down on to the floor and wrapped his arms around the dog's neck, curling his body as close as he could and burying his face in Napoleon's smooth fur. Then he cried. Uncontrollably. Alec sank down to the floor beside him and hugged them both, dog and boy, trying to tell them it would all be fine and not believing a single word.

Twenty-Seven

The footage on the lunchtime news was dramatic and frightening. For the first time, Alec heard what Ted Harper had to say.

'You see this woman?' Harper yelled. 'Anyone tries to come in here and she's the first to die, I promise you that.'

Naomi, Alec realized, was furious. It wasn't fear that kept her twisting in Ted Harper's grasp. It was sheer rage. He had one arm curving about her waist and she clawed at it with her nails. Alec saw that she'd drawn blood. Her feet alternately dragged on the ground or flailed back, kicking out at the man. Her feet were bare and had little impact. But he could see she was determined, that he wasn't getting the better of her. He just prayed that her cussedness would not be paid for once they got inside. The bruising on the left side of her face, where he had struck her earlier, was clear to see.

'So far,' the reporter said in her piece to camera, 'police have been playing a waiting game. It's unclear what triggered this violent response, but what is becoming clear is that time is running out and the police may soon be compelled to act.'

Mari gently lowered the phone on to its cradle. The news report played out on the television, but the eyes of all three Emmetts, Lillian, Samuel and Simon, were fixed upon her.

'Patrick's escaped,' she whispered. 'He's with Alec. Alec's been relieved of duty. Neither of them want to come away but he says he'll bring Patrick here very soon.'

The relief was tinged only by anxiety about the others. Mari could tell them nothing more.

'Patrick can tell us all he knows when he gets here,' Lillian reassured her. 'And you'll both stay until this is finished.'

164

'Thank you,' Mari told her gratefully. 'I don't know what I'd have done.'

'Oh, what are friends for?' Lillian told her. She got up and kissed Mari affectionately on the cheek.

'They want him to go to the hospital to be checked over,' Mari went on. 'He'll need some clothes too and I don't have Harry's key.'

'Hey, don't fret,' Simon told her. 'I know the sort of stuff Patrick wears. I'll go shopping. I promise, only the deepest black will do.'

Mari smiled gratefully.

'But,' he half teased, 'I expect an exclusive when this is through. That a deal?'

'Simon, when this is over, you can tell as many tabloid lies as you like and we'll put our name to it,' Mari told him. 'Now, we just need some good news about the other two.'

Alec had been about to leave the incident room and escort Patrick home to Mari when his phone began to ring. Automatically, he took it from his pocket and glanced at the display. Patrick's phone, it read. Alec stared.

'Hemmings!' He gestured the new SIO to his side and then answered the call.

'Um, it's Harry,' a voice said.

'Harry! Patrick's all right. I've got him here.'

'Oh, thank God. Look, Mr Harper wants to speak with you.'

'Put him on.'

Harper's voice was loud. Hemmings leaned in to listen. 'I want my bus and I want my plane and I want them now. A half hour you've got, copper, that's all – and this time, no concessions and no delays.'

'I want to speak to Harry Jones,' Alec said, trying to keep his voice as calm and level as he could.

'You're in no position to want anything. Half an hour. No more time.' Then he was gone.

Alec made to call back, but Hemmings stopped him.

'What, then?' Alec questioned.

'We do as he wants,' Hemmings said. 'We take them to the airfield and we hope for a break. There are only two gunmen

165

now. If we can take them down before they get on the bus, so much the better. If not, we wait until we can.'

Alec nodded. 'Blick authorized this?' he asked. Hemmings had spoken to him a little time before.

'He told me I called the play,' Hemmings said heavily.

Alec almost laughed. 'So, it goes right, Blick covers himself with glory. It goes wrong, it was down to you.'

Hemmings shrugged. 'It was ever thus,' he said. 'You know that, Alec.'

'Then I want to stay,' Alec told him. 'I want to be there.'

'You know I can't say yes to that.'

'Why not? Look, you're wasting time. Half an hour, he said, and we know he won't wait.'

Twenty-Eight

'It's here! It's bloody here.' Alan didn't quite believe it.
'Good, so they've seen sense at last.' Ted Harper climbed
on to the table and peered out through the broken glass. A
minibus sat close beside the steps. Its driver, wearing full flak
jacket, visible inside.

Ted Harper stepped down and then took Patrick's phone
from his pocket. He'd watched Harry use it last time and knew
who to call.

'Your bus is here, Mr Harper,' Alec said.

'I want a different driver. Tell him to shove off.'

'Who do you want to drive, Mr Harper?'

'How about you?'

Harper listened to the silence his words provoked.

'I know about you. I know you're a friend of that kid's,
and you're a copper. I know you're a friend of our Naomi's
too, because she told me. She wasn't keen on telling me, of
course, but there you go. So, I want you to drive. Is my plane
ready?'

'It's ready, but it's only a four-seater, Mr Harper. You, your
son, the pilot, and one other, if you insist. Our local airfield
isn't cleared for anything but light aircraft.'

Harper said nothing, but scowled angrily.

'We could arrange to take you to a larger airfield, of course,
but that would take more time to arrange and we thought that
time might be of the essence.'

'Don't you get clever with me.' Harper considered. 'It'll
do,' he agreed. 'I'll let the pilot know our destination once
we're in the air.'

'That might not be possible,' Alec told him. 'Pilots need
clearance from air-traffic control. They have to register a route.'

'Well, air-traffic bloody control better make an exception, hadn't they? Now. You – get your arse down into that driver's seat and we'll get ready to come out.'

Hemmings wasn't happy.

'I don't see as we've much choice,' Alec said.

'Given the situation, neither do I,' the ARV commander agreed. 'Look, we talked to someone at the airfield and they gave us some useful details. Try to pull up just before the main runway in front of the tower. There's really only one building on site, so you can't miss it. I'll have men stationed in the tower and we've called in extra support from the army base just up the road. You might not see anyone, but there'll be snipers in position.'

'Just make sure they know who to shoot at,' Alec told him.

'Oh, that's easy. We only aim for the ones with the guns. If shooting starts, hit the deck and make sure the hostages do the same. Naomi knows the score, she's already proved that with her instructions to Patrick.'

Alec nodded. Patrick was watching anxiously. Alec managed to smile at him. 'It'll be over before you know it,' he said. 'I'll have to get someone else to take you home.'

Patrick nodded. 'It's OK,' he said. 'Just, you know, take care of my dad and Naomi.'

Nothing felt real, Alec thought as he went downstairs and was fitted with his stab vest. He crossed the street, aware of the many eyes on him again. He wondered if Mari would be watching the news. If this would go out live. If she would be annoyed that he'd not taken Patrick over to her first. He almost laughed at the stupidity of that last thought. The oddest things occur, he thought. None of it was real; none of it made sense.

He got into the bus and took his seat, hoping he would be able to drive the thing. It was an automatic and he'd only driven an automatic *anything* once before, and that had been his Aunt Billie's silly little car.

There was another stupid thought. Great-Aunt Billie – Wilhemina, if she didn't like you – had been dead these past five years.

168

A sound from the bank caused him to look towards the doors and the next minute they opened. The two gunmen had surrounded themselves with a human chain of hostages. They held hands and kept in close, prompted by the guns held to the heads of two. One was a woman Alec guessed must be Dorothy Peel and the other was Naomi.

Thoughts that this might come to a swift resolution here and now were dashed once and for all.

The windows on the bus had been hastily blacked out. Cardboard boxes cut up and taped in place. Logos for baked beans and washing powder where a view should be. The hostages shuffled aboard, urged into their seats at the barrel of a gun. Alec tried to talk to Naomi, but he had no chance. Ted Harper took position behind the driver's seat, the shotgun against the back of Alec's head, and told him to keep eyes front and mouth closed. His son crammed against the bulkhead on the other side, sawn-off pointing backwards towards the rest of the passengers. Alec did not like to think what damage it could do in so confined a space. The younger man looked pale and tired and nervous. Dangerous.

Alec closed the doors.

'Now drive,' Ted Harper said. It was two o'clock on the Wednesday afternoon.

Twenty-Nine

A lec drove so carefully he could have been carrying a load of nitroglycerine. He'd never reckoned that driving with a gun to your head would make you more aware of road conditions, but it did have the effect of focussing the mind. He had no wish for Ted Harper's finger to slip on the trigger.

It occurred to him for all of thirty seconds that, being the driver, he might be able to swerve and throw Ted out of the way. He abandoned the idea immediately. Had Ted been the only gunman, there might have been the chance of that working. But it would only take a fraction of a second for Alan Harper to turn the gun on him and fire, and Alec, trapped in the driver's seat, had nowhere to go.

Up ahead were two police motorcycles. Two more followed behind. Alec was glad they were there; it gave him something to follow. For some reason – fear, lack of sleep, a combination of the two – he was not able to both concentrate on the route and keep his focus on driving. He was actually glad that this was an auto. He truly didn't think he'd be able to change gear as well as point the vehicle and accelerate at the appropriate time.

The journalists at one end of the street had been moved back to allow the bus to move through. Long lenses peered at him. Sound men chased their presenters. He caught sight of Simon standing at the end of the row with a photographer. Simon looked shocked to see him. As they drove away, Alec glanced into the wing mirror. He could see Simon talking animatedly to his photographer. Maybe, Alec thought, he was making sure he'd got the picture.

He wondered if any of them would try to follow, and what safeguards had been put in place to ensure that they did not. He ran a checklist in his mind of things that should be done, then remembered that these tasks were no longer his to carry out.

He was, for the moment, just a driver. He should just drive.

The motorcycles had picked up the pace and Alec accelerated to keep his distance from them. 'Keep it steady,' Ted Harper warned him. 'No funny business. We set the pace, not them.'

Alec allowed his speed to drop off and the bikes fell back to keep with him. He wasn't sure why Ted Harper wanted to slow down. In his position, he'd have pushed for speed. Maybe, he thought, Ted wanted to savour the moment. A police escort that had nothing to do with a prison van – and a police officer at the wheel, compelled to do his bidding.

It was about fifteen miles, if Alec recalled correctly, to the airfield. It backed on to the village of East Rydon, a prosperous little place beloved of the wealthier retired. A couple of miles beyond that was an army training camp and, if Bill Priestly was to be believed, they'd currently be positioning their own people as back-up for the police riflemen.

Alec didn't know whether to feel happy with that arrangement or anxious, but then, he rationalized, that was simply because Alec had a strong dislike of guns in any form.

'We'll be on the dual carriageway in a few minutes,' he told Ted Harper. 'Do you want me to keep to twenty miles an hour, or can I keep up with the flow?'

'Just drive,' Ted Harper told him.

Back on the High Street the reporters at both cordons had something to watch as a team of armed officers entered the bank. The building made safe, Hemmings entered with Sarah and Sam and others of his team.

'You must be Danny.' Sarah knelt beside the barely conscious man.

'Good guess,' he smiled weakly. 'You Sarah?'

'Yeah.'

'Pretty as you sounded,' Danny said.

She returned his smile. 'Save your breath. There's an ambulance on the way.'

Gently, she peeled away the fabric adhering to the wound and examined it with gloved fingers. She had a first-aid pack with her and she strapped a pad tightly in place, wadding both the entrance and the exit wounds.

'Bad, isn't it?'

'You look as though you've lost a lot of blood. I'm no expert, but the shoulder joint's a right mess. You're in for the long haul, I think, Danny.'

'Long haul both ways,' he said. 'We'll be going down for a while, I reckon.' He grinned suddenly. 'Will you write?'

Sarah laughed. 'You're no longer my worry, Danny. Another hour or two and I'm headed back home.'

He grimaced. 'Never get me a nice girl,' he complained. Then he frowned. 'You really letting them go? Ted and Alan?'

'That's not up to me.'

'Ah.' He closed his eyes. 'Look, Ted deserves all he gets, but the kid, Alan, he was just trying to prove himself to his old man. All he did was wave his gun about a bit and do as he was told.'

'And what did you do?' Sarah asked him.

'Me, oh, I behaved like the fool my mother always said I was.' He closed his eyes and Sarah thought he might have passed out. She was relieved to see the paramedics coming through the door. Hemmings had been adamant they should not be allowed into the street until the building was declared safe.

'Over here,' she called.

'Sarah?'

'Yes?'

'Tell them about Alan. Tell them if they take his dad out, he'll be quiet as a lamb.'

'Why should you care?'

'I don't know. Maybe 'cos there's no one else ever has.'

In the manager's office, Hemmings was surveying the damage. He tugged on the desk and raised an eyebrow. 'Wouldn't have thought the kid could move that on his own, never mind drag it across the room. It weighs a ton.'

'Stronger than he looks,' Sam agreed. 'Though I guess being shot at does tend to give you an incentive.'

The police surgeon was bending over Ashwin's body. 'Well, he's dead,' he confirmed. 'You can tell SOCO they can take over.'

172

'Like to make a guess as to when?'

'Get in touch with the insect man. He'll have plenty of raw material.' He shrugged. 'I'd say sometime on the first day.'

'Insect man?' Sam asked.

'Forensic entomologist. There's a job title for you. Flies have a pecking order. The first lot arrives within minutes. According to what eggs have been laid and their state of development, he can give you a pretty accurate timing. But I expect your man out there will be able to save you the expense anyway.'

Hemmings nodded. 'Probably so.'

'So,' Sam asked. 'Now what?'

'Oh, you should know,' Hemmings told him. 'You've a talent for it.'

'We wait,' Sam guessed.

'Got it in one.' He stared at the broken glass fallen on to the tarmac in the yard. Jagged teeth of it still clung to the double frame. 'Patrick was more than lucky,' he said. 'His guardian angel deserves a commendation.'

Simon was getting over his shock at having seen Alec. What was going on? His mobile rang. It was his editor. His increasingly impatient editor. Film of the bus leaving had apparently been on the television, and he wanted to know what Simon had.

'There's going to be a statement made in a few minutes,' Simon told him.

'And everyone will have that. Simon, you promised me something special here. I'd hate to think you were losing your touch.'

Simon stepped back from the crowd so he could speak without being overheard. 'OK, how's this? The mother of one of the hostages is at my parents' home right now,' he said. 'Her grandson managed to escape earlier on today and is going to be taken to join her any time now. And the man driving the minibus with the hostages on board – he happens to be a good friend of mine. Clive, I've already been promised an exclusive on this one . . .'

'How much?'

Simon rolled his eyes. The glass was always half empty for this guy.

173

'Favour to a friend,' he said. 'That cheap enough for you?'

'Nice one, Simon. Don't cock it up.'

Simon folded his phone and slid it back into his pocket, then looked round for his photographer. His mind was working overtime. Something on the Parker interview stuck in his mind. They'd wanted a plane, Mrs Parker had said. She'd overheard them discussing it and how they could take their money out with them. She'd rambled on then about a lot of other things, elaborating on the robbers' demands until her husband had begun to contradict her. But it made sense, and Simon, being local, had an advantage. He had a good idea where that plane might be taking off from.

'We're leaving,' he told his photographer.

Bobby Rowe looked at him as though he'd gone mad. 'We leave now, we'll miss the press statement.'

'I can guess what's in the press statement, Bob. We don't need to listen to it. Look, I've a shrewd idea where that bus went to. Now, you coming or what?'

Bobby Rowe took one last look at his rivals and colleagues crowding the barrier and followed Simon.

Andrews had been fielding calls from anxious, angry relatives. The situation had run ahead of police communications and many of the relatives had seen the newsflash showing the hostages being herded on to the bus.

Where were they going, what was happening? Why hadn't they been told?

Calmly, Andrews told them what he could, but it wasn't much more than they'd gathered from the newsflash. In the end he called the hotel where the press conference had been held and asked if he could borrow one of their meeting rooms.

Better, he considered, to have everyone possible in one place as the dénouement to this unfolded. He left his assistants calling the relatives and telling them to come to the hotel. The hotel had cable and Andrews thought he could probably convince the manager to lay on a television in the room they'd been loaned. There might not be a budget for this, Andrews knew, but he figured the hotel manager would make his money back in good will and paid interviews later on.

As he was leaving, one of his constables called out to him. 'I've just been talking to a Mari Jones. She's waiting for her grandson to be brought over to her. Reckons Inspector Friedman was going to do it. Any chance of an ETA?'

Andrews hesitated. Should he tell her that Alec was on the bus? He took the phone. 'Mrs Jones, PC Andrews here. I think DI Friedman must have been delayed. Things started happening at a hell of a rate.' He paused. 'You saw the newsflash. Look, I'll collect Patrick myself and drop him off. I take it you don't want to come to the hotel? No, look, I'll be with you in, say, three quarters of an hour.' He ended the call and stood thinking for a moment, calculating the time. Then turned to the young officer who had taken the call.

'Got to make a detour, Jenny. You get over to the hotel and see if you can sort out a TV set in the room, greet the relatives. They'll have their liaison officers in tow, so you'll be all right. Got that? Oh, and Jenny, don't mention where DI Friedman is just now, the super wants that kept under wraps.'

No one had spoken much since they boarded the bus. Naomi, sitting close to the back, heard Alec say something to Ted Harper, but the engine was noisy and she couldn't make out the words. Hearing his voice was comforting though. Comforting and, at the same time, upsetting. To have two of the people she loved most in the world in such danger was almost more than she could bear. She comforted herself with the thought that Patrick, at least, was safe. Maybe that gave some hope to all of them.

She was exhausted and her mind wandered in random directions. For an instant it nagged at the thought this might be her final day alive. The next thought was that at least this would be over for Patrick's birthday. Then she had to figure out if that was tomorrow or the following day. This was only the third day of the siege, she told herself, but already she was so disorientated. How did people manage who were subjected to this for weeks or months or years? Did it assume a kind of normality? Did the outside world take on a greater sensation of threat and captivity become almost comforting?

Right now, all she wanted to do was sleep. For a day, two days, a week. How much sleep would cure this need?

175

Beside her, Harry thought about his son. Sixteen years. And it seemed like yesterday when he'd first held Patrick in his arms. That tiny, squalling bundle he had loved with a passion from that first moment. A passion he wasn't always sure he was able to convey. Did Patrick know how much he loved him?

'Do you think he knows?' he asked Naomi. 'Patrick, I mean, just what he means to me?'

'He knows,' she told him. 'Of course he does.'

Did his mother know what had happened, Harry wondered? Mari, surely, would have informed her? Had their places been exchanged, Harry would have been on the first flight. Was she on her way?

Harry still didn't understand how he and Caroline had come to marry in the first place. Looking back, divorce seemed an almost inevitable conclusion. That they had been intimate for long enough to produce a son was little short of a miracle.

Maybe, he thought in a woozy, unconnected way, *that* had been the purpose of it all. Some divine plan to produce Patrick.

He glanced across at the seats opposite. Tim and Megan held hands, bodies leaning in towards each other, heads almost touching.

Ask her, Harry thought. You want to so much. Ask her to marry you, now, while you've got the chance.

Dorothy and the brigadier sat in front of them, eyes forward, backs straight. 'They're just as scared as we are,' Harry breathed.

'Who?'

'Dorothy and Peter Hebden. The brigadier. Do you really think he was a brigadier?'

'Why not?'

'I don't know. Tim should ask Megan, you know.'

He didn't need to explain. 'I know,' she said.

He caught Alan looking at him and he fell silent.

Would they be released once they got to the airfield? What would happen then? 'If we get the chance, we run,' he said to Naomi.

She squeezed his hand. 'You'd have a better chance without me.'

'Never,' Harry told her. 'That I'd never do.'

*   *   *

Hemmings had called everyone together for his statement. He stood atop the bank steps, the crime-scene tape a demarcation line behind him, the half-open doors revealing movement as the white-clad SOCOs moved in their painstaking search for evidence.

'I've got a brief statement,' Hemmings said. 'I'll tell you what I can, but in order to protect the hostages, there are limits on what I am able to say.

'As you are all aware, at two p.m. today a minibus carrying six hostages and two gunmen left this bank for a destination I cannot yet reveal. I am able to confirm that the seventh hostage made a successful escape bid earlier this morning and is now safe and well and back with his family. I'm not yet at liberty to reveal his name.

'I can reveal, however, that the other two gunmen were left behind here in the bank. One is seriously injured. The other is dead and the evidence leads us to believe he was killed shortly after the raid began. The wounded gunman is in police custody. He is being treated for his injuries, but is expected to recover.'

'And the condition of the hostages?' someone shouted. 'Shots were fired. Are there any injuries?'

'Shots were fired, resulting in the injury of the third gunman and also the shattering of a rear window within the building. No hostage was injured by shots fired during the siege. I'm sorry,' he went on, 'but that's all I'm prepared to say at present. I'll ask you now to return to the barriers. Further details will be given out as the situation becomes clearer.'

'Mrs Parker said they asked for a plane. Is there any truth in that?'

'Mrs Parker, in her interview, stated that she believed the robbers had made a number of requests. We are not in a position to verify that. Now, as you can appreciate, there's still a hell of a lot to do.' Ignoring other shouted questions, Hemmings crossed the road to the greengrocer's shop and went back inside.

Patrick had been watching from the window. Someone had wrapped a blanket round his shoulders and he no longer shivered. Napoleon nuzzled at his hand and he stroked the dog's head.

Patrick felt numb and lost. He couldn't get his brain to work

177

properly. He couldn't get it out of his head that he should be revising for his exams, and he kept having to remind himself that they were long past and he was just waiting for the results.

Was his father all right? What about Naomi? Did his mother and his other family in Florida know what was going on? He could imagine his stepdad and brothers wanting to come right over and storm the building. His mum would probably be too busy sunbathing.

He should have phoned them last night. He called them every Tuesday and they spoke to him again on Thursday. They would wonder why he hadn't called.

He wanted so badly to go home to Mari, and while he didn't in any way blame Alec for not taking him, he now felt so bereft and alone he could hardly bear it. He almost wished he were back with his father, leaving on that bus.

Would he see any of them again? Mari would know. Mari would be able to tell him. His grandmother's house was only a mile away. Maybe not that far. He thought he could remember how to get there.

Everyone seemed busy and no one took any notice as Patrick made his way downstairs with Napoleon in tow. The back door was unlocked and Patrick slipped through. In a moment of surprise when his feet burned against the hot paving, he remembered that he was without his boots. Then he decided it didn't matter. It wasn't that far and he just wanted to get home. At least get to Mari.

Wrapping his blanket around him, oblivious to the heat of the afternoon, Patrick set off down the road, Napoleon trotting obediently at his side.

Alec had reached the village of East Rydon. It was some five miles off the dual carriageway, situated on a broad area of flat land that had once upon a time been marsh. Deep dykes bore witness to its past, but unlike most fen land, which was given over to massive fields and monocultures, East Rydon and its environs still boasted small farms and copses of native trees.

The airfield could be seen from the road leading into the village, though it lay on the other side, and Alec wondered what the locals must be thinking when they saw a battered old minibus, its windows patched with corrugated card and advertising slogans, escorted by four police outriders.

He drove through East Rydon and a half mile on up the road, followed their escort through the gates and on to the airfield.

The ground here was absolutely flat. Scarcely a thicket to interrupt the monotony of long grass, broken only by the grey concrete of two runways running parallel to one another in front of an octagonal control tower.

The tower itself was painted white, with its angles and corners picked out in a faded green. It looked almost art deco in its shape and style, and Alec thought of Agatha Christie on television. The tower was central to a wider building. Flat-roofed, with what looked like observation platforms fenced in on top, and ladders leading upward, clamped to the white walls. It extended backward in two surprisingly large wings with their own separate entrances. The one they passed had *Conference Facilities* emblazoned proudly above the door and a bicycle propped against the steps.

Aside from the bike there was no sign of life anywhere.

Three single-engined planes sat on the tarmac to the side of the building and Alec spied others on the far side of the field. One somewhat larger, with twin engines, was already on the runway. The pilot in the cockpit turned to look at the minibus as it pulled up where Alec had been instructed to stop in front of the control tower.

Ted Harper had other ideas.

'I never said stop here.'

'You never said anywhere.'

'Don't be smart. Pull right up to the plane.'

'I told you, you can't take everyone on board.'

'I don't need everyone. Do what I told you.'

Sighing, Alec started the engine again and drove out on to the runway.

Thirty

Hemmings returned to the incident room. He'd sent officers to bring in Nan Harper, threatening her with arrest for obstruction if need be. If anyone had an idea where Ted Harper might want to go, she was his best bet.

'Any news from the airfield? Has Alec arrived yet?'

Alec was at that moment just entering the village of East Rydon.

'The control tower says there's a storm front moving in. If they don't take off soon and keep ahead of it, they'll be grounded until it's passed over.'

Hemmings glanced out of the window. The first heavy drops of rain had begun to fall as he'd crossed the street. Now the clouds were thickening rapidly, darkening in a way that threatened more.

DCI Travers came pounding up the stairs. 'Well?'

'Alec's almost at the airfield.'

'Good, everyone's in position that end. I've got men coming in from the other way to block the entrance once they're on site. The pilot is briefed and armed.'

'Is that wise?'

'Not my decision,' Travers said. 'We've borrowed him from divisional HQ. He's been on standby, as you know, since early today. They insisted he be armed. He's ex-RAF apparently, now a DI.'

'It might be academic if the weather doesn't change again,' Hemmings told him. 'The tower warns of a storm front, looks like we're picking up the start of it now.'

'Well, the building's been locked down. We don't want another siege situation developing.' He frowned anxiously. 'Alec's a good man, but I'd sooner he wasn't involved in this.'

180

'Sir, they're on the airfield now. The escort has pulled back as instructed and the second team are moving into position.'

'Second team?' Hemmings asked.

'Blocking the gate and watching the perimeter. If they make a run for it across the fields, there are armed officers already in place with orders to try and bring them in without violence, but if they shoot first, the response is at their discretion. It's too big an area to deal with any other way.'

Hemmings nodded. Sarah had been listening. 'I know this isn't relevant,' she said, 'but I promised Danny Mayo I'd pass his message on. He reckons Alan isn't a player in this. He's just out to impress his dad. Take the father out and Alan will put his gun down.'

'Noted,' Travers told her, 'but those decisions have to be made by officers on the ground. There's nothing I can do.'

Sarah nodded solemnly. 'We're all packed up, sir,' she told Travers. 'If you'll release us, we'll be heading back to base to be debriefed.'

Travers shook her hand, then turned to Sam. 'You did a good job,' he said.

Sam shrugged. 'Maybe. It isn't the resolution I'd have wished for. You'll be getting our report in due course, I'll leave you to judge from that if we could have done things differently.'

'Do you think you could?' Travers asked.

'Always,' Sam told him. 'In my choice of scenario, no one ever winds up dead.'

They had just departed when PC Andrews arrived looking for Patrick. He explained his errand to Hemmings and then told Dick Travers that he'd borrowed the hotel conference room.

'I'll send you the bloody bill,' Travers told him.

'Well, I shall have to have a whip-round then,' Andrews retorted.

'No, but it's sound thinking to get them in one place. Events caught us on the hop this morning. It doesn't look good when the families are left out of the loop. Play it as you think fit.'

Andrews nodded, acknowledging the trust of his superior officer. 'Where is the boy?' he asked.

181

Hemmings was puzzled. 'Asleep? Have a look in the back rooms. Poor bugger was knackered enough to drop off anywhere.'

A brief search informed them that Patrick was nowhere to be found.

'He's got the dog with him,' Hemmings presumed. 'He'd nothing on his feet. Where the hell would he go? My fault,' he acknowledged. 'He was in a hell of a state, and when Alec went off, it must have been the final straw.'

'His grandmother is staying with friends,' Andrews said. 'I'll get her and we'll go and find him. A barefoot kid and a black dog should be easy enough to spot.' He glanced out of the window. In the minutes since he'd arrived, the clouds had begun to shed their load of rain. It fell against the windows in a heavy curtain, blurring the view of the street and making the bank across the road impossible to see. 'He's going to get bloody soaked,' Andrews said.

Fifteen miles away, Alec drove out on to the runway and halted the minibus beside the plane.

Thirty-One

Nan Harper was not a happy woman. She was slightly relieved to have been brought to the incident room and not the police station, but she was still determined to give Hemmings a piece of her mind. So far, he was letting her rant and taking very little notice.

Finally, when the worst of the rage had passed, he sat down opposite her and steepled his fingers in front of him on the table. Hemmings came straight to the point.

'Your ex has six hostages plus one of my colleagues in a minibus and has demanded to be driven to where he can be put on a plane. Now, we're all hoping he won't get that far. That we can put a stop to this before he gets in the air, but, if he does manage to take things that far, where would he want to go?'

'How the hell would I know? I've not seen the bastard in years.'

'Nan, I know this is uncomfortable. I know your knowledge of Ted is likely out of date, but we don't have anyone else to ask.'

'What about those names I gave that other one?'

'Steve McGuire is in custody. He copped to driving the getaway car but he's admitting to nothing more. Frankly, I don't think Ted regarded him as a confidant.'

Nan snorted. 'Confidant! That's a word Ted never knew the meaning of. He didn't go in for friendship.'

'Yet you married him. There must have been something.'

'There was a baby on the way. That's what there was.'

'But you had a relationship with Ted. You must have had for there to be a baby.'

She looked at Hemmings as though he were stupid. 'I never

said it were his,' she advised him. 'Look, the dad was a married man. Ted seemed OK. I'd been around with him. He didn't know about the other fella, he'd have killed him if he had. I knew he could be difficult. Violent, even, but he was never like that with me. Not till after.'

'After you were married?'

She nodded. 'Then, as far as he was concerned, he owned me. I so much as looked at another man and I got a pasting for it.'

'And he had family?'

She shrugged. 'He had a brother come to the wedding. He lived in Ireland somewhere. Seemed a nice chap. I knew when I met him I'd chosen the wrong one, but it was a bit late by then.'

'Ireland. North or South?'

She frowned, thinking. 'County Clare. Like the girl's name. Wherever that is.'

Hemmings nodded. 'He have a name, this brother?'

'Ted called him Jimmy. I suppose it must have been James. He wanted us to visit but we never did.'

'You have an address for him?'

She shook her head. 'It was years ago. Why would I keep in touch?'

'Anyone else you can think of? We've been on to his prison governor. He had visits from his son and his probation officer. Refused to see the prison visitors. No one else.'

'Doesn't surprise me. Ted wasn't a man for friends. I told you that. When I first met him he hung around with a gang of lads, all a bit wild. Rode bikes too fast, one or two that stole cars or lifted stuff from the off-licence. They've all straightened themselves out. Got families, jobs, all the stuff I wished Ted would do.'

'Did he ever talk about wanting to live somewhere else?'

She shrugged again. 'Spain, mebbe. Had this thing about all the top men living in Spain. You think he'll want flying out there?'

'It's not the place it used to be, Nan. We could still extradite him from there.'

She laughed. 'You think he'll know that? Lived in the past, Ted did. Some time that never existed, if you ask me.'

184

Hemmings thought about it. The plane would have to refuel two, maybe three times if it had to go that far. No, this was a no go. He didn't believe that Ted had the foggiest notion of where he wanted to be. He was just in love with the idea of escaping custody. A dramatic aerial escape. Once in the air he'd probably be asking the pilot where *he* thought they should be headed. Eire was a better bet. A remote airfield somewhere, and a fast car. Even so, he'd be easy to track. They'd have a helicopter on standby . . . but this didn't solve the problem of the hostage he might take with him or the pilot he might well see as an adequate substitute.

No, Hemmings decided. They had to end it now, at the airfield. He glanced out of the window at the broken weather. At the airfield; in the pouring rain.

Simon and his photographer had arrived at the airfield only five minutes or so after the minibus. They could see activity at the gate as they approached the village, but it was only as they rounded the final bend that they realized just how many police vehicles had been assembled.

A police officer waved them down.

'What's going on?' Simon asked.

'Can I ask where you're headed?'

Bobby Rowe, the photographer, leaned forward. 'Millfield,' he said. 'The army base up the road. Back from leave.'

The officer eyed them suspiciously and Simon cringed inwardly. He might just about pass for a returning recruit, but Bob had hair hanging past his shoulders.

The officer came to a decision and waved them on. 'Keep on going,' he said. 'If I see you here again, I'll pull you on suspicion.'

'Suspicion of what?' Simon questioned.

'Impersonating an army officer. That do you?'

He had a point, Simon thought as he drove on. 'What kind of pathetic excuse was that?'

'Didn't notice you come up with anything.'

'I would have done,' Simon protested. He glanced sideways towards the airfield, catching tantalizing glimpses through the hedge of the plane on the runway and the minibus beside it.

'Keep going round the next bend,' Bobby told him. 'You see that copse over there. Pull on to the verge and we'll work our way back. It comes out behind the second runway.'

'How come you know so much?'

'There's a fishing lake just up from the woods. I bring my kid brother sometimes. Carp the size of German Shepherds.'

'You ever catch any? What would you do with a fish that size anyway? Not that I believe in fish that size,' Simon added, concluding that he was having the mickey taken.

'I kid you not! Nah, they're wily old brutes, but it's fun trying, and if I did, I'd just have me picture taken with it and lower it back in, gently. Very gently.'

'That's assuming it hadn't taken your arm off first. This the place?'

A track ran down at the side of the wood, disappearing into the heart of it as far as Simon could see. He pulled his car as far on to the verge as he could without sliding into the ditch.

'Looks like rain on the way.'

Simon looked back the way they had come. The sky was black and moiling cloud was racing towards them. 'Oh,' he groaned, 'this just gets better.'

Patrick was lost. Quite how he could get lost in so short a distance, he couldn't understand, but he was lost all the same.

He stood in the middle of a street that looked the same as the last three streets he'd stood in the middle of, and turned slowly around, trying to get his bearings.

The rain soaked his hair and it hung down over his face. He tried to flick it out of his eyes, finally bringing one hand from beneath the cover of the blanket for long enough to push it away.

Napoleon whined. He hated being wet – unless it was the fully submerged and swimming kind of wet – and, worse still, he could sense Patrick's distress and did not know what to do about it.

Patrick bent and stroked him. He should ask someone where to go, he thought, but, on that front, his options seemed few. People had hurried in out of the rain and those he had approached had looked at him as though he'd dropped from another world and scurried away.

He looked down at the rain puddling around his feet as though suddenly aware that they were soaking wet and also very sore. The pavement had worn his socks through.

'This way,' he decided. 'I think it's this way.' He began to move again.

Travers had taken over from Andrews, freeing him up to look for Patrick. He called in when Travers had just reached the hotel, to say that he was with Mari and they were setting out to find the boy. He asked for news. Travers had none to give him. The last he'd heard, the minibus had pulled on to the runway beside the plane and remained there, doors closed as though those inside could not decide what to do.

'By the way,' Travers asked him before going through into the conference room. 'Did we ever find anyone for the brigadier?'

'No,' Andrews told him. 'We tried but there seems to be no family, and as for friends . . . It's not right, is it, gov?'

'No,' Travers agreed. It wasn't right.

Alec was unsure what was happening. Ted Harper had been sitting motionless for the past fifteen minutes. He'd said nothing and he'd ignored his son's questions. Alec had almost begun to wonder if he'd fallen asleep.

'You could end this now,' he said softly. 'It doesn't have to go any further than this, Ted. Show you're the man and give it best.'

'Start the engine,' Ted Harper told him. 'I want this wreck turned around so that the exit is next to the plane. Do it.'

He jabbed the shotgun into the back of Alec's head to reinforce his last words, just in case Alec should fail to comply.

Alec started the engine and manoeuvred the minibus slowly into position. It took him several frustrating minutes. Either, he decided, he was losing his touch or the vehicle had the turning circle of an overladen freighter. Finally, though, he was in a position that Ted Harper approved.

Harper got up on his feet and gestured at his son. 'You, out first.'

'But, Dad . . .' Alan peered fearfully out of the front wind-screen. 'What if . . .?'

'You see anyone out there?' Harper senior demanded. 'Stay between the plane and the bus.'

'You, Naomi, get your backside down here.'

He waited for her to conform. Alec half turned, but Harper caught the movement and swung the shotgun back his way. 'Eyes front!' he demanded. 'Hurry it up or I'll shoot the old woman.'

Dorothy Peel tutted beneath her breath. Alec heard. He closed his eyes and bit his tongue, trying to restrain the totally inappropriate impulse to laugh. She sounded as if she disapproved of some small social faux pas. He heard Naomi getting up and moving forward.

'What do you think you're doing?' Ted Harper demanded.

'I'm helping her.' Harry's voice was firm.

'She need help to walk, does she? Sit back down.'

'It's all right, Harry. I'll be fine.'

Alec's heart almost stopped at the sound of her voice. His chest felt so tight it was hard for him to breathe. He heard her soft footsteps. She was barefoot, he remembered. None of the hostages had been wearing shoes.

'Now, open the door and you get out first.'

Alan pressed the button that activated the doors. There were two. One on the dashboard and a second, beside the doors themselves, that was marked *Only for emergency use.*

Alan stepped out cautiously, swinging his gun from side to side in some bad imitation of a soldier on patrol. Ted Harper motioned Naomi to follow, forgetting for a second that she could not see. He muttered something in exasperation and Alec said, 'Take me, not her. It doesn't have to be her.'

'No? Well, copper, you're not the one making the decisions here, are you?'

Alec noted that the pilot was now out of his plane and standing on the runway. He was watching Alec through the window. Catching Alec's eye, he patted his side and nodded. He was armed, Alec thought. Just what they needed, another man with a gun. Alec looked past him at the thickening cloud. As Naomi emerged and came past the front of the vehicle, the rising wind whipped at her hair.

He waited until he could see Ted Harper outside, then he turned on the ignition, praying that it would catch first time.

Furious, Ted Harper stepped back, intending to return.

'Harry,' Alec shouted. 'Get them out of here. Now.'

He sensed, rather than saw, Harry rising from his seat. Alec threw himself out of the door and into Harper's path. The big man shouted in rage and struck out at Alec, who was clinging terrier-like, to his arm.

Harry had his foot on the accelerator. He missed the struggling pair by mere inches.

'Shoot the bastard!' Harper senior yelled. Alan raised the sawn-off and fired. He hit the bus, but Harry had his foot to the floor.

Then there was a second shot. It shocked them all; Alec letting go of the arm and Ted Harper stumbling back. For an instant they both stared in disbelief. Alan Harper lay stretched out on the floor. A tiny entrance wound marked the centre of his forehead. The massive exit wound had spread the contents of his skull in a widening pool upon the ground.

Thirty-Two

'Christ, he shot him!' Simon was incredulous. 'You get that!' he shouted at Bobby Rowe.

'Course I bloody did. Shit. The way he just went down.'

'Where did the shot come from? I don't see anyone.'

The photographer turned his head just long enough to deliver a look of complete contempt. 'Don't you think that's the whole point?' he said. 'Wouldn't be much of a sniper if you could see where he was.'

'OK.' Simon wasn't used to this. He'd known people who were. War correspondents and photojournalists whose lives were spent avoiding being shot at, but that wasn't him. 'We stay put. We don't try to get in any closer. How many do you reckon there are?'

'Enough. I thought I told you two to keep moving?'

Simon swung around and groaned as he came face to face with the officer they'd met on the roadblock. He had four friends with him and they didn't look impressed. Simon held up his hands in mock surrender. 'You can't blame us for giving it a try.'

'This isn't a game. You get shot, we look bad, and, frankly, I don't think you're worth any of my colleagues being suspended over. Got that?'

'Got that,' Simon agreed. But deep down he was elated. They'd seen it. He wasn't sure he wanted to see a man shot. Not really, but they had it on film. No one else would have that.

A police officer drove his car back to the gates.

'Are we under arrest?' Simon asked.

'Not up to me. My instructions are to keep you out of the way.'

190

He turned abruptly. There was a commotion at the gate. Simon got out of the car and watched in astonishment as the minibus hurtled towards the cordon. His first thought was that the second gunman had somehow regained control. He'd seen the bus take off just before the younger guy was shot, but the relevance of that hadn't registered until now, and then he saw who was at the wheel.

'Harry? It's Harry!'

Simon was jumping up and down like an excited child, all pretence at journalistic adulthood forgotten. The minibus skidded to a halt just inside the gate, scattering officers in all directions. Armed police surrounded it, covering the door.

'Don't be daft,' Simon shouted at them. 'That's Harry Jones. He's a hostage. He's Patrick's dad.'

Ted Harper was the first to recover from the shock and he grabbed Naomi, wrapping his arm around her neck and pulling her backward towards him.

Alec made to move towards him but the pilot held him back.

'Naomi!'

'Don't be stupid. Anyone gets the chance to take a shot, they will. You could well block them.'

Alec gazed at him in horror. 'They won't shoot while she's that close?'

'If they get a clear shot, of course they will. A good man could take him out and not touch the girl at all.'

'Stay back!' Ted Harper warned. 'You want to see what she looks like with her head blasted off?'

'You kill her, you'll have nothing to protect you,' Alec told him.

'Want to take that chance, do you?'

A crack of thunder startled them all. The rain followed fast on its heels.

'You. Fly me out of here.'

'I can't, not in this.'

Alec looked at the pilot. He had no idea if that was true or not, but he knew for sure that he had to keep Ted Harper there. That once he took off, he'd kill Naomi and he'd have himself another hostage in the form of the pilot and, frankly,

191

Alec didn't think the fact that the pilot was armed would make much difference to that scenario. It's hard to fight a gun battle and fly a plane.

'He's right Ted. He can't take off in this. If the lightning hits, you're all finished. Ted, let her go. You're making it worse for yourself. Just let her go.'

'Oh no, I'm getting out of here. One way or another I'm getting out of here.'

He's lost it, Alec thought. He's completely off his head. He doesn't know what's real any more.

Naomi whimpered, her feet scrabbling against the ground, her fingers pulling at the arm across her throat. Ted started to back up, heading towards the tower. He turned abruptly as he went, shifting left and right, jinking like an aircraft in a dogfight.

Alec watched him in despair. The rain fell so heavily that Ted Harper and Naomi disappeared from view within ten feet, no way was anyone going to fire with that restriction on visibility. Alec could hear the pilot talking and realized he had a radio.

'The bus is at the gate,' he told Alec. 'They're getting ready to board it now.'

Naomi had warned them that if the police came into the bank, they would have to treat everyone as suspicious until proven otherwise. It was not unknown, she said, for hostage-takers to pose as hostages in order to escape.

Lie flat on the floor, she had said. Arms out to the side to show you're not armed, and identify yourselves immediately.

It was this that Harry remembered now. It wasn't possible to lie flat on the floor, but he raised his hands and told the others to do the same. 'I'm Harry Jones,' he said. 'Don't shoot. Please don't shoot.'

Two armed officers came on board. One by one they escorted the hostages off the bus and patted them down and checked their names against a list they had. Harry saw that they also had photographs. His was an unflattering picture that he used on his work ID. 'Couldn't you have found a better picture?' he asked, then giggled like a child at his own stupidity.

He held his face up towards the sky, feeling the cold rain on his face, and he laughed aloud until he cried. Someone gently wrapped a blanket around his shoulders and led him to one of the waiting cars.

'Naomi? What's happening with Naomi?' Guilt at that brief moment of elation overwhelmed him. 'Oh God. She's still out there.'

'Drink this.' A paper cup of scalding tea was placed between his hands.

'Is everyone all right?'

'Everyone is fine.'

'And Patrick? My son. He's all right?'

'Was your son on the bus?' Sudden concern and confusion.

'No. He got away before we left the bank. Alec told me he was all right, but I've heard nothing after that.'

'I'll see what I can find out. You just sit tight.'

The man went and a few moments later the car doors opened once again. 'We thought you might not want to be alone,' Dorothy told him as she clambered into the front passenger seat of the car. The brigadier got in the back beside Harry.

'They'll be all right, you know. Your friends. We've all come this far.' Dorothy spoke with authority. 'Providence and young men with guns will take care of that.' Then her lips trembled and she put up her hand to cover her mouth. 'Oh look at me. What a fuss I'm making.'

'Not at all,' Paul Hebden told her kindly. 'You've been wonderful. I was wondering, in fact, when this is all sorted out . . . maybe the cinema, or dinner somewhere?'

'That would be nice. Yes, in fact, that would be more than nice.'

Harry closed his eyes and chuckled softly. 'Dorothy, will you do something for me? I should myself, but I don't think I have your style.'

'Anything. Of course.' She sniffed emphatically and wiped her eyes.

'Go and tell Tim that he must propose to Megan.'

Patrick had found Mari's house, but she wasn't there. And the neighbour who had the spare key, she wasn't home either.

Patrick didn't know what else to do. He sat down on Mari's doorstep and pulled Napoleon under the now soaked blanket, trying to protect them both from the freezing rain. He thought that summer rain was meant to be warm, but this must be coming off the ocean. Naomi always told him that the rain was cold when it came from out at sea. He closed his eyes, drawing up his knees and curling into a tight little ball in the corner of the doorway. Napoleon edged closer and lay his head on Patrick's raised knees. Glad he was there when the rest of the world seemed to have abandoned him, Patrick rested his hand on the big dog's neck. Then he fell asleep.

Patrick dreamed. In his dream it was his birthday and it was early morning. He was just a little kid and his dad was carrying him on his shoulders. They were going to the park, and then into town to buy something special and then to Mari's to have his birthday cake. But there was something wrong with the park. It was dissolving before his eyes, melting in the sun and then sliding into the river as the rain got heavier and heavier and the river began to rise. Patrick woke up in panic to find someone bending over him. For a moment, he was back in the bank and the shadow was Ted Harper. Ted Harper with a gun.

'No!'

'It's all right, lad. No one's going to hurt you.' The man crouched down eye level with Patrick and he saw the uniform and the sunburnt face of PC Andrews and behind him two women, one black and one white, gazing at him with a mixture of fear and relief.

'Gran? Lillian?'

Mari bent down. 'What possessed you to go off like that? You're soaked through. Oh, for goodness' sake.' They pulled him to his feet, pausing to fuss the dog that wriggled tail and body at them, almost beside himself with excitement.

Patrick allowed himself to be chided and loved and calmed as they led him towards the waiting car.

'Your dad and the others are all right,' Mari told him as she settled him in the back seat and helped Napoleon in beside him.

'They're freed?'

'Yes?'

But there was something wrong. He knew there was something wrong. 'And Naomi?'

Mari bit her lip. 'Patrick, I'm sorry. Ted Harper still has Naomi.'

Patrick closed his eyes. There was still the rest of the nightmare to endure.

Thirty-Three

Naomi could hear Alec calling to her.

Ted Harper's breathing sounded ragged and uneven and she could feel his heart hammering against her body. His arm around her neck forced her chin high and her head back and made it hard to breathe. She grabbed at his arm, digging her nails deep and twisting against him to try to free her airway, but he seemed not to notice. Blood pounded in her ears and she was certain she'd pass out. Almost wished it. Ted Harper would then have her dead weight to contend with and he'd either have to drop or carry her; neither would be a good option for him.

A clap of thunder startled her. Ted Harper seemed oblivious to it. The lightning that followed was bright enough for her to see, triggering what little residual vision she had left. It left her feeling even more exposed and just increased her sense of panic. Up until now, she had remained in control. Most of her ordeal she'd actually coped with well, but now she could feel herself letting go of what little control remained. She clawed harder at his arm, digging her nails into the tough, hairy flesh until she felt the blood flow, warm against her fingers, then chilled by the rain.

Her feet stubbed against the concrete, bruising her toes as she fought for purchase. Much of the time, Ted carried her along, suspended by her neck and the grip she tried hard to keep on the steel of his arm.

'Armed police. Put your weapon down!' The shout seemed muffled by the force of the rain, or was it just the surf-like pounding in her ears?

'Like hell!' Ted Harper fired the shotgun, both barrels. She felt the recoil in his body and heard herself scream. Only, she didn't have the breath to scream. It sounded in her ears like a pathetic choking and left her more faint and breathless than before.

'Shut up, bitch,' Ted Harper told her.

'Officer down,' she heard someone shout. Ted Harper laughed. He threw the shotgun to the ground and for an instant, as she heard its metallic clatter, Naomi thought that might be it. He was now unarmed. But then he reached down to pull the pistol from his belt and fired again. She had forgotten about that, or not known about it, she could no longer be sure. Harry had told her they had handguns; preoccupied with the larger weapons, she'd just not remembered it until now.

The surface beneath her feet had changed. Smoother, slippery, like polished granite or limestone. She felt the drag of his arm tighten against her neck and found herself being lifted bodily. Steps.

Trying to get her footing, she trod on Harper's foot. He grunted and shifted her weight sideways. Naomi took that moment of opportunity. She struck backward with the heel of her hand, but he was too fast for her. He snapped at her wrist with the butt of the pistol, hitting the bone at the base of her palm. Numbness and then pain spread through her hand.

'Keep still,' he told her. 'Remember, I could enjoy myself hurting you.'

They'd reached the door and Harper kicked out at it, then tried the handle. Encumbered by Naomi and the need to keep his weapon free, it was no easy task.

'Naomi!' Alec calling to her again. Or was that just her imagination? The wind, channelled along the contours of the building, skittered round. It blew the rain hard in her face. 'Naomi. Stay calm, we're with you.'

She heard Ted Harper swear and then he was pulling her down the steps again, moving sideways now, crabwise, as though protecting his back.

'Any closer and I'll shoot another,' he yelled. His voice sounded small and weak against the storm.

'Just put the weapon down and let her go. You've nowhere to run to. Nowhere to go.'

'I told you. Keep back.'

197

Naomi had tried to count the steps they'd taken, but her brain wouldn't function. He must be keeping close to the building, she guessed, because the feel of wind and rain against her face and body had changed as though they were in partial shelter. She was desperate not to let him take her inside. Alone with Ted Harper . . . the thought terrified her. She sensed that he'd gone beyond reasoning. Never a stable man, he seemed to have lost what residual hold he had on reality. Now, he was cornered and he was responding as a cornered animal would do. Back to the wall and snarling at the world, ready to attack and not discriminating over the size of its foe.

He was right up against the wall now. She could hear the scraping of his belt against the stone or concrete and the heels of his boots against the brick. He was feeling his way. They must be in close, the armed officers, she guessed. So close, he dare not take his eyes from them for long enough to examine his surroundings.

She heard a chink of metal as he kicked something, and then felt him pause. His breath seemed even more laboured and hers more strained. She noticed a change in him then, his breathing quickened as though suddenly excited or relieved.

The arm moved from her throat. For an instant, he cupped his hand against her chin and pulled back. 'You move and I swear I'll blast your brains out.'

She felt the cold metal against her temple and she froze.

'That's good,' Ted Harper told her. 'Now just hold it there.'

Naomi dared not move. She felt him drop his hand to his waist and unbuckle his belt, pull it from the loops. He lifted his hand again and fumbled against her neck. At first, she did not understand what he meant to do, then she felt the leather against her neck and she knew.

'No!' She lifted her hands to pull the belt away but he jammed the pistol more tightly against her head and she dropped them down.

It wasn't easy and it took him some little time, but eventually he had the belt slipped through the buckle and pulled tight against her throat.

'We're going to climb,' he told her. 'Any trouble and I'll just pull.' He demonstrated with a painful jerk.

198

'You see this?' he shouted. 'We're going up there. I'll go first and she'll come on behind. Any of you buggers shoot me, I'll bring her down too. You got that?'

'Ted, what will you gain by taking Naomi up there?'

She didn't recognize the voice.

'You can't get anywhere from the roof and that's where the ladder leads to. It's just an inspection ladder, Ted, they use it to check the water tank and the heating vents. You can't get down from the other side and you can't get off. You'll just sit up there and we'll just sit down here.'

'Suits me. Now move.'

Somehow, he managed to wedge them both on to the ladder. Ted a step above, keeping tight hold on the leather belt that wrapped around her throat. Every time he moved higher, he pulled painfully on the loop. Naomi had had trouble breathing before, but now she could feel her head swimming and the effort it took to grip the rungs was unbelievable. She tried to wedge one hand between the belt and her neck, but he just jerked harder and pulled it tighter, and the difficulty of climbing with just one hand in contact with the ladder, when she couldn't see where the rungs were, proved to be more than she could handle. And her feet were bare, slipping and sliding against the cold, slick metal.

'Move it! Move faster!' Ted was shouting at her.

Naomi sobbed in desperation. Her feet slid again. Hands didn't seem able to grip. Lungs on fire. Body cold and drenched with freezing rain. Naomi came close to just letting go.

'Naomi. We're with you. Naomi it'll be all right. You just hold on.' She heard him, his voice dim and fuzzy in ears that were filled already with pounding blood and the sucking in of half breaths. Alec. She had to make it down. She had to make it back to him. She couldn't die. Not now.

Somehow she reached the top and Ted Harper dragged her down over the low parapet and on to the roof. He released his grip on the leather and she slid her fingers behind the tightness of it, pulled the soaked and tightened belt a little away from her throat. Enough to breathe.

She felt him move away from her and reached out, trying to get her bearings, judge how far from the edge she might be.

'Come and bloody get me!' Ted Harper was exuberant. 'Who's a loser now, copper?'

He fired his gun in the direction of the armed men. Once, and then again, and Naomi knew that he had only one thing on his mind. To inflict as much damage as he could on anyone unlucky enough to get in the way.

The armed response units had pulled their vehicles into a tight formation and were using them to give cover. Two police and one army vehicle, Alec noted, though in the gloom and pouring rain it was hard for him to differentiate between the well-armed men. The pilot had joined them and Alec sensed that the man was angry at not having been able to do more to stop Ted Harper taking Naomi. Alec didn't know if more had been possible. In the situation, at the time, he would not have said so. What insight hindsight would reveal, he knew from experience would be another matter.

'Did you know he had a second weapon?'

Alec shook his head. 'I knew they had handguns, but not who had them.'

'Well, we've one man down. Not seriously wounded, I'm thankful to say, but, from the look of Harper, he'd like to try for a few more.'

Alec nodded. He could barely see Ted Harper dancing on the roof. Rising to fire a shot, then ducking down again.

'Will she have the sense to stay down?'

Alec nodded. 'I believe so. She can't see where she is, remember. She'll only have a rough idea of where the edge of the roof is. I doubt she'll want to move.'

He hoped she wouldn't want to move.

The man beside Alec had a scope on his rifle that looked fit to see Mars, not just Ted Harper. The red beam was diffracted by the torrential rain. It ran down his nose, into his eyes. He remained amazingly still despite that, only occasionally raising a hand to wipe the pouring water from his face. 'Can you see him?'

'I can't predict where he'll pop up next is the trouble, and there's always that chance it'll be the lady and not him. Split second makes all the difference.'

Alec gnawed at his lower lip. He wanted to be up there, with her. He wanted to kill Ted Harper.

Naomi was listening to him move. He was taunting them. He'd fired six shots so far. She'd counted them and she'd heard him replace the clip. Did the gun just hold six rounds, or was the clip capable of a forced round? Did he have more ammunition?

She noticed that he moved in quite a restricted plane around her. Not so far away that she might be out of reach. She noted too that, so far, no one was returning fire, and guessed she must be the reason.

'You see?' Ted Harper was delighted. 'Cowards, the lot of them. Just don't have what it takes. Try and pick off your boyfriend, shall I? I can see him. Oh yes, hiding out down there, but from up here I can see him well. She had dragged herself slowly to the parapet, feeling her way along, so she had some sense of where she was in relation to the ladder. Ted was taking little notice of her, pausing in his dance only to crow over the fact that he was up here, the hero in his own head. They were down there, poor sods in the pouring rain, waiting for him to see how many he could kill.

Suddenly, Naomi knew she could take no more. The thought that anyone else would be injured by this crazy man appalled her. More than that, the thought that he might, by some freak chance, really hit Alec was more than she could cope with. Ted Harper had lost his mind, she was certain of that, and he'd pushed Naomi to the edge of reason.

She was tired and cold and had gone beyond being afraid for her own life. She just wanted this to be over. She waited until he had fired the next shot, waited while he moved into his new position for the next. She'd got the measure of him now, could tell by the sound of his booted feet exactly where he was. She waited a moment longer till he rose up again, gun raised, laughter bursting from his crazed mouth. And then she hauled her weary body to its feet and she launched herself at Ted Harper. Pushing him with all her strength and all the force of will that she possessed, catching him at that moment of unbalance as he leapt to his feet ready to fire again.

201

Ted Harper stumbled forward and Naomi dropped down, ready to throw herself again, the thought that she too might fall entering her head only for long enough for it to be dismissed.

Before she could rise up again she heard the sharp report of a rifle shot. Instinctively, she dropped on her belly and pressed her face into the floor. She felt him tumble past her, his leg catching her shoulder as he cartwheeled down. He was dead already. Long before he ever hit the ground.

Thirty-Four

On the morning of his sixteenth birthday, Patrick slept late. It was almost noon when the household finally stirred and decided it really was time to rejoin the world.

They'd camped out at the Emmetts' house, gravitating there because of Mari's presence late on the night of Naomi's rescue. Lillian had put Naomi and Alec in the spare room, Mari being housed in their younger son's bedroom, he being away at university.

Patrick and Harry slept on sofas downstairs. Lillian had been worried about them having enough room and being comfortable, but in truth they would have slept anywhere by then.

Simon, interview safely in the bag – in reality a tape of random recollections and impressions and reactions that he'd have to put in some kind of order before it could be used – had been shooed off home, or wherever else he needed to be. Lillian, disapproving of her son's methods, made it plain she didn't want to know.

Simon had departed cheerfully enough, knowing that Lillian's irritation would not survive a good night's sleep.

They cooked breakfast at lunchtime, crowding into Lillian's cheerful kitchen and all getting in one another's way, barring Naomi, who sat at the table, Napoleon by her side, drinking tea and saying very little while Alec fussed around her.

'And what will you do today?' Lillian asked Patrick. 'Go home and unwrap your other presents?'

Patrick shook his head. 'I want to go to Morton Park,' he said unexpectedly. 'I want to sit in the sun and be quiet and not think about anything, and then later, I want to go to the cinema. I don't care what's on and I want everyone to come. And then . . . then I want to go out and eat somewhere, really late at night – anything but pizza.'

Harry laughed at that.

'We should get a cake,' Naomi said, trying to make an effort to join in.

'Mari – Nan – already has one,' Patrick said.

'And how would you know that?' Mari asked him.

Patrick shrugged. 'I just know. Dad, he bust up my skateboard. You think I could get another? I've got some money saved and I've been given some for my birthday.'

'Before or after the park?' Harry asked. 'Better go before, I think, then you can take it with you. Finish breakfast and we'll go to . . . oh, that strange shop you like in Pinsent.'

'OK. Thanks,' Patrick said. 'Then we'll come back and get everyone. Yeah?'

Naomi nodded, though all she really wanted was to go home and sleep some more. She'd spent the night curled up as close to Alec as she could get, his arms around her, her face buried in his shoulder. She'd cried herself to sleep and had a shrewd idea he'd done the same. All of the emotion kept so tightly controlled over three days spilling out.

'What happens now?' she asked, after Patrick and Harry had departed.

Alec held her hand. 'We help Lillian clear up this mess. You wash, I'll dry. Then we go to Morton Park and I give you a live commentary while Patrick does unspeakable things on his board and Harry cringes.'

'Ordinary things,' she said.

'Ordinary things,' he confirmed. 'I think we need ordinary things. And then, when Patrick's day is over, I'm going to take some leave and we're going to the travel agent and we're going to slam some money on the counter and say, "How far away can you send us for this?" and when we get there, we're going to lie in our hotel room and sleep for as long as it takes.'

'I don't want to close my eyes. I feel so dark inside.'

'Then we'll lie on the beach. Somewhere hot and bright so that you can see the light. Naomi, will you marry me?'

She smiled and leaned against him, her head resting on his shoulder. Napoleon nudged the pair of them with his nose.

'Maybe,' Naomi said.